A RIGHT

FACE-OFF

SIMON EDGE

Lightning Books

Published in 2019
by Lightning Books Ltd
Imprint of EyeStorm Media
312 Uxbridge Road
Rickmansworth
Hertfordshire
WD3 8YL

www.lightning-books.com

Cover by Ifan Bates

British Library Cataloguing in Publication Data
A catalogue record for this book is available from the British Library.

Printed by CPI Group (UK) Ltd, Croydon CR0 4YY

ISBN: 9781785631306

In memory of
Nick Decalmer

1

The Duchess, it was easy to see, enjoyed being looked at. This was just as well. As the most scandalous woman in England, it was her fate to be the centre of attention wherever she went, whether she liked it or not.

At thirty-four, she was long past her prime. Even in the flickering candlelight, more lines were visible around her eyes than had been there when she last sat – more precisely, stood – for Tom, and she wore a thicker layer of paint on her face. Nevertheless, her allure remained immense. Her eyes, behind those legendarily long lashes, spoke of love to any beholder lucky enough to have them rest upon him. Her mouth seemed permanently organised into a pout of such coquettish power that strong men were enfeebled. Today she wore a gown of sensuous crimson silk, in the same shade as the ermine-trimmed robe strewn ornamentally over the tall plinth next to her, alongside her coronet. Her petticoats exploded out of the front of her gown in a dazzle of silver brocade. Her hair, powdered a fashionable iron grey, towered majestically towards the ceiling, and her gleaming white arms and breasts nestled in teasing lace flounces. She was ravishing still, and she knew it, which was undoubtedly why she was content to stand nearly an hour in the same pose, her rouged cheek resting on one slender finger, her eyes fixed somewhere over Tom's right shoulder, as he worked barely a foot away.

The Duke, her husband, had also arrived in full royal fig, the gold chain around his neck clanking against the gold buttons of his waistcoat. Two or three years younger than his wife, he had put behind him his days as the worst rake in town, and his regard for her was absolute. That they had arrived in tandem was a mark of this devotion.

Unlike his wife, the Duke was a fidget, unable to stay still for more than a few moments at a time. In the past hour, he had paced around the studio, causing havoc in his wake as his sweeping velvet train knocked over boxes, jars and a pile of empty frames. Eventually, the Duchess had successfully enjoined him to remove his cloak, and since the couple had not brought their own footman, she had taken it upon herself to lay it neatly on a side-table. But still the Duke had tripped over an easel as he persisted in trying to peer at the faces looking back at him from their shadowy frames on the walls. Every time he knocked into something, he cursed loudly at the darkness that Tom insisted on maintaining in the studio, even though it was bright noon outside.

'Can't you open the blasted curtains, man?' he demanded. 'A feller can't see a perishing thing in here.'

Tom stood firm. Years of experience had taught him that it was easier to capture a precise likeness when only the face was lit, and all its surroundings were in the deepest possible gloom. If that meant a member of the Royal Family tripping over everything because he could not remain at repose for more than a few seconds, so be it.

The Duke of Cumberland was the younger and more disgraceful of the King's two surviving brothers, although both were too much for His Majesty. The middle brother, the Duke of Gloucester, had already visited the studio, as Cumberland now discovered with a shout of surprise.

'Damn me, if it isn't Brother Billy! It's so damned dark, I didn't notice him before.'

The full-length canvas was leaning against the wall just behind where Tom stood, which meant that this cry was delivered very close to his left ear. He hoped the Duchess did not notice his own involuntary wince at the outburst. She was still looking over his right shoulder, but her pouting lips twitched in amusement.

'How is it, my dear? Is it very like?'

'Hard to see in this damned gloom.'

Tom could sense the Duke peering closer towards the portrait.

'What the devil are these trees? A child could do better!'

Tom coughed discreetly.

'The picture is unfinished, sir. It is customary to finish the setting last.'

'What of the face, my dear? Is it like?'

'Behhhh…passing like,' the Duke conceded.

Tom sensed that his visitor did not bestow compliments lightly.

'Damned tricky for you, though,' he continued, prodding Tom on the shoulder with his cane.

The jolt made Tom's hand jump, so that a dab of crimson

from the Duchess's right cheekbone now spilled onto what ought to be the distant background.

'How is that, sir?' he asked, mopping away the rogue colour with a damp piece of sponge from a saucer beside him, and hoping the irritation did not sound in his voice.

'Let's face it, he's an ugly blighter, and ye'd be mad not to try and pretty him up a little, wouldn't ye? Eh? Ha!'

Tom cleared his throat. 'His Royal Highness is a man of distinguished aspect, sir. One would expect nothing less from a member of such an illustrious family.'

The Duke sniffed.

'Devil take me if I'm that ugly. Always thought he had the look of a sheep, old Billy. It's the way his nose starts too high up his face. Ye've caught that, indeed ye have.'

The truth was, he was right, and Tom had thought much the same when he was working on the painting. Not that he could possibly say so. If blood was thicker than water, royal blood was thicker still.

The Duchess came to his rescue.

'I believe there is also a portrait of Maria, my dear. I think I saw it as we entered the room.'

'Where?'

'Next to your brother. Just to the right.'

'O yes, bless me, there she is, the old girl. Yes, ye've certainly caught her. Not a looker, bless me, but what can ye expect when her husband has the face of a tup?'

There now came a series of adenoidal snorts from immediately behind Tom. The Duke was laughing.

Without moving her head, the Duchess turned her eyes on her painter.

'Did they also sit for you together?'

'No, ma'am. The picture of Her Royal Highness, the

Duchess, was painted previously, when she was still Lady Waldegrave. At least, when we thought…'

He stopped, for fear of saying the wrong thing.

It was the Duke's turn to help him out.

'Before the world knew that my brother had married the old stick in secret?'

He snorted again, even as the Duchess tutted a gentle rebuke.

'And you painted His Royal Highness on a later occasion?' she asked.

'Yes,' said Tom. 'They both visited me here, but it was only the Duke of Gloucester who sat.'

'I don't believe I've seen either picture before. Did you not show them at the Academy?'

'As I say, ma'am, the portrait of the Duke is not finished. I did endeavour to show Lady Waldegrave – that's to say, Her Royal Highness, the Duchess – the very year I painted her, ma'am. I regret to say that I was…obstructed.'

'Obstructed?' boomed the Duke. 'Who the devil by?'

Tom used a cloth to daub some black shadow along the outline of the Duchess' nose.

'I submitted the picture to the Academy, sir, but the council, in its wisdom, declined to exhibit it. The picture was returned and it has remained here ever since.'

'Damned cheek! Why the blazes did they do that?'

Again, this was sensitive.

'I believe the president of the council feared that the picture of Her Royal Highness, as we had recently learned her to be, might cause embarrassment to His Majesty when he visited the exhibition.'

Which might have caused embarrassment in turn – he thought, but did not say aloud – to the president himself.

'Ha!' said the Duke. 'Ridiculous business, the whole perishing thing. If the King would only mind his own damned business about who married who in his own damned family, nobody would need to be embarrassed at all.'

Tom suddenly found it necessary to focus very minutely on the set of the Duchess' left eyebrow, using his finest brush and leaning right into the canvas.

'My love, you mustn't speak of your brother so,' she said, her amused pout as intact as ever. 'You're making poor Mr Gainsborough uncomfortable. In any case, it was not the King who refused to show dear Maria's portrait, but the president of the Academy.'

'Damned fool thing to do. Who is the president? Do we know him?'

'We sat for him, my dear. Do you remember, we went to his house in Leicester Fields.'

'The feller with the blasted ear trumpet?'

'Indeed, my dear. Sir Joshua.'

'Ridiculous feller. Don't know why he needed the trumpet. I had nothing to say to him. Just get on with it and paint, man: that's my view.'

Tom wished the same rule might apply in his own studio.

He turned his attention to the Duchess' mouth. Those lips would have to be made to pout a little less, for her sake and his own. Picking up the mauve chalk that he used for all his initial sketching on the canvas, he traced the outline a little wider, and at once she was more serious; languid, even. The likeness was of course what mattered but, when a subject had such a surfeit of vivacity, there was no harm in holding a little of it back in the studio, and keeping it from the world at large.

He gulped in distaste as a blast of noxious breath passed over his left shoulder. The Duke was standing even closer behind him now, inspecting his work. Tom's instinct was to reach for a perfume-soaked kerchief and press it to his nose, as he might when he walked passed a reeking mess of soil in the street. In this case, it would hardly be wise. He did his best to breathe only through his mouth, trying discreetly to move his head away from the Duke's line of breathing.

'Why's her bally head so close to the edge? Seems an irregular sort of composition to me. Is this the modern way? Damned idiotic, if it is.'

'That, sir, is just while I'm working. As you can see, the canvas is still loose. That enables me to move it around the easel to bring it as close as possible to the element of the subject I am painting – in this case, Her Royal Highness' head. In that way, I find can get the likeness much better.'

'Hmmm,' the Duke considered. 'There's not much there yet, but it's not bad. He's beginning to catch you, my angel.'

'Of course he is. He is famous for the quality of his likeness.'

Tom inclined his head, accepting the compliment. It was true. Nobody else could come near him in that respect. Certainly not Sir Joshua.

'At least he isn't making us dress in damned silly costumes like that other feller wanted. I remember now. I refused. Told him it was beneath a man's dignity. Why the devil does he do that?'

Tom shrugged.

'I believe he learned it in Italy. He calls it the Grand Style. He likes to elevate his sitters, make them into characters from ancient history and legend, even if they are elevated enough already, as Your Royal Highnesses so obviously are. If he makes a big fuss over the clothes and the setting, he hopes that nobody will notice that the faces are nothing like.'

The Duchess laughed, a clear peal of merriment. As she

tilted her head back to do so, Tom caught a glimpse of the soft, white skin under her chin.

'Is it true that you and Sir Joshua are great enemies?' she asked, returning to her proper pose.

Tom stood back from his work, hoping it would encourage the Duke at his left flank to back off too.

'Not at all, ma'am. It's true that I was in a fury with him when he refused my picture. As Your Royal Highness may know, I have refused to send work to the Academy in the years since then. Rather than subject my pictures to Sir Joshua's petty-fogging prejudices, I have mounted an annual exhibition here at my home instead. But I am still a member of the Academy, and I have been away too long. I have decided it is time to show my face – and, therefore, your faces – there this year.'

'Of course you must. You have sulked quite long enough.'

Tom smiled.

'Do you hear, my dear? Mr Gainsborough plans to send our pictures to the Academy this year. We will see if my face is too shocking to put before the King, as dear Maria's was.'

'If he won't see you in person, he can damned well see a picture of you, to remind him you exist. Gainsborough, did you know the King won't receive my wife?'

Tom did know. All of London did. The Duke and Duchess lived in crenellated splendour in Windsor Great Park. They had their own private palace – inherited from the previous Duke of Cumberland, the notorious Butcher of Culloden – which they filled with gamblers and libertines to make up for the snub of not being welcome at Court.

'His Majesty is a terrible jealous feller,' the Duke continued. 'He puts himself about as a simple, saintly soul, but the truth of it is, he's eaten up with envy. He decided that my brother and I should each marry a dumpy German princess from a runtish little kingdom the size of Berkshire, just like he did, and when we refused to do so, he couldn't forgive us. If he thinks that's where his duty lies, so be it, but why must we all suffer? I was never going to be king and I married for love, damn me. I won't apologise to a soul for it.'

'Nor should you, sir,' said Tom, wondering how he might nudge the subject onto more loyal ground, when protocol demanded that he only speak when spoken to.

Once again the Duchess came to his rescue.

'Is it true that Sir Joshua is too miserly to mix the proper colours?'

She turned to glance at him for a second, and he thanked her with his eyes.

'Whether it is for meanness or for want of knowledge, I cannot say,' he said. 'But it is true that his colours are apt to disappear. Especially the reds. However much rouge you wear when you sit for him, you will have none left in six months.'

His guests both laughed – she with her musical peals, he with his animal snort.

'He shouldn't paint his own face then,' boomed the Duke. 'Red is the only damn colour he needs for that.'

Tom allowed himself to join in with that one. It was not bad, for the Duke.

The shape of the Duchess' face and hair were in place now. She would need another sitting to get her eyes right, and the full texture of her skin, after which he would rearrange the canvas and set to work on her silk finery. For the moment, it was time for husband and wife to change places. If nothing else, it would stop the Duke breathing over his shoulder.

He rang for his footman, a spotty youth who had recently arrived in the household from Suffolk. Tom had taken him on as a favour to his sister, who was on a mission to help the lad's family. He provided board and lodging, and half a crown a week, but it was not obvious what he gained in return, particularly with the new tax of a guinea a head to be paid on male servants. The lad tugged constantly at his collar, as if his new livery were choking him, and he had flatly refused to run errands out of doors, so convinced was he that he would be press-ganged into service in the American war. He could at least earn his keep indoors.

To his surprise, the lad appeared in an instant – almost as if he had been hanging around outside the door.

'Fetch a chair for Her Royal Highness. And when you've done that, help His Royal Highness into his cloak.'

The Duke's top layer of ermine was rearranged around his shoulders, with his golden chain over it, and Tom placed him where his wife had been, this time facing in the opposite direction, so that his face was pointing over Tom's left shoulder.

The face itself, he now observed properly, was not displeasing. The Duke's nose was straight, his brow was high under his white-powdered wig and his eyes were comfortably set, neither too close together, like the Duke of Gloucester, nor too wide apart, like the King, who had been handsome as a young man but in middle age, from what Tom had seen in paintings, had come to look like a bullfrog. While handsome, the Duke of Cumberland had a famously vicious character, and it was hard not to see that in his cool, grey eyes. Tom must make an effort not to let that aspect show through. In his early days, it had amused him to emphasise the curl of a lip or the stiff spine of some country panjandrum, who was too caught up in his own self-regard to notice the slight. With the Royal Family it was different, because everyone was watching and the stakes were potentially a good deal higher.

As usual, he would begin with the head, which meant

slinging the loose canvas over his easel so that the place where the head was due to go was as close as possible to the Duke's own features. These were now neatly illuminated in the candlelight.

'Will you look directly at me, sir?'

'Like this?'

This time the blast of foul breath hit Tom full on from the front.

'That's it exactly, sir,' said Tom, turning his nose into his sleeve as if he were rubbing an itch. From behind him, he heard a soft giggle. The Duchess, at least, was enjoying herself.

The Duke himself did not seem to have noticed. He was frowning faintly, with a distant look in his eyes. He appeared to be thinking.

'I say,' he said after a moment. 'Once you've done these pictures, you could send all of them to the Academy: the Duchess and meself, and Brother Billy and Maria. Show 'em all together, hey? That would stop the King in his tracks. Ha! I tell ye what would happen then. 'Pon my soul, he's so jealous, he'd want ye to paint him too. Mark my words, man: before ye know it, ye'll be the Court Painter!'

'I fear that office is already taken, sir,' said Tom.

'Really? By who?'

'His name is Ramsay, sir. He is Scotch.'

'Never heard of the blighter. Has he done me?'

'I don't know that he has, sir. If you do not recall sitting for him, perhaps not. He has of course painted their majesties, but I understand it has become impossible for him to paint these days. He broke his arm falling from a ladder, and now he is quite crippled.'

'What was he doing up a ladder? Stealing apples? Ha, ha!'

'I understand he was showing his family how to escape onto

the roof in the event of fire.'

'He had an accident while he was showing 'em how to avoid an accident?' That adenoidal snort sounded again. For the Duke, the best jokes involved the misfortunes of others. 'But I don't see why he can't paint. What's wrong with his other arm?'

'If he is right-handed, my dear, he cannot be expected to paint with his left,' said the Duchess.

'Hmmm. 'Spose you're right. Feller shouldn't still be Court Painter though, if he can't paint. Stands to reason. Sounds like a job for you, Gainsborough, hey?'

Tom merely smiled.

To my dearest Ma

I know you cannot make out my scratchings on the page, because you never learned how. But I trust our Richard to read this out to you. It shall be one of his duties now he is become the man of the house in my absence. He is good with his school learning and 'twill be no trouble for him.

'Tis full two weeks that I am here in this great city of London. I cannot tell you if this town is a fair place or a foul one, because I have taken your instruction to heart, and when my master asks me to leave the house on some errand, I tell him nay, I dursn't, because I will not be press-ganged into no army, whether His Majesty wills it or not. My master vents his rage on me and tells me I am a witless numbskull and a coward, but I tell him I am too afeared and he does not force me to go, so I think he is a kind man really. In consequence, of London I have seen precious little.

I can tell you that my master – that is the brother of Mrs Dupont, although he seems so much finer than her – is a great gentleman. He is much given to carousing, but he has a worthy Christian soul too, and although he is quick to temper, he is right afeared of my mistress, as we all are.

He has such a house, you never did see the like. It is full five floors high, and while it is narrow from the front, it is of large proportion inside, because it goes back farther than you would imagine. From the street, you go into a parlour, and from there into a hallway with a great circular stair with light coming down from windows in the roof. 'Tis so different from our narrow little stairway at home.

Upstairs there is a drawing room and a dining room, and above that a large chamber for my master and mistress, and two smaller ones for my master's daughters, Miss Molly and Miss Peggy, who are grown up and like to become old maids because they have not yet found husbands.

I sleep in the top attic which I share with Mr Perkiss, the groom. I have my own little bed, we have a wash-stand between us and there is a little oak chest to keep my clothes and my private things. There is also a cook and a parlour-maid in this house, but they sleep below stairs, next to the kitchen, and the cook says she will have my guts for sausage-skins if she catches me down there when I should not ought to be. I did not understand why she spoke to me so stern, wagging her fat finger before my eye, but she has the countenance of a woman who does not waste words in jest, and I have no inclination for any part of me to be made into sausages, so I will obey her ban most diligently.

From our little window you can see St James's-palace, which is very close by, and Buckingham-house, where the King actually lives. I swear they are no further hence than your own little cottage from All Saints-church. I have not yet set eyes on the King or Queen, but I keep looking out for them. I can also see Westminster-abbey very close, which is the most magnificent church you ever saw, far finer than St Gregory's or St Peter's, which afore I came here I should never have thought possible. One day, if I ever dare venture forth from this house, I should like to go to the abbey to see it for myself.

The name of our street is Pall-mall. 'Tis such a smart place to reside that, if you throw an apple over the back-garden wall, it will land in the garden of the Princess Dowager, that was the King's mother, only she is dead now and the house stands empty. I have heard from Mr Perkiss that there is also a temple of ill-virtue in the house next to ours, but this great city London is like that, Ma, and you must not worry, I will never venture there, I swear. I do not know if my master goes, but 'tis not my business to enquire nor to wonder neither.

Every day I rise afore dawn. My duties are to carry coals up to the rooms, clean the boots, trim the lamps, lay the table for meals, answer the front door and discharge any other task that my master or my mistress desire to be done. I do perform them all to my best ability, so as Mrs Dupont will think me worthy and she will not regret sending me to my master, her brother. I have a fancy coat of red velvet, with knee breeches and stockings, and I must wear powder in my hair. You would be so proud if you could see me. I do not have much time to call my own but my mistress sometimes allows me part of a candle, as she has done this night, so I can write my tidings in this letter to you.

I have made the time to write to you now because I have such news to tell you. Can you guess who came to this very house yesterday? I know you will not, so I will tell you: not just one Royal Highness, upon my life, but two of them: the Duke of Cumberland, that is His Majesty's youngest brother, and his wife the Duchess, that was Mrs Horton afore. They came wearing so much gold, you would not believe it. The Duchess had an actual crown with her, although it was only a little one. Mr Perkiss says she is famed for being a great strumpet, but I do not think that can be fair, because she looked very elegant and fine to me.

If I am truthful, I had never heard the name 'Duke of Cumberland' afore, but Perkiss told me His Royal Highness was the talk of all London a few years back, because he had what is called a 'criminal conversation' with a lady called Lady Grosvenor. I do not rightly know what a criminal conversation is, but whatever they conversed about, it must have been exceeding bad, because the King himself had to pay thirteen thousand pounds to Lord Grosvenor, on account of the Duke having spent all his own money already. Can you imagine such a sum? I would need to work for my master two thousand years to earn it.

Any road, Lady Grosvenor is all forgotten now and the Duke does not chase petticoats no more, says Mr Perkiss, because he has found Mrs Horton, and she is now a Royal Highness too, even though she was once a commoner just like us. Although maybe not quite so common as us. She is such a great beauty, she can make any man do most anything she wants. Not in a bad way, I do not believe. That would make her a witch, and she is not one, I am sure on it. Her eyes are too kind.

There was great to-do in the household all the morning on account of these two great personages being expected. I was dispatched to polish the door plate and sweep the step, and Miss Molly and Miss Peggy spent hours putting on their best gowns and trying to put their hair up in the high fashion. 'Twas a wasted effort for them, because they stayed upstairs the whole time, and they only saw the top of the Duke's wig from where they were spying over the second-floor landing.

My mistress also put on a good gown, but she was fretting more about other matters than her dress. She said she would be pleased to curtsey to the Duke, but she would not know what to do if the Duchess wished to be presented to her. It would put her in an uncomfortable position, she said, because the King does not receive the Duchess at his home, so it would be disloyal for my mistress to receive the lady at hers. She looked as if she had not slept for the worry, with bags like potato sacks under her eyes, but she might as well have slept sound, because the Duke and Duchess never asked about her at all. The only room they visited was my master's painting room at the back of the house, and my mistress was not presented to no one.

In all this fussing, my master himself was the calmest person in the house. Mr Perkiss says this is no surprise, because he is used to the society of the highest people. He has painted all the most beautiful ladies in the realm and he could dine every night with dukes, if he chose, but he don't chuse, for he prefers the society of actors and musick-makers so they can carouse together.

As I explained to Mr Perkiss, 'tis an amazing thing that someone from our little town, whose father, as you always told me, was always in debt, can now enjoy the society of the finest folk in all England. But Mr Perkiss says my master do not find it so fine. He told me he is always grousing how much he hates the face-painting business, because it means he must doff his cap and watch his tongue with high-born folk, the like of which he does not respect but he has to pretend as how he does, else they and their friends will not come back to sit. It is a chore for my master, Mr Perkiss says, and he would rather spend his days painting trees and meadows and streams, which is called landskip. I tell you, Ma, he has bits of rock and twig in his studio to make the likenesses. If you saw one of his finished paintings, you would never know that a great tree trunk was copied from a bit of stick no bigger than your hand.

Mr Perkiss asked me if I had noticed that my master's humour is always worse when he has passed the day in his painting room, copying the face of some fine lady or gentleman. I had not, but when I thought on it, I saw it was true. This day sennight, just after I came here for the first time, my master was locked away all day with a titled lady. Her society was evidently not to his taste, because when she was gone, he asked me to fetch his burgundy slippers and I was too long about it, whereupon he cursed me so fierce, I feared he would send me back home to you in the instant. He even shouted at Fox, his collie-dog, who normally has the run of the house, along with a bright little spaniel called Tristram, who belongs to my mistress. My master spoils Fox with meat and fish from the table, and my mistress spoils Tristram, so that to lead a dog's life under this roof is normally to lead a most comfortable one. However, on this day that I am speaking of, my master was so vexed that he shut poor Fox out of doors to scavenge for his supper in the street. Then the next morning, he was as cheerful as you like, as if nothing had happened. When he called me into his painting room to help him lift down a frame, I saw he had been copying a little stump of vegetable called brockolly, which is like a green colly-flower. On his canvas, it became an oak tree. It is genius the way he can do it, Ma, honest it is.

Mr Perkiss says my master is considered the second-best painter in all England, only I must not ever say those words in his presence, because he would fain be the first-best and we must all behave like he is. If it displeases him to doff his cap to high-born people, it stands to reason that doffing it to royal people should displease him the most, especially as the Duke of Cumberland has the reputation of a scoundrel and his wife that of a strumpet (even if that reputation is not deserved). So when he called me to attend him in the painting room while their Highnesses were still with him, I expected his humour to be terrible. I was so afeared, my hand was shaking as I opened the door, and I waited for him to chide me for arriving too slow. But he did nothing of the sort. He just bade me fetch a chair for the Duchess. I was still shaking a little as I fetched it, but nobody seemed to think anything of it, and the Duchess sat down very nicely. When my master enquired after her comfort, she told him the chair was soft and she was content, so she was not dissatisfied with my service. Then my master required me to help the Duke on with his gown, which I also did, and nobody cursed me or told me I was a numbskull, so I must have done it right. I even helped smooth it over his shoulders, so now you can tell everyone back home, Ma, that your own son has laid hands on royalty!

In all this visit, there were no cross words directed at me or Mr Perkiss at all, and after the Duke and Duchess had gone, my master was in such fine humour that he gave me and Mr Perkiss a bottle of beer to drink in the pantry. While we drank it down, I said to Mr Perkiss that maybe my master don't hate face-painting as much as he used to. And Mr Perkiss, he says: it all depends, my boy, on who the face belong to. We both had a good laugh at that.

Any road, Ma, the candle is almost burnt out and my poor brother will likely have no voice left after reading such a long letter out loud to you. So I will bid you a good night and I hope that you will send some news from home by the hand of my brother Richard to your ever loving and affectionate son

David

3

Gemma looked at the queue of mainly elderly hopefuls snaking down the gentle slope of the wedge-shaped town square, and wished she were somewhere else.

She had dreamed of a television career since the age of twelve. As far as her mother was concerned, boasting to family and neighbours, she had achieved that ambition. She worked in the industry, her name was on the end credits, even if they were always shrunk down so small while the next programme was trailed that nobody could read them, and she knew the coffee preference of a number of individuals whose screen appearances placed them somewhere in the lower foothills of celebrity.

It was not, however, the career that Gemma had foreseen.

In her original vision, she was a foreign correspondent, reporting with integrity and a rare sensitivity from troubled yet exotic parts, before returning to some more sedate, studio-based position and ending her career by revealing a hitherto unnoticed flair for light entertainment and fronting a tasteful but potentially cultish panel show.

Instead, a combination of bad luck, poor planning and inferior connections had brought her, at the age of twenty-seven, to a blustery square in East Anglia in the middle of February, where she was attempting to marshal two or three dozen increasingly impatient pensioners.

The show they were making was completely new and had no name recognition. Gemma tended to explain it in terms of more familiar brands: they were adding a twist to an old format, she said, a kind of *Antiques on the Road* meets *The X-Factor* or *Britain's Got Talent*. That twist was a competitive element. No, she patiently explained while setting up episodes in Lincolnshire, Cheshire and South Wales, Ant and Dec were not involved, but she was confident that the show's own, unique presenters would one day be stars of a similar class. She believed nothing of the sort, but blatant untruths were so normal in the world of light entertainment, she barely noticed she was lying.

It was her job to book accommodation for crew and talent, liaise with the venue and ensure there was enough publicity in the area to generate a good turnout from locals – because without the public, they would have no programme. In each location so far, a good crowd had turned out on the day, all clutching attic heirlooms wrapped in bubble-wrap or old blankets, and there had been a good mix of decent finds, honest near-misses and laughable junk. That last part was vital for the show's comedy twist, which its creators hoped would be their ticket to the international franchising jackpot.

And now she was in Suffolk, standing outside the disused

church they were using for the shoot, welcoming and directing the would-be participants. Above her, with his bronze, frock-coated back to her, the town's most famous son stood contemplating them too, brush in one hand, palette in the other, as if he were about to commit them to canvas. Not that Thomas Gainsborough ever had any interest in such a composition: it was far too urban, from what Gemma had seen of his work in her preparatory research. Comely peasants at woodland cottage doors were more his thing; these pensioners in headscarves and anoraks, clutching takeaway coffee from Greggs were better suited to Lowry or Beryl Cook.

Her main task this morning was triage. That was what Fiammetta, the series producer, called it, but it was an unfamiliar word to Gemma. As far as she was concerned, she was sifting: sorting antiquarian wheat from landfill chaff, with the twist that there was also a perverse premium on the absolute worst of the rubbish.

At first, she had been daunted by the responsibility.

'I don't know anything about antiques,' she protested.

'Trust me, darling, you'll know more than Ethel,' said Fiammetta.

'Ethel' was the in-house nickname for the generic punter – elderly, female, under-educated – without whom they would not have a show. The term dripped with snobbery, and Gemma had refrained from using it at first, but she became so used to hearing it that she abandoned her resistance.

'Just have a look at what they've brought,' said Fiammetta, gold bangles jingling as she hooked a rogue strand of red hair out of her face. 'Nobody will bring Ming, I promise you, and it will be much easier than you imagine. Think of it as an algorithm. One: is it broken? If yes, it's junk, if no, it's still in the running. Two: is it older than you? Seriously, just because they find it in the attic, they think it's old, and they forget they only moved in ten years ago. If the answer's no, it's junk. If yes, it's still a possible. Three: if you found it, would you take it to Christie's or the car boot? You'll know the difference. And that's all you have to do. After that, it's up to the experts.'

The 'experts' were what counted with a venture such as this. Memorable personalities in the line-up would make all the difference between standing out in the schedules and fading into the mist of daytime mediocrity. To the viewing public, they were the arbiters, the gimlet-eyed professionals who could distinguish at a glance between treasures and dross. In reality, actual expertise was of minor importance. They needed just enough knowledge, or the semblance of it, to be plausible. It would be embarrassing if they were exposed as ignorant, but none of the programme was live, so any such embarrassment could be edited out. Much more important was *presence*, the kind of quality that made viewers at home think of people on their screens as their friends. Few of those viewers ever grasped what was an axiomatic truth for all those working behind the camera: the qualities that made a TV personality likeable on screen made them largely unbearable in real life.

Britain's Got Treasures featured four front-of-camera performers. The one with the most TV experience was in the anchor role. Regina Oxenholme, a tiny, ferociously ambitious brunette, was a Channel 5 news presenter with an unfortunate inability to pronounce the letter 'r': it came out as a 'v', introducing a jarring note into news items about roads, railways, robberies and Russia, but most notably playing havoc with her own first name. She seemed to have no idea she was doing it, and cheerfully complied with requests to introduce herself for every sound-check, oblivious to the hilarity it caused behind the camera.

Of the rest of the 'talent', only one had ever appeared on the screen before. Kaz Kareem, the first of the trio of supposed experts, was a midway evictee from one of the last seasons of Big Brother, when even *Heat* magazine and the *Daily Star* had lost most of their interest in the tired franchise. Kaz had started his working life on his father's bric-à-brac stall in Romford. On this basis, he ought at least to have the antique dealer's gift of the gab, if not the entire knowledge. Unfortunately, he seemed to have spent his whole time on the stall dreaming of escape, and his instincts were more those of a pantomime dame than a market trader. In front of the camera, he had developed a mannered repertoire of eye-rolling and facial jiggling, and had already evolved, through incessant repetition, a catchphrase. 'But whaddo I know? I'm just a fat poof from Essex!' he would exclaim, as qualification to every opinion he offered. This self-deprecation worked wonders with Ethel, triggering immediate grandmotherly instincts that transcended more obvious barriers. On a professional level, however, it did not inspire confidence.

The second expert, Lavender Weston-Taylor, was an old friend of Fiammetta's. She wore mauve suits and ties, had a violet rinse in her grey, bobbed hair, and owned a Georgian townhouse in Spitalfields which was reputedly crammed with eclectica from all eras, with the only proviso that it had to be purple. Gemma at first assumed that this thematic mania was inspired by her name, but in fact the connection was the other way round: Lavender was originally Louise. Her collecting was a qualification of sorts: she had spent thirty years scouring sale-rooms and junk shops, and knew much about many things – so long as they were purple.

The final member of the trio was Vivian Morris, who was a

genuine antiques dealer: he had a shop in a village popular with second-homers on the north coast of Norfolk. Tall, thin and florid, with a pencil moustache, he was always immaculately turned out in tweed jacket, waistcoat, plus-fours and deerstalker, smoking what appeared to be ultra-thin cheroots. On closer inspection, these were roll-ups made with liquorice-flavoured paper. This visual incongruity was reinforced when he opened his mouth: instead of the far-back bray which his outfit seemed to herald, he spoke with an elongated East Anglian burr, somewhere between Cockney and wurzel. Vivian, Gemma wanted to believe, was the real deal: a quirky character with a genuine knowledge of carved oak furniture and Regency porcelain. Unfortunately, he was too gentle for the camera, which rendered him hesitant and limp. He would grow into it, no doubt; that was what Fiammetta promised, anyway. Gemma hoped it would not ruin him.

If they had been making a more conventional antiques show, these three would have offered their best guess at a valuation of the objects set before them, and that would have been that. The key innovation of their own format was to introduce an element of competition. In every locality, each expert would choose a favourite object from the episode to champion. By the end of the season, they would amass a collection of items – dubbed the Treasure Trove – which would then, in a supposedly nail-biting grand finale, go under the hammer at a real auction which, in an eye-catching flourish, would be screened live. Having seen what price they achieved, the owners of the items would be allowed to decide whether to keep the object or take the cash, while the expert who achieved the highest bidding total for their Trove would claim the series crown.

The idea was to create an energy, driving the season to an

exciting climax and bringing unaccustomed adrenaline to the antiques show genre. Gemma was not convinced. The auction might well be exciting for the owners of the objects, but the competition between the three experts was too contrived, with nothing of substance at stake for any of them. More to the point, she was not sure the genre needed shaking up. It was indeed cosy and undemanding, but that was just how its audience liked it.

The show had one other talent-show trick up its sleeve: public humiliation. Just as the singing contests had their audition rounds, where caterwaulers without a shred of talent were mocked for thinking they could be contenders, the equivalent on *Britain's Got Treasures* was the anti-treasure, a piece of such obvious junk that the very act of bringing it in was laughable. Fiammetta encouraged the experts to nudge and gurn for the cameras, but most of this could be added later in the edit, and with the voiceover. The victim would not know they were being played for laughs until the programme went out.

It was Gemma's job to look out for candidates for this Grot Slot, as it was informally known. She felt guilty at first, but some of the offerings were so inappropriate, she concluded their owners must be impervious to mockery or shame, so there was little harm to be done. A woman in Skegness had brought a chipped glass vase that clearly had an Ikea imprint on the base. In Nantwich, someone had turned up with a plastic life-belt, fairly obviously made within Gemma's own lifetime, on which the letters TITANIC had been stencilled. An elderly man in Caerphilly had brought them a badly framed reproduction of Degas' Dancer on the Stage; he had read in the *Daily Express* about a Degas – he pronounced it 'dee-gus' – reaching a record price at Sotheby's, and could not understand why there was no knock-on effect for his print.

She had set up a welcome desk just inside the church doorway. Here she would spend the rest of the morning greeting the hopefuls, inviting them to unwrap whatever junk they had brought – while being careful always to refer to it as their 'treasure' – and then assigning them a place in the queue for whichever expert she thought best-placed to value it. Any obvious candidate for the Grot Slot would be directed inside in the same way, but Gemma would also alert Fiammetta, who would come over for a discreet look and take the bearer aside for pre-assessment filming if she agreed the object was sufficiently awful.

It proved to be a slow morning on that score. There was a chipped Willow pattern tea-set that deserved putting out of its misery in a skip, and a marquetry view of Sorrento which, she remembered from a family holiday, could be picked up for ten euros in souvenir shops all round the Bay of Naples; but nobody brought anything downright laughable.

When the church clock struck noon, she realised it was time to go in search of lunch for the talent and crew. It would only be sandwiches, but Fiammetta liked them arranged on platters in a form of buffet, as if they had proper catering. Gemma had recce'd the area on her phone the previous evening and, fortunately, there was a Waitrose, which would help keep any tantrums at bay. Waitrose was Fiammetta's comfort blanket, easing her panic at journeying outside the M25. Gemma was not convinced that anyone would notice if she arranged Gregg's sandwiches on the same platters, and she kept a few spare Waitrose plastic bags as an emergency disguise, but this was one location where she would not have to use them.

She was already on her feet when the church door opened and the tiny, stick-thin figure of an elderly woman appeared.

Her hair was dyed jet-black and cut into a girlish bob, but her face was deeply lined and she was bent arthritically; she looked as if she was pushing eighty. She peered up out of her hunch as she entered the church, glaring around her.

'Is this *Antiques on the Road*?' she demanded. Her voice was unexpectedly high and girlish.

'Not quite,' said Gemma, putting on her most indomitable smile. 'We're *Britain's Got Treasures*. Almost the same, but a different channel. Have you brought something lovely for us to see?'

She nodded her head encouragingly towards the large carrier bag the old woman was clutching. Iceland, she noticed, trying not to judge in the way that Fiammetta would. Inside it, she could see a bulky rectangular object parcelled in newspaper. A mirror, perhaps, but more likely a picture, which was a shame. Having already had one charity-shop Degas, another similar would be too repetitive.

'It's for the experts,' said the woman, clutching the bag to her chest.

'I know, but I'll need to see it first, and then I can point you in the right direction.' Gemma increased the wattage of her smile. The punters were not usually this truculent. 'Can I start by taking your name?'

The old woman looked her up and down suspiciously.

'It's Mudge,' she said, with evident reluctance. 'Muriel Mudge.'

She had the same accent as Vivian: unfamiliar, elongated, mashing up rural burr with London vowels.

'Right then, Mrs Mudge. If I could just have a look…'

'It's Miss.'

'Sorry.'

In London, Gemma would never dream of making that kind

of assumption. She was embarrassed to have been caught out.

'Right then, Miss Mudge. I'm just going to need you to pop your address on this form and sign here, which gives us your permission to use any film we take.'

'Why?'

'Well, it's a requirement, I'm afraid. Everyone else taking part has signed one. It just gives us your consent to broadcast the footage.'

Miss Mudge scowled for a moment, considering her options, then carefully placed her precious cargo on the floor at her feet, pulled a pair of reading glasses out of a grubby tote bag slung over her shoulder, and proceeded laboriously to print her address and sign her name.

'That's lovely. Thank you so much. And if I could just have a quick look at the treasure you've brought today…?'

Miss Mudge glared at her. Then, with a sigh of acquiescence, she lifted the Iceland bag, deposited it on Gemma's table, and removed the paper parcel from its outer wrapping. As she took away the newspaper layers, one side of a heavy, wooden picture frame emerged. She seemed to be deliberately making sure the picture faced away from Gemma, as if building for a big reveal. As the full frame now came free of the paper, all Gemma could see was the back, which was covered with brown paper, darkened and blotched with age, and what seemed to be a framer's label in the bottom right-hand corner. Gemma leaned forward to get a clearer look at the label, but before she could read it, Miss Mudge flipped the frame around.

'There,' she said.

Gemma's eyes widened and her mouth fell open.

What she was looking at had once been the head-and-shoulders portrait of a man in late middle age, in period dress. The brushwork was loose and hasty, so it was hard to make out the detail of the clothing, but it looked like a blue velvet coat, with some kind of lacy cravat at the neck. The face was round, with a cleft chin, broad, almost bee-stung lips and a wide nose, and the hair was grey and curled. It was a thoroughly believable portrait – or it would have been, if it had not been grotesquely defaced. The head was surmounted with a pair of hairy animal ears: slightly pointed, dark on the outside, lighter and fluffier on the inside, like furry pouches. They were like the kind of instant bunny ears or devil's horns for a hen-night posse or a Hallowe'en costume, only this was some kind of eighteenth-century version, where the sitter had been made to look like…what? A horse?

The vandalism was vicious, clearly designed to ruin the portrait, but it was also skilful, and now Gemma realised what it called to mind. In a school production of *A Midsummer Night's Dream*, she had been given the part of the fairy Peaseblossom, commanded by Queen Titania to wait on Bottom, who was played by a fat boy with a knack for comedy called Marius. These were just like the asses' ears that Puck magicked onto Bottom's head to humiliate him.

What made the picture all the more grotesque was that it seemed to have been cut into four quarters and then repaired with black thread. The stitches crossed at the sitter's nose, leaving unblemished the two ears in the upper quadrants.

'It's… It's…'

'Valuable?' said Muriel. 'I should say so. It's been in my family for a long time and we don't let many folk see it.'

'Has it really?' said Gemma. 'It's clearly very…unusual.'

She was already viewing it through Fiammetta's eyes, and she knew already what she must do. 'Miss Mudge, would you excuse me just a second?' she said.

Turning away, she looked into the body of the church. There

was no sign of Fiammetta in the nave. But she caught a glimpse of red hair at the far end of the building, under the chancel arch. Walking as quickly as decorum allowed, she wound her way through the groups of punters and crew crowding the south aisle, scarcely able to contain her excitement.

Her producer was in conversation with the lead cameraman, but Gemma knew she could interrupt.

'Sorry, Fiammetta,' she said, touching her boss on the elbow to get her attention. 'You're going to want to see this. Urgently. And I promise you, you're going to really, really like it. I've got something wonderful for the Grot Slot. It's perfect, the owner's perfect, it's... Well, you'll see. Just try not to laugh in front of her, OK?'

4

Tom examined himself in the entrance hall glass. Almost fifty summers old, and every one of them etched in his face as deep as the engraver's cuts on a copper plate: drooping skin under his eyes, lines around them, red mottling all over his cheeks. What could he do? Life was for living, and every line told a tale that was not fit for telling in most company. He drew himself up and brushed a fleck of dust off the lapel of his cornflower-blue silk coat. He did, at least, cut a dashing sort of figure still, for all his advanced age. Plenty of his contemporaries, and junior, were stouter, goutier, lamer than he. He adjusted his wig to sit a fraction lower down his brow, and carefully placed his cocked hat on top, pressing down firmly enough to put it in place, but not so firmly as to displace the hairpiece. He dusted his lapel one more time, to banish any powder that had fallen from the wig, and was satisfied. He was ready for his great return.

A clatter of heels and rustle of skirts alerted him to the arrival of his wife.

'Have you not gone?' she demanded. 'I thought you were away this past quarter hour!'

'I am waiting for that lazy coxcomb of a driver to bring the carriage round, although I could have covered the length of Pall-mall twice over in the time since I sent for it.'

'You are right to wait, sir. You must on no account go on foot. It would be beneath your dignity to do so, on such an auspicious occasion, aside from the filth you will tread in on the way.'

Tom bowed his head in acquiescence.

'You are right, madam, you are indeed right, and we are of one mind.' That did not often happen, so it should be celebrated. 'Ah look, here he is at last. And now, where is that useless nephew?' He shouted down the corridor that ran the length of the house towards his studio. 'Mr Dupont! Stir yourself, man. The carriage is here.'

His sister, Mrs Dupont, had christened her first-born Gainsborough, which was a fine tribute to her line, but it sat strangely on the tongue for the rest of the family. Tom had called him 'Gainie' as a child but, now that the lad was under his roof as apprentice, assistant and potential heir to the studio, he had been elevated to 'Mr Dupont'.

'Will Sir Joshua be in attendance this morning?' asked Margaret, as young Dupont appeared, brushing his girlish curls out of his nervous, brown eyes.

'How am I to know, madam? And why should I give a fourpenny fig?'

'You should care. He should greet you, to welcome you back. You are doing him a favour, gracing his exhibition with your work. Do not forget that!'

'I will not, madam, I will not. And where's that dratted David, now?'

'Here, master. Holding the door for you.'

The footman was indeed holding the front door open. It was a mark of Tom's nerves that he had not seen him. Fox and Tristram were wagging their tails in and out of everyone's feet, and now his daughters were there too: Molly, with her long, sad face, who was always such a worry, and the Captain, as he had always called bonny young Peggy. They each plastered him with the kisses that they ought to bestow on husbands by this age, but there was no time to fret about that now. Peggy held Fox by his scruff so he would not follow his master out into Pall-mall, and now Tom was climbing aboard the carriage with Dupont, as David stepped up behind.

Neither he nor any painting by his hand had entered the portals of the Royal Academy these past four years. He did not regard himself as having an unnaturally thin skin, and he was as capable of shrugging off a slight as any man. That year when the committee – effectively Sir Joshua – had seen fit to refuse his full-length of Lady Waldegrave, he had kept his irritation under control. The Duke of Gloucester had, not long since, revealed his secret marriage to the lady, and the news had made a fool of the King because it showed him ignorant as to the composition of his own brother's household. It was not difficult, by general consent, to make a fool of the King, which undoubtedly heightened the sensitivity of all concerned at the prospect of His Majesty confronting the Duchess' portrait during his annual visit to the exhibition. Tom could, to that extent, understand the committee's point of view, and he was prepared to reconcile himself to the removal of this one, troublesome picture.

It was only once the painting was returned, parcelled up in hessian and twine, that its rejection began to rankle. For weeks he did not unwrap it and it sat in his studio, a constant reminder of the wrong that had been done him and the insult he had suffered. For that was how, with the passage of time, the episode now appeared to him. Was the King really so delicate that he could not contemplate the image of his own sister-in-law? Even if he was, was it beyond the wit of the hanging committee to place the portrait in some obscure corner, where the King could feign not to have seen it? They were certainly more than capable of hanging Tom's pictures in barely visible places; that, too, had long rankled with him. So now his irritation grew, intensified by the fact of his living at Bath for all this period, not in London, which meant he had no personal contact with the Academy. The sense of being excluded, of a great snub, grew and grew. The following spring he wrote to the committee to say that he would not be sending anything for exhibition that year.

It was a bold statement of rebellion, making him all the more the outsider and, for the ensuing three years, his great sulk had persisted. His name had even gone forward, at the urging of another malcontent among the membership, against Sir Joshua for the presidency. The vote was a humiliation for Tom – he won the support of just one fellow member – and did nothing for his relations with the committee.

In the course of this time, he reached the point where he had painted all the faces at Bath whose owners could afford his fee. Since Bath was the second-most fashionable town in England, there was only one place left to go: it was time to settle the family in London, where he had not lived for nearly thirty years.

He took a house close to the royal palaces and he could scarce believe the grandeur of his station. It could only be sustained if fashionable people continued to sit for him, paying thirty guineas for a head, sixty guineas for a half-length or a hundred for a full-length. There had been no shortage of them to date, but he could not help noticing that they all asked if their faces would be sent to the Academy show. He began to acknowledge that it was time he let his dudgeon go, if his business were to thrive and he were to maintain a household with its own cook, groom, footman and parlour-maid – albeit a footman who was frightened of his own shadow and a parlour-maid who cost more in broken tea-cups than she did in wages.

Some correspondence passed back and forth, in which he sought assurances that he would never again be subjected to the gross indignity of having a canvas returned, and the Academy pointedly failed to provide anything of the kind. This was galling, but his need to return was too acute – as the committee doubtless well knew – so he did not try to hold out for more. If he lost face in private, he must make up for it by presenting the best possible face to the public. So he sent the two full-length Cumberlands: the Duke in ermine, with an elegance and poise for which he must thank his painter, rather than his maker; the Duchess more languid than amorous, discovering a relaxed serenity with her new royal status that belied the coquettishness of her earlier career. He was confident of making a stir with another full-length, which he had coyly titled 'A Lady' – the subject was a doe-eyed seventeen-year-old, newly married to a Scottish landowner called Graham, who had brought her to sit for him during their honeymoon in London. Tom dressed her in sumptuous Vandyke costume, with ostrich plumes on her hat and in her hand; those delicate, translucent fingers were his proudest part of the finished picture: elegant, dainty, exquisite. He hoped they would aggravate Sir Joshua, who painted hands like plates of meat, and thought that if he hid them inside gloves or within the folds of a coat, nobody would notice how bad he was at them.

Tom had also sent a full-length portrait of Abel, his dear friend, seated in a chair (although the painting itself stood seven feet tall) with composing paper at hand, the neck of his viola da gamba laid across his knees, and his white fox-dog nestling lazily at his feet.

'You have put Mr Abel on a diet, Papa!' said Molly, and it was true, he had scaled down the vast expanse of gilt waistcoat, which in real life struggled to contain his friend's immense gut. He did not think of himself as a flatterer, but in this case he had shown a kindness, for friendship's sake.

He had also sent a landscape: a scene of cattle and goats drinking at a woodland stream in the evening sunlight, with a group of country folk taking their rest in the shade next to the animals. He was pleased with the harmony of the composition, with the beasts in a patch of light in the right foreground, the peasants and the trees forming a more sombre frame, and a gap in the woodland leading the eye off towards a village and the hills beyond. He was especially pleased with the cattle: his scene did not bring to life any classical legend or reproduce any precise natural location, but he defied anyone to look on those tranquil beasts and not feel calmer in the soul. Tom himself would feel calmer in his own soul if he could induce some patron to pay properly for landscapes like this, and not just for the infernal portraits with which they insisted on cluttering their walls; if there was sufficient enthusiasm at the exhibition, a decent customer might perhaps emerge.

The exhibition itself was not yet open to the public. His present visit was to show his face and make sure his pictures had been hung to his satisfaction. He lifted the curtain to peer out of the carriage window. They were nearly there.

'When we arrive…' he began, tapping his nephew on the knee.

'Yes, uncle?'

It was awkward. He did not want to show how nervous he was.

'When we arrive, I want you to go up first. Take that good-for-nothing footman with you. I will stay here.'

His nephew blinked, a look of uncertainty on his face. 'Lest Sir Joshua should be there?'

'Good God, no! Why does everyone assume I am afraid of Sir Joshua?'

Embarrassed in his presence, perhaps. Uncertain how to play their encounter, assuredly. But afraid? Never!

The carriage had stopped.

'Just go up,' he said, wafting his hand in the direction of the Academy building. 'And make sure everything is where it should be. Every painting in its rightful place.'

'Ah! That nothing is refused. Now I understand.'

Young Dupont was out of the carriage now, standing in the street.

'You understand nothing of the sort! They will not refuse me.'

Tom was leaning out of the carriage window. He pulled his head back in, mindful that it would not do for any other member of the Academy to see him lurking here.

Nephew and footman adjusted their hats and turned to face the Palladian mansion outside which the carriage had stopped.

Dupont turned back to the carriage.

'Uncle, which is the place?' he called.

'First floor,' hissed Tom through the curtain. Confounded

boy. He might as well paint a sign to say that the great Mr Gainsborough was hiding in his carriage.

It was true, of course. Deep down, he was anxious that not all his pictures would be there: that fault would have been found, if not with that deplorable sitter the Duke of Cumberland, then with his delicious Duchess, or that some other way had been found to insult Tom, to label him wanting.

Five minutes went by. He reached a finger between the curtains to create a spy hole, and ventured a glance into the street. There was no sign of his nephew or his footman. Amid the clattering of carriage wheels and the clack of hooves, however, he could hear a commotion to the rear: his carriage was causing a blockage, and a coachman behind was berating his own driver.

'Hold your ground, man,' shouted Tom through the little window behind his driver's head. 'It is a public carriageway. We will stop in it if we want to.'

Another five minutes passed. Fortunately, his vehicle was anonymous enough not to be recognised by any of his fellow painters. Molly and Peggy had nagged at him when they were younger to paint scenes on the doors: it had tickled their fancy to imagine themselves swanning around in a decorated carriage. Their mother had put a stop to their campaign, saying it was a mode of transport, not a box at Ranelagh or Vauxhall. Tom had been more than happy to take his wife's part in the argument. How his present embarrassment might have been compounded had he not!

Finally there was a brisk tap at the door of the carriage and it opened a sliver, revealing his nephew's pointed nose and watery eyes.

'Well?' Tom demanded. 'Is everything in order?'

'No reason for concern, uncle. The pictures are all present

and Sir Joshua is not. Will it please you to come up with us now?'

Tom was on the point of snapping back that he was not concerned about Sir Joshua's presence, one way or the other, but he did not have the energy to maintain the pretence.

Instead he said stiffly: 'If you would open the door for me, perhaps I might be able to do so.'

His footman stepped forward to perform this office. Did Tom detect a smile on his nephew's face as he climbed down? Had it really come to this, that he was an object of private mockery for the young? He might be more affronted were it not for the niggling knowledge that he was indeed behaving in a ridiculous and unreasonable manner.

His nephew was correct: all his pictures were there. It had been five years since Tom had stood in this room. More than five for, before the breach, he had sent his pictures from Bath without always attending in person. The space was smaller than he remembered, and the walls more crammed than ever. What the hall lacked in length and breadth, it made up for in height, and the pictures were hung from top to bottom as well as from side to side, so close they touched at each edge. The lowest began at knee-height and the highest could only comfortably be viewed from the opposite side of the room. This was where his full-lengths were: the Duke and Duchess, the slimmed-down Abel, the ravishing Mrs Graham and a politician called Gage. They were shown to their best, and he was satisfied.

He was searching for his landscape when he heard his name called. He turned to see a dandyish figure with rouged cheeks, a pointed nose and flaring nostrils hailing him with arms thrown wide in apparent delight.

'Good to have you back, my friend,' the figure cried, bowing deeply.

The voice was unmistakeable because of its outlandish accent: Benjamin West was a native of Pennsylvania.

'We have had too easy a time of it without you,' it continued. Now the rest of us will have to raise our game.'

Tom returned the bow.

'You tease me, West. As if anything from my humble brushes could ever come near your glorious…' He scanned the room, looking for one of the overblown history paintings that were West's trademark, then waved his hand in a relieved flourish when he spotted an obvious example, all gaudy figures in epic poses, on the far wall, '…come near your glorious tableaux!'

West showed his teeth and bowed to accept the compliment. Tom bowed in return, to acknowledge West's acceptance of it.

'You have been away too long,' the American continued. 'We were the poorer for it.' He dropped his voice and leaned towards Tom confidentially. 'And not just artistically.'

'Surely you have been in capable hands. I read with great interest that our esteemed president is to present another of his lectures, so that those of us who do not know how to paint can learn not just from his example, but also from his rules. Such generosity!'

His nephew, who had been lingering at the fringe of this conversation in evident hope of being presented to West, raised his fist to his mouth and coughed, widening his eyes at Tom as he did so. It was not the most discreet of warnings, but it served its purpose, for now Tom turned to see a florid face, with pugilist's nose and the trace of a hare lip, looking up at him.

'My dear Sir Joshua,' he cried. 'I was hoping against hope to encounter you, of all people, here today!'

'Mr Gainsborough,' bowed Sir Joshua. How odd that he still had his Devon burr, for all his grand title and the company he liked to keep with dukes and statesmen. Tom had been at pains to erase all trace of Suffolk from his own speech almost as soon as he arrived in London for the first time, for his apprenticeship to a French engraver, as a youth of thirteen.

'It has been too long, sir, far too long. I am mighty cheered to see you returned. Are you well, sir? And your good lady? And your lovely girls?'

Before Tom could reply, the other man turned his head, presenting his right ear in Tom's direction and pressing to it the conical object that he had been clutching at his side.

Tom duly leaned down and spoke into the ear trumpet.

'They are passing well, thank you, Sir Joshua. We are all passing well.' As the trumpet remained in position, he continued: 'My poor wife is frequently obliged to point out my manifold shortcomings, for my own correction, and then she is forced to repeat her admonitions, because I am too sorry and wayward a figure to reform to her satisfaction.'

The aperture of the cone traced an arc back and forth in the air, as Sir Joshua nodded his head – either to confirm that he had heard, or by way of sympathy – and the trumpet nodded with it. But still it remained in place, with the effect of encouraging further confidence.

'Such is the price we pay for the blissful state of marriage,' Tom continued. 'A condition whose joys you continue, Sir Joshua, to deny yourself? The position of Lady Reynolds still remains vacant, does it not?'

Now, finally, the trumpet returned to Sir Joshua's side as he turned to face Tom. The gambit of the direct question had paid off.

'There is still, it is true, no such lady,' Sir Joshua replied, with a sigh. 'Who would accept such an unappealing figure as I?'

Tom had heard on good authority that several candidates were more than willing to become the president's consort, and that, since this situation operated to Sir Joshua's considerable advantage, he had no intention of putting an end to it by awarding any one of them the prize they sought.

'I know you keep them keen, Sir Joshua,' he said.

He had forgotten to wait for the trumpet to come back into place, but Sir Joshua bowed his head graciously, either because his hearing was not so bad after all, or in pretence of understanding what he assumed would be a compliment.

'I trust everything is to your satisfaction here?' the president asked, wafting his free hand in the direction of the Duke and Duchess of Cumberland on the wall behind him.

'Indeed. Completely,' said Tom. The warmth of the welcome put his five-year-old bitterness quite out of his head. It would be unworthy to continue to hold a grudge. 'However, I have not yet had the opportunity to view the rest of the work. Won't you show me your own paintings?'

The trumpet had been in place for that, and the president seemed to grow in stature as a proud beam flashed across his ruddy face.

'An honour, my good sir. Won't you step this way?'

He offered Tom his arm. Their difference in height made them an ill-matched pair, more like man and wife than two gentleman boulevarding together. Nevertheless, in this spirit of friendship they now proceeded to examine Sir Joshua's own entries.

There were two full-length society beauties. Lady Bamfylde had been captured in a pose that recalled a clothed Venus de' Medici; she was arrayed in flowing white draperies, which were matched by the trails of white lilies and daisies beside her, emphasising a purity that was sharply at variance with the reports of the lady's reputation that had reached Tom's ears. The other was the Countess of Derby, leaning on a plinth, apparently in conversation with a parrot.

'Such originality, such flair!' enthused Tom. The disposition of the figures in the Derby picture – the countess, the bird, and a stone statue looking on in the background – was undoubtedly arresting. 'How did you keep the parrot still? Is it stuffed?'

He meant no slight. If he could use vegetables and pebbles as models for the trees and rocks of his landscape, he had nothing but admiration for any similar tricks of the trade that allowed a resourceful colleague to study an exotic creature from the wild at leisure in his studio.

'It is a macaw, not a parrot,' said Sir Joshua, in a tone of rebuke. But there was a conspiratorial glint in his eye as he added: 'It would be a deceit if I denied the assistance of the taxidermist's hand. If I must bring creatures of the jungle into my studio, I would far sooner they be dead than alive, biting me and shitting everywhere.'

There was also a three-quarter length of a small figure standing in a winter landscape. Tom had noticed it from across the room. The skirted figure was dressed all in black, save for a red velvet muff in which her hands were conveniently encased, and she was peculiarly shapeless, with no suggestion of a waist or any other feminine contour, like some ancient creature who has lost all the defining graces of her sex. As they neared the work to inspect it, however, Tom saw that the subject was an infant of no more than two or three, swaddled in winter clothes.

'She is the little daughter of the Duke of Buccleuch,' said Sir Joshua proprietorially.

'Again, what a remarkable composition!' shouted Tom into

his companion's hearing aid. His every instinct was to pick up the poor mite and bring her into the warm.

'You are too generous, sir,' said Sir Joshua, bowing gravely.

Tom returned the bow.

'I have no doubt she will be a great success with the public,' he said. They would certainly remember it. 'And when does the King come?' he continued.

'I am told their majesties will honour us with their visit next week,' said Sir Joshua.

'They will have a capable and erudite guide to show them the work,' said Tom.

Sir Joshua inclined his head.

Tom could have laid odds they were both thinking the same thing: this was the role that he, Tom, had tried to usurp when he had let his name go forward for president. But all that was over and done with now, and he had been deservedly thrashed in the election. The two of them had effected an effusive public reconciliation with this encounter and he was glad the rancour was behind them.

It was time to take his leave. His nephew was dawdling in front of Lady Bamfylde, leaning in to examine the detail.

'Did you notice her hands, uncle?' he whispered, as he hastened after Tom down the grand stone staircase.

'Like claws,' muttered Tom. 'And I'll wager the complexion of that strange child in the winter scene will become stranger yet once the carmine in her face fades. It will be like chalk in six months.'

Young Dupont sniggered, and Tom felt a twinge of remorse at bad-mouthing Sir Joshua's work within two minutes of wishing him good speed. Was it not his duty, though, to draw his apprentice's attention to bad technique, that the youngster could profit from the lesson? Satisfied with the justice of this argument, he had banished all trace of guilt by the time they emerged into the sunlit pandemonium of Pall-mall.

It was only once they had found their carriage and were rattling back in the direction of home that he realised he had completely forgotten to check on the hang of his landscape.

Pall-mall,
April 22nd, 1777

To my dearest Ma

My heart was glad to receive the letter which Richard wrote
for you, although the tidings it contained made me sore at
heart. It pained to me to think of the ague that ailed you after
I was first gone, and I only rejoice and give thanks to the good
Lord that the malady has now passed.

I have now settled into this city and am becoming more used
to its ways. I hope you will pardon me but I have also begun to
venture forth alone from my master's house, as I will tell you
presently, because I had begun to fear that he or my mistress
would turn me out of their service as a footman if I refused to
run a footman's errands. I have now discovered that this place
is mayhap not so dangerous as you did make me fear.

I do not have the chance to explore this great place on my
own account, because I am at my master's beck and call from
afore sun-up till the stroke of midnight, or e'en thereafter if

he is out carousing and needs letting into the house when he returns in his cups. However, it is often my master's wish to send me hither and thither, and it has now been my great honour to attend no less a place than the Royal Academy.

I don't expect you have heard of this place, Ma, but it is a sort of club for the most esteemed artists, with the King's name above the door. Every year the members of this Academy have a display of their own paintings, which all the smart folk in the city pay half a shilling to look at. You would not believe the finery. If I say you could not find an inch of wall without a painting, I wager you will not believe me, but that is the truth.

When a painter like my master does the portrait of a great lady or gentleman, like the Duke of Cumberland that is the King's brother, and his wife that was known before as a strumpet but is now a Duchess, he calls them 'face pictures', but he don't just paint the face. He does the whole figure, from the tip of the slipper to the top of the hairpiece, and some of the ladies in London pile their hair astonishing high, so that is a fair distance. The painting of the person must always be the same size as the actual person, and then my master includes all kinds of things above and below, such as dogs or flowers at their feet and long views of mountains or forests behind them, and the sky above their heads, so a whole picture can be a full eight foot from top to bottom.

What you have to imagine, Ma, is that my master sends four or five of these full-lengths, as they are known, and so do all the other members of the Academy, who number more than three score, so all these great gentlefolk in their frames on the walls are pushing and shoving for space in no less a fashion than the publick paying their sixpences to look at them.

Not all the paintings are full-lengths. Some just show the head and shoulders of the sitter (as the person in the painting is called, whether they are sitting down or standing up), so they take up less space on the walls. Others go in the other direction: great scenes from history, of battles and such, painted broader than they are tall, full of people that are all so life-like, you fancy you are in the battle with them. And all these pictures come in great gold frames, carved and modelled almost as fine as the paintings inside them. These frames are packed in so tight that if you was to ask me what colour was the wall behind, I would not know the answer.

It has been my honour to see this show of pictures not once, but twice. The first time, I went with my master and his nephew, Mr Dupont, that is the son of our Mrs Dupont, who lives with us as my master's apprentice, and has the room next to me and Perkiss in the attic.

You may not believe me when I tell you, Ma, but it is the Lord's honest truth: at first, my master was too afeared to go inside, and would rather skulk downstairs in his carriage, while Mr Dupont and I checked to see if the placing of the pictures would be to his liking. I had no idea what would vex my master and what would not, but Mr Dupont thought he knew, and he said he reckoned the pictures were arranged to advantage, which was good. So we went back down to the carriage to bring my master upstairs, with him feigning there was never nothing amiss and he was not afeared, although Mr Dupont and I both knew he was really.

When he saw his pictures, he was right pleased. There was a big smile on his face, and he bowed and waved his hand at all the other gentlemen in their wigs, who were the other painters. He greeted one of them special friendly, a gentleman as talked in the strangest way you ever did hear, like he had a spoonful of porridge in his mouth and had forgot to take out the spoon. He was called Mr West and he talks like that because he is from

America (I only knowed this because Mr Dupont explained it). If they all speak like that, I wonder how any of them ever understands each other.

Then my master talked to a very little gentleman with cheeks as red as our Jack's mouth after he has been scrumping mulberries. Any person who wants to converse with this gentleman must needs direct their talk into a funnel that he holds up to his ear, else he cannot hear a word. My master was grinning and bowing at him like it was the best friend he ever had, and you could have knocked me over with a willow frond when I heard him call him 'Sir Joshua', which is short for Sir Joshua Reynolds, the greatest painter in the realm (only I must never say so in my master's hearing) and the president of the Royal Academy. My master and he are said to despise each other most bitterly, but I could not see any hate in the face of either.

After that we returned home, but my master fretted all the way about his picture of a herd of cows in a wooded glade. Do not ask me why he chuses to paint such a subject: if you forget what a cow looks like, you can easily go down to Fullingpit Meadow to see one for yourself. That's what I think, but my master likes to paint cows in his landskips, only he was talking so much to his friend Sir Joshua that he clean forgot to look out for this one. Mr Dupont forgot too, and I could hear my master inside the coach telling him he were a great blockhead.

My master was still fretting about it the next morning, which was the day the exhibition opened to the publick. He did not want to show his own face to the general mass, so he gave Mr Dupont and me sixpence apiece and bade us go back there, just so he could rest easy that his landskip were in a proper place.

You never did see such a multitude indoors, all of them dressed as fine as you like. They were all trying to look at the paintings and getting proper peevish with any persons obstructing their view. Honest, Ma, you would imagine these fine folk would have the highest manners and behave in a nice way, but they do not. They were all a-prodding and a-poking each other with their fans and canes to make them shift out of their way, as bad as any ill-bred folk, so it is not true that gentlefolk is gentle.

Mr Dupont is better used to London ways than I, and he was not too shy to push his way through. Also the ladies let him pass because he is pretty, with his lashes and his curls, and some of them put their fans to their faces, which is what fine ladies do in this city when they are no better than they should be.

I was slower following him, but it was no time afore I saw him coming back. He was biting his lip, like he does when he has a worry on him, and he acquainted me as how he had found my master's landskip, and its position was not so good at all, viz. it was quite high up, so it was hard to see what the cattle were about. 'Twas a bad discovery for Mr Dupont and me, but mainly for Mr Dupont, for it fell to him to break the tidings to my master, and we both knew he would not take it gladly.

We dawdled back home very slow and, when we reached the house, I made myself scarce and let Mr Dupont proceed, unhindered by my presence. I knew by the shouting when he had done it, and the whole house could hear as how Sir Joshua Reynolds was a coxcomb. My master was bellowing it so loud, I would not be surprised if Sir Joshua himself could hear it at the other end of Pall-mall, without the need of his funnel. That evening he stayed out very late drinking gin, for that was what I smelled on his breath when he came a-banging on the door in the early hours of the morning, and he was most ill-tempered in the morning, for he cried a pox on me when I tried to enter his chamber to take his cup of chocolate.

A little after that, my mistress called me aside and said as how she had an idea that might help. She bade me run out and fetch all the morning prints. That meant I must go out alone, and I obeyed, for I had no choice. I comforted myself that the King's press-gangs were not likely to be abroad at that early hour, and I am happy to say that I returned safely from my mission without mishap. I saw other footmen in their livery about their own errands and I began to form the opinion that perchance I had been too strict to follow your instruction, if you pardon me, Ma, and this city is not so hazardous after all.

On my return, my master had roused himself and was sitting nicely at breakfast with my mistress, the Misses Molly and Peggy and the dogs, who are treated as full members of this household. My mistress told my master that she had sent me to fetch the prints, but he was still in an ill humour. 'A pox on the prints, madam, a pox on the pictures, I do not give a fig,' said he, and I noted Miss Molly and Miss Peggy a-blushing at the ripeness of his phrase. My mistress told him fie, that was no way to speak or think, and she set about opening up the papers to find something that might lift his spirits.

The first one she picked up was the *Public Advertiser*. Despite his grousing, my master decided to go along with this notion, and he picked up another of them, the *Gazetteer*. As ill-fortune would have it, he found the notice before my mistress could find hers, and it was a bad one. We knew this from his cry of rage, which was so loud it sent poor Fox fleeing out of the room. We all learned the reason as my master read aloud from the newspaper: the gentleman from the *Gazetteer* thought that, aside from works by Sir Joshua and another painter whose name I forget, but 'twas not my master, this was the meanest collection of pictures ever seen.

My master threw the paper down on the table so it near upset his chocolate, but my mistress piped up that she had found the notice in the *Advertiser*. That one was much more favourable. It said how glad the paper was to see Mr Gainsborough once more submitting his work to publick inspection, which could not fail to add to the entertainment of the town. They said 'twas hard to know in which branch of the art he most excelled, landskip or portrait (which is face-pictures).

My master was still snorting through his nose, but not quite so angry, more like a horse when it is in a good humour.

Then Miss Molly, who has a very doleful countenance (and, between you and me, Ma, is not always quite right in the head), took up the *Morning Chronicle*. She read out the notice, and it started out most promising, saying that, as a landscape painter, my master was one of the finest living. This was good, of course, but I could sense what Miss Molly could not, that there might be something not so good coming. And when it came, it was this: that he was almost as fine with portraits as Sir Joshua, and it was not always clear that Sir Joshua was better.

Now the writer of this notice clearly wanted to pay my master a compliment, but you can only give a compliment to a person who is in the mood to receive it, and my master was not. He was in the contrary humour, looking for offence where none was meant.

Now he shouted, 'So I am sometimes as good as Sir Joshua, am I?' and he snatched the *Morning Chronicle* from Miss Molly's hands. I could see her lip begin to quiver, which is always a sign that a young lady is about to cry (although Miss Molly is not so young any more, she is a grown woman of nearly thirty years old). He set to read the notice, and I could see the side of his temple start to throb under his wig. He began to read aloud the harshest parts of the notice, which said his flesh tints were too purple and his Duke of Cumberland was inferior to Sir Joshua's. To show his disgust he rolled the whole *Chronicle* into a football and threw it into the grate. 'Twas just as well it is April and there was no fire, else it might have set the chimney ablaze, and it would have been my job to put it out.

Miss Molly was still quivering, but my mistress, who is never one to give up, took up the last of the papers I had brought, which was the *Morning Post*, and cried out 'Look!' in such a mighty voice that it made e'en my master pay attention. She was pointing at the words at the top of the notice. Where you would expect to read 'Royal Academy Exhibition', or some such, instead it said 'Thomas Gainsborough'. I could see as how this was a kick in the teeth to Sir Joshua and all the other painters who had their pictures hung on the walls of that room.

My master's mood changed in an instant. Ah, Bate, said he, all smiles. What does the fine fellow say? It turns out that Reverend Bate, the editor of the *Post*, is a good friend of my master, and he said in his notice that my master's picture of Mr Able is the finest modern portrait he remembered seeing. Mr Able is a famous player of musick, and a friend of my master, so he comes often to this house. He is German and he speaks in a most peculiar way, even more peculiar than the American gentleman Mr West – although in Mr Able's defence, he already has a language, and he has mastered English as a second one, when Mr West has no such excuse.

Now Miss Molly piped up, saying that the picture of Mr Able was almost as fine as the picture of Mr Fisher. As she said it, a light came into her face that made her almost pretty. The same remark, though, put a black cloud on the face of Miss Peggy. You see, Mr Fisher is another German player of musick who is often in this house, but as much to cast glances at Miss

Molly and Miss Peggy as to drink chocolate with my master, or so it seems to me, and the young misses are jealous of each other in consequence.

Normally such a remark would enrage my master, because he is mighty jealous where his daughters are concerned, but on this occasion he did not even notice. He was all puffed up like a turkeycock, his previous rage quite forgot. You know how our Jack can bawl his eyes out over some hurt or grievance one minute and laugh like an idiot the next, with all the injury forgot? My master is the same, and he does not have the excuse of being five years old.

My mistress continued to read from the notice, telling my master that his landskip was a masterpiece, in the opinion of Mr Bate. My master was very pleased at this, but not so pleased by the next line, which Miss Molly read over her mother's shoulder, saying that the landskip was viewed to every possible disadvantage from the situation in which the directors of the Academy had thought to place it.

My mistress pulled the paper away and jabbed her finger into Miss Molly's arm, making her cry out, but the damage was done, and my master was in a rage again, saying that Sir Joshua could go to the D___l. He worked himself up so much that he bade me fetch his hat and coat so he could go round to the Academy that very minute and demand the picture be moved.

My mistress tried to calm him, saying it was too late to intermeddle with the arrangement of the pictures now that the exhibition was open, with the multitude in the room all the day and every inch of the wall covered. He would surely be refused, she said, and she warned him that refusal would enrage him all the more, which I am certain is the truth.

Now Miss Peggy, who had been silent all the while, piped

up to ask if the *Post* did not mention Sir Joshua at all. I fancy she knew it did, for she is a sharp one. My mistress put her head back in the *Post* to check, and then started laughing, so much that in no time at all her cheeks were shining wet. This was quite a sight, for my mistress do not laugh much as a rule.

Now, of course, my master wanted to know what was so comical. And it turned out that this Reverend Bate had been exceeding rude about Sir Joshua, making sport at his expense, saying he was so anxious for his faces not to fade away, as they have done in the past, that he had started to paint his sitters dark, like Hindoos. I thought my master would rupture himself, he laughed so hard. His face turned red as a boiled beet and he smashed his fist on the table so that the cups jumped out of their saucers, and everyone else laughed too.

So you see, Ma, that is how things are in this house: the mood changes like the weather, and it can rain and shine three times in the same hour. I have told you this story at length, and I hope I have not been too tedious, because I wanted you to understand the world that I am now living in.

How different it is from your own quiet little world with Richard and Jack, although I know of course that life is much harder for you than it is for my master and my mistress, because you do not have servants such as me to perform all your duties for you, and you must either do them yourself or leave them undone. This is our lot, when we are base-born, although I swear to you I am not ashamed of my humble station in life.

Which subject reminds me: I have learned from Perkiss the reason for Cook's zeal in banning me from her kitchen, except when I am taking my dinner and my supper. In my innocence when I arrived in this house, I fancied she took me for a light-fingers who would thieve her bread and pies, and thus bring the wrath of the mistress down on her own head, a trial which no right-thinking person would suffer willingly to happen. Since then, however, I have come to realise that was not it at all. 'Twas not her loaves and her sweetmeats that Cook was so keen to safeguard, but the virtue of Annie, the little parlour-maid as breaks my master's china every time she is called to serve tea. Cook is convinced that any young man entering this house will have designs on Annie's purity, but I will take my oath, Ma, as I hope to be saved, that no idea could be further from my mind. You raised me in a decent Christian way, so I am not the kind of ill-mannered young rascal who would ill use a member of the fair sex, even in this wicked city where sin is all around. I own, though, that this is not the only reason that Annie's virtue is safe. I do not wish to sound ungallant, Ma, but the poor creature has the face of a dormouse, with little teeth that stick out at the front, and the shy manner of the same. There may be a thousand parlour-maids in this city whose presence in a house would tempt a young footman into naughty conduct, but our poor Annie is not among them. I tried to explain this to Cook, but her zeal was not abated and she told me warmly that she would box my ears if ever I spoke of the subject again. I fear as how she means it, which is a pity, for I yearn to set foot in that kitchen more often, not on Annie's account, but because Cook do make the most tasty pies.

Now I have made myself hungry just thinking about them, but there is nothing to be done about it. The hour is now late and I must stop this letter, else I will be too tired for my duties tomorrow and my master will call me a numbskull more times than usual. So before I blow my bit of candle out, I send big kisses to everyone, and most especially to you, from your ever loving

David

6

Muriel Mudge was being filmed for her preview interview, before her formal encounter with a *Britain's Got Treasures* expert, and it was not going well.

The reticence she had shown with Gemma was compounded by her obvious discomfort in front of a camera. Theo, an assistant producer with exaggeratedly geeky glasses, who was asking the questions, was doing his best to put her at her ease and make her forget the lens was there. As soon as the camera started rolling, however, she visibly stiffened, panic in her eyes. Her answers, hardly forthcoming even without the camera to inhibit her, became more forced than ever, delivered through a rictus of concentration. And so far Theo had only asked her name and where she was from.

'Relax, Muriel,' he said.

Muriel's jaw tensed as she clenched her teeth.

'Let's try it again from the top. In fact, let's try a little rehearsal, just to get you comfy in front of the camera. Why don't you start off by telling me what you had for breakfast this morning?'

'Why do you want to know that?'

'I don't particularly. I mean, it's not important. If you don't want to tell me what you had, it doesn't matter. I don't want to invade your privacy. Just make something up, I really don't care…'

Gemma, watching from just outside the shot, stifled a giggle.

'OK then,' said Theo. 'Let's go back to Plan A. Can you tell me your name and where you live?'

The rictus of concentration returned.

'My name is Muriel Mudge, that's 'Miss' not 'Mrs', and I already gave my address to the young lady when I came in.'

Theo bit his lower lip.

'Yeah no, it's not actually your address we need. Just the town or village, wherever you've travelled from to be with us today.'

'I a'n't travelled from anywhere. I only live in School Lane.'

'No problem. Just say the name of the town. "I'm Muriel Mudge, and I'm from…" That's all we want. All-righty, from the top?'

Eventually, Muriel was induced to identify herself and her home town in one complete sentence, without freezing or looking at the camera.

'And why have you come here today, Muriel?'

'Well, because it's *Antiques on the Road*, innut?'

Theo's smile faded.

'It's actually *Britain's Got Treasures*.'

'Shall I say it again?'

'Not to worry, because that wasn't quite the answer I was looking for, if I'm honest. My fault, I should have been clearer. You've brought us something today which is very special to you, haven't you? Tell me why you thought we should see it.'

'Well, I saw the notice in the free paper, and it said if we had any old treasures, we should bring them. So I have.'

Theo nodded frantically and gave her a thumbs-up. 'And that treasure... no, you don't need to unwrap it, I think you're going to show it to Kaz shortly, and we can film it properly then... Just tell me why it's so precious to you.'

'It's precious because it's been in my family for a long time. I had it from my father when he passed on, and he had it from his, and so on, all the way back.'

'And how old do you think it might be?'

'I don't think, I know. Two hundred years odd. Stands to reason.'

'And you're certain of that?'

'Course I am. It's been passed down.'

'And you're hoping to sell it for a lot of money?'

'Sell it? You're jokin'! Not after it came down to me from my father, and to him from his, all down the generations. I just thought your experts might like to see it.'

'And... cut!' said Theo. 'There, we got there in the end, didn't we?'

Having got into her stride, Muriel looked bewildered to have been cut off.

'Don't you want to see it?'

'Of course we do,' said Gemma, stepping forward and guiding Muriel by the arm towards the corner of the nave, where she could see Fiammetta briefing Regina and Kaz. 'I'm going to introduce you to Regina, our presenter. Perhaps you've seen her reading the news? And you're also going to meet our expert, Kaz Kareem. You may remember him from *Big Brother*. No? He's going to have a proper look at your treasure and give you his evaluation. Happy so far?'

Behind her wide smile, guilt was stabbing at her conscience. Muriel had seemed so defensive and hostile at first that Gemma had no qualms about exposing her grotesque picture to ridicule. Now that she had begun to open up, however, Gemma had seen a more sympathetic side to her, and she was not proud of her own role in the woman's eventual humiliation. She took a deep breath and told herself that she was only a very small cog in a machine that would be grinding up people's delusions and vanities whether she was part of it or not. If she wanted to get on in this industry, this kind of stuff had to be done. She just had to woman up and get on with it.

Having seen them coming, Fiammetta now turned to face them with a wide, treacherous smile.

'Muriel, isn't it? My name's Fiammetta and I'm the producer. We're so pleased you came to see us today. Can I introduce you to Regina, our presenter?'

Regina, who was only a fraction taller than Muriel, held out a tiny hand, impressively tanned for February. Behind her immaculate plum lipstick and ferocious bronzer, she too was beaming for all she was worth.

'Veally pleased to meet you, Muviel. And veally, veally looking forward to seeing your tveasure. Yes, if you wouldn't mind unvapping it, I would vey much like… Oh my! Oh, I say…!'

Gemma had worried she might have oversold her find. The two women's reaction dispelled any such concerns.

'It's very old,' ventured Muriel.

'It's remarkable,' said Fiammetta. 'I can honestly say I've never seen anything like it.'

A small crowd had gathered, as Vivian Morris and a couple of technicians stopped what they were doing to take the object in. One of the technicians clapped a hand to his mouth, setting a wristful of bangles jingling, in a poorly disguised attempt to smother a laugh. Vivian's expression was more serious. It was a house rule that the expert to whom an object had been designated was not allowed to see it until the on-camera reveal. Since this one had been assigned to Kaz, there was nothing to stop Vivian having a look. He leaned closer, tilting his head back to examine the detail of the image through the bottom part of his bifocals.

'Now, Muriel,' said Fiammetta briskly, loosely folding the wrapping back around the picture and returning it to its owner. 'If you'd just like to pop yourself over there for a sec, we'll set up, and we'll come back to you very soon. All right?'

Muriel did as she was told, clutching her precious possession to her chest within folded arms and making her way over to the institutional plastic chair to which she had been directed.

Gemma noticed that Vivian was still standing in the same spot, his chin cradled in his hand, lost in thought.

'Gemma!'

Fiammetta was beckoning to her with a crooked forefinger held close to her face: an instruction to go over for a discreet word.

'Is everything OK?'

This was a constant worry, where Fiammetta was concerned.

'*Au contraire*, darling, it all looks fabulous. You were quite right to bring this straight to me. I just wanted to know how the preview interview went. Did she say anything interesting?'

Gemma pulled a 'meh' face.

'She was quite hard work. She's really stiff and guarded in front of the camera. Theo was trying his best to relax her, but it was all a bit painful. One thing, though: she did say this painting has been passed down her family from generation to generation, and she's certain it's at least two hundred years old. I don't know how she knows that, but she's adamant. She got quite stroppy when she thought Theo was doubting her.'

'In a way it's so sad,' Fiammetta sighed. 'I've seen people like her before: I bet she hasn't got a bean to her name, so she's fixating on some hideous old tat that has been passed down through the family like an heirloom, with no inkling that it's completely worthless.'

'Actually she doesn't want to sell it. That's one thing Theo did manage to get out of her. She says she'll never part with it, and she seemed really irritated at the suggestion she would.'

Fiammetta raised a pencilled eyebrow.

'I guess it takes all sorts. Anyway, it looks like they're ready for her over there. Can you take her over?'

In a pool of lights in the nearest corner of the nave, Kaz Kareem was finishing up with the previous hopeful, a cheerful-looking woman in a fleece and sensible shoes, who was returning some item of brassware to her jute bag-for-life. From her shrug, it was clear that Kaz's valuation had not been encouraging, but she seemed to have taken it in good heart.

As she moved way from the lit area, Kaz called after her: 'But whaddo I know? I'm just a fat poof from Essex!'

The woman winced. Seeing Gemma watching her, she rolled her eyes and shook her head indulgently.

Muriel was sitting waiting patiently. Gemma offered a hand to help her to her feet.

'And who do we have next?' Kaz was saying, peering off-camera in their direction.

Gemma guided Muriel towards the pool of lights by a quivering elbow, gently nudging her towards him.

'Hello, my dear,' he beamed. 'And you are?'

'Muriel, Muriel Mudge. Miss,' said Muriel.

She looked smaller and more stooped than ever under the white lights.

'And what treasure have you brought to show us, my darling? Is that it? Yes, please, you unwrap it. I love this part,' he mugged as an aside to the camera. 'It's like Christmas, innit, only they're doing the unwrapping!'

The small group of onlookers who had either shown their own treasures already, or had only come to spectate, tittered obligingly.

Muriel was fumbling with the wrappings.

'Here, let me take that off of you,' said Kaz, relieving her of a bundle of newspaper and handing it discreetly on for disposal off-camera. 'It's exciting, innit? I can see a frame. I'm guessing a picture, am I right? Oh yes, definitely a frame, definitely a picture. So go on, turn it round. I'm dying to see… Oh my giddy fucking uncle!'

He clapped his hand over his mouth in histrionic penance for his profanity. There might be a token slapped wrist later, but Gemma knew that Fiammetta would adore the spontaneity, and a judiciously inserted bleep would add to the comedy of the moment.

Recovering some of his composure, he took one side of the picture while Muriel held the other, so that the camera could get in closer.

'So, Muriel,' he said. 'Tell me what we're looking at.'

'It's a painting,' said Muriel.

'Of…?' said Kaz, making a rotating motion with his hand to encourage her to continue.

'I don't know who it's of.'

'But we can say it's a man of…what sort of age? About fifty?'

'I don't rightly know. Maybe fifty. Maybe forty. Maybe sixty.'

'Right. But he's also got…erm…' He made the rotating motion again, but she looked at him blankly, so he was obliged to finish his own sentence. 'He's got ears like a donkey, hasn't he? I mean, they're hard to miss. And they're not a feature you see on many men in real life, are they? Am I being fair?'

'They're unusual,' Muriel conceded.

'And why would you say the painter has put them there? Was this man some kind of freak of nature, a circus exhibit? Was he on his way to a costume party?'

'I've no idea. That's why I brought it. I was hopin' you might tell me.'

'I see,' said Kaz, flashing an eye-roll at the camera, which had pulled back from the picture and had both of them in its frame again. 'And there's one other thing that immediately hits the eye, if you don't mind me pointing it out, Muriel. It's quite damaged, this painting, isn't it? It looks like it's been cut into four pieces and then stitched together again.'

'Yes,' Muriel agreed. 'Someone has repaired it. Long before I got it, though.'

'They haven't done it very skilfully, to be fair.'

Muriel blinked at him.

'Can I be honest with you, Muriel?' said Kaz, placing his palm flat on his own chest to emphasise his sincerity and looking at her with wide-eyed sorrow. 'I'm afraid it's hideous. It's a complete mess and, I'm not gonna lie to you, I just can't understand why you've brought it.'

Gemma caught her breath, wondering if Muriel might burst into tears on camera. She wished she could make this cruelty stop. She glanced at Fiammetta, whose eyes were shining. Regina was actually hugging herself. Next to them, though,

Vivian was frowning.

Muriel was now staring at Kaz in disbelief.

'I brought it because it's a…'

Kaz bent down closer to hear, as her voice dropped.

'Because it's a what, my love?'

'Because it's a Gainsborough.'

'A what?'

'A Gainsborough.'

Kaz's eyes widened.

'A Gainsborough! One of England's greatest painters! Is it? Are you sure, Muriel? Are you really sure?'

He flashed another look at the camera, tapping the side of his head with his index finger as if to say, we've got a right one here. This time, Muriel saw him doing it.

'Yes I am sure, but this has been a mistake. Pearls before swine.'

She pulled the picture away from Kaz and, before he could react, she was pushing her way past Fiammetta and Vivian towards the door of the church. Her face was red with emotion and her lip was trembling.

'Don't be like that, Muriel!' called Kaz, with the cameras still rolling.

Muriel had already got as far as the porch, with her head down and her precious picture clutched to her chest.

Now Fiammetta was hissing at Gemma: 'Get after her! Bring her back!'

How was she meant to do that? If Muriel had no wish to be humiliated on camera, Gemma did not see how she could talk her round. There was no point in trying to say that to Fiammetta, however, particularly with a bunch of stunned-looking spectators watching their every move. She had at least to look like she was trying to get Muriel back. She hurried after her.

From the doorway of the church, she scanned the square. It was busier now, with more shoppers, and at first Gemma could not see Muriel. Surely she could not have gone far? Then she caught sight of the small, dark figure hurrying along the pavement outside Boots.

'Muriel! Miss Mudge!' she called.

She ran down the pavement, mouthing 'no thank you' at a *Big Issue* seller with a plaintive, East European accent, and hopping into the road to get past a harassed-looking dog-walker in a tangle of leads.

Muriel was at the bottom of the square when she caught her up.

'Muriel, please. Miss Mudge,' she panted, touching her on the elbow. 'Stop a minute.'

To her surprise, Muriel did abruptly stop, and now she stood peering up out of her arthritic hunch at Gemma, with an expression of unalloyed hurt.

'Why would he talk to me like that?' she said. 'What have I ever done to him?'

'I know,' said Gemma. 'He was horrible. It's just… That's how television works. It wasn't personal. I think Kaz was just a bit shocked by… Well, you must admit, your painting is quite strange looking.'

'I know it's a mess, of course I do,' said Muriel sadly. 'It's been cut up and badly repaired, and I've no idea why the man in the picture has asses' ears. To know the answer to that, we'd have to ask Gainsborough' – she nodded in the direction of the statue at the top of the square – 'but we can't because he's been dead more than two hundred years.'

Gemma took Muriel's hand and squeezed it, hoping that this was not too presumptuous.

'Can you really believe it's a Gainsborough?' she said. 'I won't lie, I don't know much about him. Like Kaz said, though, he was one of this country's greatest-ever painters. And this picture… I'm sorry, but it is a bit of a monstrosity.'

Having permitted her hand to be held, Muriel now slipped it free.

'I know it is, but it has been handed down in my family for generations, to my father from his, to his father from his, and so on, and I've always been told it's a Gainsborough, because that's what they said. That's why we kept it. Who am I to say any different? I'm not an educated person, but I would like to be treated with a little respect. Is that too much to ask?'

'No,' said Gemma miserably. 'No, it isn't. But why don't you come back and explain all that to Kaz? We can film it all again, if you like.'

She wished that were true, but she also knew that Fiammetta would regard the existing footage as gold dust, and would want to build on it, not throw it away.

Now it was Muriel's turn to take Gemma's arm, pulling her closer as she continued: 'Can you promise me, if I go back in that church with you now, that I'll be treated with decent, human respect?' She pronounced it 'hoo-man'. 'Can you?'

Gemma sighed.

'You know what? In all honesty, I can't. And I actually don't blame you.'

Fiammetta would be furious, but she was not prepared to talk Muriel back under false pretences.

'If you don't want to come back, don't. Unfortunately, I can't guarantee that we won't use the footage we've already got, so the programme may well show you walking out, and there's nothing I can do about that.'

'What if I don't give my permission for it to be shown?'

'I'm afraid you've done that already, on the form you signed when you came in. All I can tell you is that my boss is really keen for you to come back, because she wants to make your painting into a big element of the programme. And if you go back, they may not treat you with any more respect. Or perhaps they will to your face, but they can change things afterwards, when they edit it. I really shouldn't be telling you this, so please don't say I did. But if I were you…'

As she spoke, she looked around to check that no one from the production team was within earshot, because talking like this was probably a sacking offence. She did not expect to see any of her colleagues: it was more of an instinctive thing. So she was amazed to see a tall, thin figure in tweeds striding towards them.

'Muriel,' he called as he neared, offering a long, ruddy hand in greeting. 'I'm Vivian Morris, another of the experts. I'm sorry for the way you were treated just now.'

Muriel accepted his hand, but she remained guarded.

'They must really want me to go back in there to be laughed at, if they've sent you after me, as well as her,' she said.

'Nobody sent me. I came because I wanted to. If they had asked me, I 'ud've said no.'

They shared an accent. No wonder he instinctively sympathised with her.

'I came to ask if you'd mind showing me your paintin'. You showed it to Kaz, but I'd like a proper look too, if I may. That's not too much to ask, izzut?'

'I'm not going back in that church under them cameras,' said Muriel, clutching the painting to her chest. She had not had time to wrap it again, but she pressed it with the image to her clothing, so that only the ageing backing paper was visible.

'That's fine. I'm not asking you to. Show it me here, if you like. Let's get off the pavement, where it's a bit more private.'

He ushered her into the wide, covered doorway of an estate agent's, out of the path of buggies and shopping trolleys. As Gemma followed, Muriel slowly turned the picture around.

'Thank you, Muriel. I appreciate this,' said Vivian. Steeped in decades of liquorice roll-ups, his voice was rich and soothing.

He took the picture from her, holding it close to his face and tilting it towards the sky to catch the grey February light. In this fashion, he allowed his eye to travel all over the damaged canvas, from the sitter's sketchily painted coat to his chin, to the rough stitching that crossed at the subject's nose, and then up to his eyes and the alarming furry ears, to which Vivian paid particularly close attention. Finally he held the picture at arm's length so he could see the whole thing.

'Would you allow me to take a photograph, Muriel?'

She lifted her chin at him by way of grudging assent.

'Thank you. Would you hold it for me?'

She took the picture back, and he pulled his phone from the pocket of his jacket.

'Now if I can just find the right setting…' He held the camera up. 'There now…and there…and one more…and one for luck. Thank you, Muriel, for showing it to me.' He slipped his phone back into his pocket. 'Now, if we need to, do we know how to get in contact with you?'

'I gave my address to her, on the form I signed,' said Muriel, nodding at Gemma.

'Good. Perhaps we'll be in touch.'

He held his hand out. Again, she took it, looking thoroughly bewildered now. She was not the only one: Gemma was not sure what had just happened, either.

Vivian turned to her.

'Gemma, if Fiammetta asks, I'm just nipping out for half an

hour. Tell her I've gone to the pub, if you like.'

'But you're not going to the pub?'

'I've got to see a man about a dog,' he said, tapping the side of his nose. With that, he strode off towards the bottom of the square.

'Where's he going?' asked Muriel. 'I don't understand.'

'Join the club,' said Gemma.

She remembered that Fiammetta was waiting for them.

'So, just to be clear, you're not coming back inside, are you?'

'No, I am not! I thought that was settled.'

'It is, but I need my boss to believe I've tried my best to get you back. Would you agree that I've tried?'

The trace of a smile ran across Muriel's lips.

'You go back and tell her you tried your best but I'm too stubborn to persuade. It's the truth.'

Gemma nodded.

'Right, thank you. Will do. And again, I'm sorry.'

Now all she had to do was face Fiammetta.

7

On the folding oak table in front of his easel, Tom had constructed a section of countryside in miniature. In the foreground were small pieces of coal, representing rocks. In the middleground, he had spread sand. In the finished picture, this would be a river, but the grit established the lie of the land. In the background towered a forest of broccoli. The light would come from a setting sun in the distance, and he now lit a tallow candle and placed it on a stand of its own, just beyond the table. Its yellow flicker cast the shadow of the broccoli onto the darkened walls of the studio so that it really did look like a forest.

It was a bright summer morning outside but, as ever, Tom had bidden the boy David pull all the blinds down so that he could control his own light source. Working alone, with just Fox for company, was part of the pleasure of painting a landscape. If he painted a face, the owner of that face need to be entertained, flattered and generally indulged, and Fox was not allowed into the studio in case the sitter had an aversion to animals, so that a sitting of two or three hours became an interminable ordeal. This, by contrast, was blissfully tranquil. He slipped a piece of roasted rabbit from his pocket to Fox, who snatched it deftly from his fingers and sat up attentively in hope of more. Tom wagged his finger to say that that was all for now, and took up a thick hog brush to block out the the middleground in a loose wash of raw umber, ignoring the two piercing eyes staring up at him, trying to wear down his resolve.

Another great benefit of landscape painting was the financial liberty it afforded him. His prices for face pictures had been widely advertised, which meant that Mrs Gainsborough, the guardian of the household treasury, knew exactly how many guineas were due to him when he painted a half- or a full-length. The cost to a client of a landscape painting was more obscure, for the simple reason that the commissions were much rarer. While any person wishing to be taken seriously in society desired to display their likeness above their chimneypiece, they felt no parallel obligation to display pictures of peasant families gathered at the doors of woodland cottages, of the sort that Tom enjoyed making. In consequence, there was no established scale of prices for the different sizes of canvas. His charge for any such commission was a more *ad hoc* affair, depending on his own estimation of the client's ability to pay. Thus far, he had managed to keep the details of all such transactions from his wife, which meant that any resulting fee was his to spend. If only the rest of life were so simple.

Two years had passed since his return to the Royal Academy.

Work was plentiful. There was no shortage of eminent – and sometimes scandalous – personages willing to visit his studio at the back of the house in Pall-mall and sit while he captured their likeness in pigment and oil.

He had not had the confidence in his standing to put his rates up, but he had learned to increase his income by working faster, thereby enabling him to undertake more commissions. In this business, the face was everything. If he could establish a strong and pleasing likeness, the rest of the picture could be finished quickly and no client would complain. Sitters were sometimes surprised to see him take up a sponge, rather than a brush, to block the colour of a silk dress, and then to capture the finest embroidery with a few zigzags or hatches, or a bright dab of impasto. When he showed them the finished work, he made sure they stood at the correct distance, where the magic of the paint made it seem as if he had caught every stitch and ruffle. When they went closer, the detail dissolved, but by that time they had experienced the illusion and were satisfied.

He had become so fast at the backgrounds and clothing that he had on occasion made pretence of needing a week of finishing-off time after the sitter had gone; otherwise they were liable to wonder why they were paying thirty guineas for no more than an hour of his time, as had been the case with the Linley boy in Bath. That was a special case: the lad had just been made a midshipman and was in a hurry to get to his ship, so Tom had dashed the picture off in forty-eight minutes flat. It showed, there was no doubt, but in this case the client was pitiably grateful: poor Sam died of a fever contracted on his first voyage, and Tom's hurried portrait was all his grieving father had left of him.

Now that he was capable of such a rapid output, he was no longer as worried as he had been about funding the expenses of the household. What did preoccupy him was the composition of that household, viz. two daughters with no husbands and no means of supporting themselves when he was no longer there to provide.

If he had had his way, they would each by now be teaching music or drawing to smart young ladies. There was no shame in that for the granddaughters of a Suffolk shroud-maker, just as there was no shame in their aunt, Tom's sister, setting up shop as a milliner. Unfortunately, their grand style of living, first in Bath and now here in Pall-mall, within shouting distance of the royal palaces, had given them ideas. The fact that they were liable to trip over the Duke of This and the Duchess of That in their own hallway had given them the notion that they were not so much the teachers of smart young ladies, as smart young ladies in their own right. It was true, they were waited on by servants and rode out in their own carriage; but they were not gentlefolk, whatever the company their father might keep. This had become all too apparent in Bath, where the avidity of their husband-hunting was beyond reproach, but its results were woefully lacking: the invitations they so craved to the smartest salons and balls, where the eligible young men were all to be found, simply never came.

Persuading them to peg their expectations to a more realistic measure of their own station would have been easier if their mother had helped temper their ambitions. Her writ was the law of the household where financial matters were concerned, and proper direction from her would have cured them of their wilder fantasies. On social questions, however, she was prone to the same delusions as her daughters, and was more likely to encourage than to quash them. She saw Tom keeping company with the finest gentlemen in the land, and she expected to do the same with their wives. In fact, she thought she was more entitled to do so than he was. She could not forget – and she would not let him forget – that her own blood was so much nobler than his.

The problem, as he could never quite muster the courage to explain, was that her origins were cloaked by a gag of secrecy, not to be revealed even to Tom's own kin. He had deeply appreciated his wife's paternity in the early days of their marriage, because of the two hundred pounds a year that came with it. It was made clear, however, that the payment would be cut off immediately if the noble gentleman in question were ever publicly identified as Margaret's father. The fact that she was only secretly acknowledged meant that social recognition would never ensue.

So the three of them continued to wait for invitations worthy of their standing, and still those invitations failed to arrive. The result was a household seething with affront, and two daughters approaching their fourth decade of existence with neither husbands nor means of independent support.

The closest either of them had come was the rapscallion Fischer, who had once been Tom's own friend, although that friendship had become impossible to pursue. Like Tom, Fischer was a fellow of the middling sort who enjoyed entry to drawing rooms far beyond his natural standing by dint of being an artist – in his case, a musician. He played the hautboy angelically, which diverted attention from the fact that he spoke English execrably. He was a favourite of the Queen, who cared little that his English was so poor, because they could speak German together.

Tom liked the society of musicians, and would spend all his time in the company of Bach and Abel, through whom he had met Fischer, if he could. What he liked about them, however – their fondness for carousing and their Teutonic bluntness when it came to the satisfaction of their appetites – was precisely what made Fischer so undesirable as a son-in-law. Besides, the blackguard was Tom's own age. At first, in his innocence, he had welcomed the grinning jackass into his own home, glad to have him call. Only when he saw the eyes the Captain was making did the alarums begin to sound. He took every care not to leave the pair alone together. Congratulating himself on his vigilance, he had thought the danger averted until he discovered a letter revealing that Molly, the other slyboots, was the real, and very willing, object of Fischer's pursuit. As a result the havoc in his household was twofold: one daughter with a heart broken because she had been overlooked; the other plotting a course that must surely break his own.

Fischer was no longer welcome, and Tom had not set eyes on his shameless, laughing face – a more handsome face than any man in his middle forties deserved to have – for several months. Letters no doubt passed between the lovers, and Tom was under no illusions about his power to prevent them meeting: any sweethearts could engineer a rendez-vous in this wicked city if they were sufficiently determined. At present, his hopes rested chiefly on that determination waning. This was quite likely on Fischer's side, because he was sure to find some other distraction in a petticoat soon enough. There were grounds for optimism in Molly's case, too, albeit with a deeply regrettable cause.

For some years she had been prone to a nervous disorder which afflicted her for a few weeks and then vanished. During one of these episodes, it had no longer been possible to keep Doctor Moysey from the house, and his verdict had come as a blade of cold steel in her father's heart: it was a family complaint, Moysey said, and Molly was unlikely to recover her senses. In fact she had recovered them, and the crisis had passed, but that phrase, 'a family complaint', haunted Tom. At first he had blamed himself: his memories of one foolish act, the fever that ensued and the concoctions he had been given to try to shake it off, were still vivid. That episode, however, was long after both girls' birth, so it could not be the cause of any hereditary malady. If Moysey was right, the culprit was far more likely to be the same wanton parent, or one of his forebears, who provided Molly's mother with her discreet two hundred pounds a year.

Recently, this disorder had shown signs of returning. One of the ways it signalled its presence was the emergence of a fantasy world, built close enough to the real one to look very like it, but with key distinctions: in the present one, Molly was convinced she was being pursued by half the most fashionable young men in London. It was harrowing to see the poor girl in the grip of such a delusion, but if it set the grinning German out of her mind, its effect would not be wholly malign.

The raw umber blocking was now complete. The stream running through this middleground would widen into a shallow ford. Here would be placed his cattle drinking at sunset. He mixed up a thin grey wash with burnt sienna, a dab of ultramarine and some white to lighten it up, and set about laying the course of the water. In the foreground, he had already sketched in chalk a family cluster which, drenched in the light of the setting sun, would be the main draw for the eye: a woman with one child at her hip, its arm outstretched towards the nearest cow, who stared back with equal curiosity, and an older girl beside her, standing very close and cautiously keeping her mother between herself and the lumbering beasts. Happy these children of his imagination. Whatever their future held, it was unlikely to include a derangement caused by the sins of their debauched forefathers.

There was a knock at his studio door.

'Come!' he called.

Without turning round, he knew it was his footman, David, from the awkward little cough.

'Sorry to disturb, Master, but Reverend Bate is here.'

'Bate?' Tom stood back from his easel and squeezing his shoulders together to arch his aching back. 'What does he want at this hour? It's barely noon!'

'It's past one, sir, and I believe he is engaged to dine.'

Tom turned around.

'Is he, by Jove? Who the devil engaged him?'

The boy coughed into his fist again, in preference to answering.

'I see,' said Tom. 'I did, did I? And I imagine Mrs Gainsborough will have something to say about it, will she not? No need to answer that.'

He put down his palette and brush, and held out his arms for David to help him out of his painting smock.

'Is there any food in the house for him to eat?'

'My mistress has already sent to inquire, sir. I believe there are some mackerel, a boiled leg of mutton and a pig's face.'

'That's not enough for Bate. The man will starve! Have we no pickled salmon? And what about dessert?'

'I believe the cook has some damson tarts, sir. And some oranges, and a melon. And she has sent Annie for the cream to make syllabub. Shall I run and ask about the pickled salmon?'

'Of course, idiot wretch. Why are you still here?'

The boy disappeared, leaving Tom to wash his hands with water from a ewer and adjust his wig in the glass. He really had no recollection of inviting Bate, but there were worse ways of spending an afternoon.

With Fox trotting behind him, he made his way to the front

of the house and up the staircase. In the drawing room, his friend was sitting with his back to him, talking to Molly and the Captain. From the artful way in which Molly was showing him her lashes, she had clearly forgotten all about Fischer, and indeed that Bate already had a fine, pretty wife of his own. Tom hoped that Bate would have the nous not to encourage her.

'How de do, my friend!' he cried, as he entered the room. 'You have kept yourself from us too selfishly. How I have looked forward to this hour, knowing that I should enjoy your society again!'

Bate was a large young man, with a high brow and slightly too thin lips but an affable demeanour that belied his public reputation. Of course, it was that public reputation that had set Molly and the Captain's eyelashes a-flutter. They knew him as the duelling editor who had been forced to take up pistols to defend his own words, and who had famously pulverised a professional prize-fighter for insulting a lady at Vauxhall. The fact that he was also nominally a parson, a calling at such variance with his popular image, could only add to his allure.

He now rose to greet Tom, his eyes shining with gentle merriment. Perhaps he knew from the frantic atmosphere in the house that Tom had forgotten the invitation. Bate was no fool: although he was no lover of book-learning, he had an ability to read his fellow men which had helped him prosper in the print business, as owner of the *Morning Post* as well as scribbler and editor. Fortunately, he could also be relied upon to see the joke, and not to take umbrage.

He grasped Tom by the hand.

'However keenly you anticipated this hour, I am confident that my own anticipation surpassed it a hundredfold.'

Tom pretended not to notice the tease.

'Where is my wife? Surely she does not neglect you?'

'Mama is in conference with the kitchen, Papa,' said the Captain, with a meaningful look that confirmed to Tom that he was in trouble.

And now here she was, breathless from the steep staircase.

'Husband, you have joined us!' she said.

She would be vexed in the extreme, he knew, at having to receive Bate in her ordinary gown, which was not suited to callers, and for not having the time to dress her hair. What could he say to her? She was right, of course. He was a terrible husband, and she should find herself a better one. He had been telling her that for more than thirty years, but she had yet to heed him.

'How could you ever doubt it, my angel? I trust the cook has everything in order?'

Murderers gave fonder looks to hangmen on the scaffold than Mrs Gainsborough gave to Tom.

The food turned out to be ample. A lobster had been found to go with the mackerel; there were veal cutlets as well as the mutton leg, which was served with caper sauce, and the pig's face; and there was a pine-apple, in addition to the oranges and the melon, the tarts and the syllabub. Bate ate heartily of it all, and was particularly taken with the pine-apple, which was the first he had ever tasted. The parlour-maid even managed to serve it all without breaking a plate or pouring sauce on their guest's breeches. Tom resolved to slip the cook an extra five shillings, and perhaps half a shilling for young Annie, when the mistress was not looking.

As he slipped titbits to Fox at one end of the table, and his wife did the same for Tristram at the other, Molly and the Captain were full of questions for Bate. They wanted to know about his parish in Essex, although in truth he was too busy making newspapers to preach sermons or bury the dead; he had a curate to do all that for him. They also asked about the newspaper, which had a coarser, more direct way of expressing itself than its rivals, so that respectable people affected to disdain it; but in reality that very coarseness gave the *Post* a much greater appeal for them than its more sober rivals.

The girls' most enthusiastic endeavour, however, was to get Bate started on the subject of Sir Joshua, whose work he had castigated so entertainingly in his reviews.

Softer spoken in person than in print, he was reticent at first. After he had drunk some claret, however, and then some Madeira, his tongue became more compliant.

'There is an admiral,' he began, 'who has lately been in the West Indies.'

'Go on,' said the Captain excitedly. 'What about him?'

'When he came back, he wanted his face painted, so he sent for our friend the president, who naturally undertook the commission. He is not the man to turn down fifty guineas.'

'Is he charging fifty now?' said Tom.

'Fifty for a head, I hear, and two hundred for a full-length.'

'Hell's teeth. They must need their heads examining to pay him that.'

'Let Mr Bate continue with his story, Papa.'

'Thank you, my dear,' said Bate, gently inclining his head in Molly's direction. 'So he put on his brocade coat and sat for his head, which was eventually delivered, and he paid his fifty guineas.'

He paused for effect, looking around the table to check he had their attention.

'And then what?' demanded Molly.

'Yes, then what?' echoed her sister.

Tom caught his wife's eye. There was a twinkle in it now. Amid this happy conviviality, he was forgiven. He winked back at her, and she looked away.

'Then he sent it back.'

'No!' cried Molly, clutching her hand to her breast in outrage.

'Why?' asked the Captain.

'Yes, why?' said Tom. 'Don't keep us guessing, man. Spit it out.'

Bate was clearly enjoying holding his audience in his suspense. His shoulders began to shake.

'Because...' he began, then broke off. The thought of whatever he was about to tell had already set him laughing, and it was stopping him getting the words out.

'Because what?' demanded Molly.

They were all laughing now, although only Bate knew what the joke was going to be.

He tried once more to get his sentence out. 'Because the sky...' he attempted, but once more it was no good. His face was as red as his claret and there tears in his eyes as he fell mercy to helpless mirth.

'Tell us, man, for God's sake,' said Tom, dabbing his own eyes from laughing too much. He could not decide whether Bate was the worst storyteller he had ever encountered, or the best.

'Because the sky turned green!' exploded Bate, collapsing back in his chair in a heap of convulsions.

Four mouths fell open.

'Green?' clapped the Captain in incredulous delight. 'But... how?' She looked to her father for guidance.

'I can imagine how it might happen,' said Tom. 'But you, Bate, are the bringer of this marvellous story. Finish telling it, pray.'

His friend composed himself sufficiently to complete the

explanation.

'He is blaming his pigment supplier. He says the man sent blue verdigris, which turns green within a month, instead of ultramarine, which does not. Do I have that right, Gainsborough?'

'Almost,' said Tom. 'It is called blue verditer, not verdigris, but in all other particulars you are correct.' He shook his head as he contemplated the story. 'The man has a brass neck, and no mistake. President of our most august body of painters, in the King's own name, and he regularly tries the patience of the rest of us with his interminable lectures on how to paint. Yet he cannot manage a simple sky.'

'You should offer yourself as president in his place, Papa.'

'I have done so twice, my dear. Regrettably, no one wanted to vote for your poor wretch of a father, who knows not how to lecture on the theory of making pictures or to cloak his sitters in the robes of antiquity, and has never travelled to Italy on the Tour. My respected colleagues clearly value such qualities higher in a painter than knowing the difference between blue and green.'

Bate laughed uproariously at that, and the ladies all did the same. Tom surveyed the table happily. Would that such merriment could always fill this house.

'And of course,' continued Bate, rising to the occasion now, 'there is the matter of their majesties' portraits. Have you seen them, Gainsborough?'

'I have not, nor yet heard any report.' Tom had been so shut away in his studio, immersed in sittings, that the comings and goings of his fellow painters had completely passed him by.

'Tell us, Mr Bate, whatever there is to tell,' said the Captain, her eyes shining with eagerness to hear it.

'As you know, Miss Peggy, the Academy will shortly move

to new apartments.'

'I did not know that. Papa does not tell us anything.'

Tom shrugged, guilty as charged. Was he expected to tell them his entire business, the business of the whole town?

'There is to be a new suite of rooms at Somerset House,' their guest continued. 'Larger and grander than the present ones. Because it is the *Royal* Academy, new paintings of the King and Queen are to grace the new rooms, and the commission naturally fell to the president. Surely you knew that much, Gainsborough?'

'I may have done,' said Tom, affecting to sound off-hand. 'I pay very little heed to such matters. You know all this royal flummery means nothing to me. Unlike Sir Joshua, who has been waiting his whole life for this honour.'

'Indeed so, but I fear the sittings did not proceed happily.'

Tom raised a curious eyebrow and the ladies all leaned forward.

'It is known,' Bate continued, 'that His Majesty suffers Sir Joshua's company under the greatest duress. He is presumed too Whiggish for Royal tastes.' That was addressed, by way of explanation, to Molly and the Captain.

'Are we not excessively Whiggish too, Papa?' asked Molly.

'In matters of politics, we are not excessively anything, my dear,' said Tom, helping himself to more madeira and pushing the bottle in his friend's direction.

Bate filled his own glass. 'Which is quite the most politic way,' he agreed.

'I am quite without party prejudice: I see a troupe of scoundrels on both sides,' said Tom.

'But what of the King's picture?' pressed the Captain.

'It seems that, during the sitting, His Majesty was conspicuously bored, and Sir Joshua painted him accordingly.

It is an immense canvas, full nine feet high, but I fear its size is its only claim to greatness. The King looks like a sulking youth, sprawled in the coronation chair with yards of ermine draped all over him, staring at the viewer with an utterly blank expression. There is no dignity, no majesty about it at all. It does not even look like him, which reinforces the impression that this is some imposter lounging upon the throne. And of course the robes and draperies are all in deepest red, which will fly away and fade to brown by Michaelmas.'

'How are the hands?' asked Tom.

Bate laughed. 'As bad as you would expect. And of course they are the first thing you notice, because he is holding his sceptre in front of your eyes as you stand in front of it.'

'And the Queen?' said Mrs Gainsborough. 'Did you not say that she also sat, Mr Bate?'

'I did, madam. The mercy, when it comes to Her Majesty, is that her hands are hidden in the folds of her gown. She is seated almost in profile, and is forced to twist her neck to look at Sir Joshua, which I might almost believe a deliberate ploy to let him conceal her fingers in her lap. The main difficulty, however, is…the face.'

'Go on,' said Tom.

'Her Majesty is no beauty, it is no crime to acknowledge that. However, it is surely incumbent upon the president of the Royal Academy, a knight of the realm, to cast her in a beneficial light, where her nose might seem a little sharper than it really is, her lips less bulbous. If anything, he has done the reverse, and the only feeling the painting inspires is one of pity, that any creature should be so unhappily endowed.'

The ladies all shook their heads in sympathy with the poor, unlovely Queen.

'What will become of these unfortunate paintings?' the

Captain wanted to know. 'Will they be shown?'

'I imagine they will have to be.'

Bate looked at Gainsborough for confirmation.

Tom shrugged again. 'If Sir Joshua wants his pictures to be shown, the Academy will show them. That is usually the way. In this instance, it may not benefit him to do so, but he will not know that, and even if he does, there is nothing he can do about it, because not showing the pictures would mean admitting he has botched them. It may, however, be politick to distract the King and Queen when they come to visit the new rooms, and not let them examine themselves too close.'

'You should paint them instead, Papa. Both the King and Queen. They would surely like you much better than Sir Joshua.'

'That may be so, dear Captain, but one does not simply turn up at Windsor with a box of pigments. One has to be asked.'

'Perhaps Mr Fischer could put in a word,' said Molly. 'He teaches music to the Queen.'

'In that case you should ask him for Papa,' said the Captain, her mouth tightening. 'You are very close to him, are you not?'

Tom had no wish to hear his daughters start squabbling about the accursed Fischer in front of Bate. He stood up.

''Tis a fine afternoon out there,' he said to their guest. 'Why don't you and I take a stroll around the park?'

Bate stood up briskly too, perhaps sensing the change in mood, and understanding Tom's intention.

'Capital idea.'

As her mother and sister stood up too, Molly looked bewildered.

'Must you go so soon, Mr Bate? Will you come back?'

'Of course I will, my dear. Whenever I am asked. Even if your father forgets he has asked me.'

Tom threw his head back and laughed, pleased to see the tension broken, even if it was at his own expense.

'So you saw through me after all, my friend. I hang my head in shame.'

Now the lad David was in the doorway, no doubt bringing Bate's topcoat, although it was unlike him to be so prompt. No, Tom realised, it was too warm for a topcoat, and the boy was not bearing any garment. All he had in his hand was a letter.

'Master, this has just…' he began, holding the letter out to Tom.

'Not now, boy. Mr Bate and I are going out.'

Although the mood had lightened, he was still anxious to get his friend away from his elder daughter, before she started flirting with him again, or taunting her sister, or both.

'But sir, I think…'

'I'll look at it when I get back, not now.'

Bate touched Tom on the arm, holding him back as he made for the staircase, and nodded in the direction of the envelope.

'Isn't that the Royal seal, old fellow?'

Tom hesitated.

'Well, lad. Where did it come from?'

'It was delivered now, sir. From the palace.'

'Why didn't you say so? Give it here.'

He took the letter, ripped open the envelope, and pulled out a single sheet of paper. His wife, daughters and guest watched him read it.

'Well?' said Margaret.

The letter was not long. He read it once, and then again, just to make sure.

'What does it say, Papa? Tell us!'

He looked up them and smiled.

'It seems that I am commanded by His Majesty to come to

Buckingham-house.'

'No!'

'Yes. And…'

'And what?'

He savoured them in suspense, holding the best part back.

'And *what*, Papa?'

He laughed.

'And… I am to bring my painting apparatus with me.'

To my dearest Ma

Thank you for your last letter in Richard's hand. It cheered my heart to hear how much our little Jack is growing up and how he is doing so well at his school-learning. In no time, I'll wager, he will be so good with his reading and writing that it will be he, not Richard, who takes up the quill to send me your news.

I know it pains you that I have been here these two years and more, and I have not been home to visit in all that time. Believe me, Ma, when I tell you it grieves me no less. As you know, I hoped to accompany my master whenever he returned to Suffolk, which I imagined would be a frequent event, but he seems to have an aversion for the place of his birth because he never goes there. He prefers to pass all his time here in London, so here in London must also stay I. This is a great trial but I hope you will understand that there is nothing I can do to change the situation, and until my master decides to make the journey home, we must content ourselves with exchanging letters.

If I must needs be all the while in this city, I have no right to complain, because my lot is a most happy one. I always take delight in conveying tidings of my great adventures in this great capital, so that you can take delight in them too, and to-day was the greatest adventure of any I have had to this date. Imagine, Ma. Your humble son has this very day been to call on the King, if you please!

I have explained to you already that there is a very famous painter called Sir Joshua Reynolds, who is held in greater esteem than any other face-painter in the realm, including my master. When the King and Queen require their likenesses recorded, they do not turn to the court painter, a Scotchman who has fallen off a ladder and can paint no longer, but to Sir Joshua. They call on him even though the King is not much partial to the gentleman personally (the reason being that Sir Joshua is very close with a politician by the name of Fox, who is a friend of the Prince of Wales but says very sour things about the King – it sounds complicated, Ma, but honest, it is no different to the squabbles our Jack has with his little friends). Also, as I think I acquainted you afore, Sir Joshua is not clever at making his paints and he has a shocking reputation because half his colours vanish six months after he has painted them. This shortcoming has all the smartest folk in London a-sniggering behind their sleeves.

Yet still the King calls on Sir Joshua and not my master. My master affects not to care, but I believe he does really. As for my mistress and the Misses Molly and Peggy, they care very much, and they do not try to hide it.

Now, all of a sudden, the situation has changed. It seems

that Sir Joshua has done a picture of the King that is very bad, and one of the Queen that is yet worse. I have not seen these paintings personally, of course, but this is what I have learned from standing a-listening. The picture of the Queen is the particular problem. Everyone says as how Her Majesty is no beauty and, from the likenesses I have seen in the prints, she seems to have the face of a garganey duck. Sir Joshua's error was to make the matter worse by rendering her even uglier in the portrait than she is in life, when normally the painter would strive to do the reverse. So, finally, the King has decided enough is enough and asked my master to paint him and the Queen, in the hope that he will do better than Sir Joshua.

The ladies of the household could scarcely contain their excitement at this news, which was of an order quite extreme. My mistress gave her husband a kiss – the first time I have ever seen her do that – and the Misses Molly and Peggy quite forgot about the quarrel they had been having two seconds earlier, and fell to jumping up and down in each other's arms as if they were a-dancing at a ball. Miss Molly tried to give a kiss to the Reverend Bate, who was present when the good tidings arrived, and even the dogs joined in the celebration, because they were allowed extra leavings from the meats on the table. Sometimes I swear those dogs eat better in this house than I do.

My mistress is never happy for long if she can find a reason to be peevish. On the morrow, I heard her ask my master if she might accompany him to Buckingham-house. He said that was out of the question and she ought to remember that he was summoned as a tradesman, not as a friend of royalty asked to sup. That stopped her tongue a while, for she knew my master spoke true; but then she started up again, saying why couldn't he ask the King to come and call on us in Pall-mall, like this brothers the Duke of Gloucester and the Duke of Cumberland had done.

Because he is the King, madam, said my master. He don't go a-calling. That's not what kings do. He said it as gay as you like, but my mistress was still vexed. I could see she was jealous of her husband seeing the King when she would not, and nothing would shake her from it.

As the date of the appointment came closer, my master fell to wondering how he was to arrive at Buckingham-house. You remember, Ma, that the King's house is very close to ours. It stands at the top of St James's-park, where all the fashionable people stroll. The park is pleasant to walk in, unlike the street, which is full of slime and stink, and from this house it would take no more than five minutes on foot. However, my mistress said it was beneath my master's dignity to arrive on foot, and he should take the carriage. He said he agreed with her, not because of his dignity, for which he does not care a fig, but because he has to take all his apparatus, like his easel and his canvas and his pigments (and between you and me, Ma, he does care for his dignity too).

Then he fell to considering the manner of his arriving in this carriage. It would look wanting, said he, to present himself quite alone, with no retinue save the coachman, therefore I should accompany him as his footman. To me, this seemed a very wise approach. I would carry his easel, canvas, paints and the like, leaving my master free of such burdens, the better to bow to the King and Queen. I fancy my mistress thought the same way too, because she did not speak against the plan. However, she cast me a look of the most disobliging sort, as if she wished all manner of bad fortune to befall me. I cast my own eyes down at the floor, as any servant must, and pretended I had not noticed anything amiss. Inside, though,

I was laughing fit to explode. My mistress was jealous of me, because I was off to the visit the King and she was not.

To-day was the day. My master was bidden to meet the King at ten o'clock, and the carriage was called for half-past nine o'clock. My master said this was too early, but my mistress did insist on it. We set off on time, but we would have been so much quicker on foot, even with the painting apparatus to carry. To reach the top of St James's-park by road from Pall-mall, you must first return to Charing-cross, which is quite the opposite direction, and we were jammed in a mess of carriages as we tried to turn back into the Mall, which leads along the park. It was ten minutes to ten o'clock when we finally arrived at Buckingham-house, and my master had become exceeding agitated with the coachman, telling him he was a blockhead and coxcomb for going so slow. It does not do to keep the King waiting, even if you affect not to care about him.

The house itself is a beautiful place, Ma. I have heard some of my master's smart friends say it is not much of a palace, because it is too small, or it is too ugly, or it is made of brick not stone but, if I were a king, I should be more than content to live in it. It is three houses really: one large red-brick one in the middle, and two smaller ones on either side, joined by curved passageways, like a man's head and two hands, with his arms held out wide. Of course, the smaller houses are not so small at all. Each one could fit two dozen cottages like yours inside it. I am speaking by the King's standards now, not of humble folk like us.

There is just a railing between the front of Buckingham-house and the park, so that the whole world can see in, but there is no gate at the front, and the coachman could not find the way inside. That agitated my master once again, and he took to calling the coachman an ignorant whoreson and an addle-pate and I don't know what else. Eventually we found the entrance, which is hidden at the side, and my master was a little calmer as I helped him down from the carriage and fetched his apparatus after him.

I did not know which door we would use, and nor did my master, since he had no more experience of visiting the King than I did. Any road, it soon became clear that the decision was not ours to make. One of the King's footmen appeared, and my master told him his name. The footman bade us follow him and we did as we were told. We were escorted through the tradesmen's entrance into a passage quite ordinary in appearance, with a stone floor and whitewash on the walls. I do not suppose the King and Queen ever set foot there. From the window, I could see we were in the part of the building linking one of the small houses to the big one. At the end of this passage was a door, and the King's footman opened it for my master to go through, but then he stood in my way and told me I need come no further. When I said what about the apparatus, he said they had servants of their own to carry that, and I was to go on back to the stable-yard and wait.

So that is what I did, and I can tell you a good deal about the stable-yard, which has six coach houses and stabling for forty horses, but that is the most I can tell you about the King's house, because that was the closest I came.

I found it most strange to spend nigh on three hours waiting in that yard with nothing to do, when my master's house was only five minutes away on foot and I could easily have run there and come back later. After the first hour, I complained of the tedium to the coachman, whose name is Spinks. He looked at me with his mouth agape and said, 'Boy, do you want to run home so my mistress can set you to work polishing boots, when you can sit here in front of the park and watch the world go by? There is no one here to scold you or box your ears for being idle, because you are only doing what you have been bidden to do by the King, or his servant, which is as good as the same. So you have perfect licence to take your rest.'

Spinks knows whereof he speaks, because he spends his life waiting until my master, my mistress or the Misses Molly and Peggy need him to drive them somewhere. I therefore resolved to heed his expert counsel, and the pair of us found a good spot where we could watch all the fine folk walking around the park. This is a strange fashion in this city, Ma: for the likes of you and me, walking is a means of getting from one place to another, but these smart ladies and gentlemen have chaises and carriages to convey them around the town, so for them it is a novelty to use their two legs. They walk for amusement, and to show off all their latest silks and embroideries to one another. Watching them promenade this way and that, me and Spinks thought how fine it would be if any person of our acquaintance spied us there, a-lounging like lords inside the King's own property. Sadly I do not have much acquaintance in London, and none of Spinks's is the sort to walk around St James's-park in the middle of the day, so it could not ever happen. It gave us a laugh just to think about it, though.

When the bells struck one o'clock, my master was still not back with us and we both agreed we were starving hungry. It was a great trial to be so weak for want of food when we knew my master's house was just five minutes thence, with a kitchen full of victuals (where Cook stands guard less fiercely these days, now that she has accepted I have no designs on poor Annie). Just thinking along those lines made our bellies groan all the more, so, after a while, I worked up the courage to knock at the kitchen door and beg a piece of bread to help us endure the wait.

A young man in livery, barely more advanced in years than myself, opened the door and heard my request. He listened very nicely and then he said if I did not mind waiting two minutes, he would command a team of under-footmen to lay a table with a white cloth in the yard and they would serve us an array of meats on silver platters.

I was overjoyed to hear these sweet words, and I was thinking what a noble thing is royalty, that it treats its guests so handsome, even when they are of the serving kind – but then I realised his promise was not sincerely meant and he was making mockery at my expense because he considered us of low station. I was left in no further doubt about this interpretation when the uppity young butler closed the door flat in my face so that it near busted my nose.

I was seething angry that he should be so hoity-toity with us simply because he serves the King and we only serve the King's painter. I wanted to bang on the door again and make this cub come outside and say the same again, so I could knock his block off but, in the instant, I was deprived of this opportunity by the return of my master.

The horses had been allowed into the stables while we were waiting, and Spinks now hastened off to make them ready and to bring the carriage round. I was afeared of how this would likely vex my master, if he were in the typical bad humour that painting faces normally brings to him. He seemed quite unconcerned, though, and he waited very nicely for Spinks, while I held his paints and brushes. He no longer had the easel or canvas, for whatever painting he had done must needs be left to dry.

I wanted to ask how the King and Queen did, were they gracious to my master, and so forth, but it is not my place to speak unless he speaks to me first, so all I could do was observe his demeanour and form my own opinion. This was not hard to do, because my master fell to whistling a merry air until the carriage came round. He was still tra-la-la-ing when he climbed up and took his seat inside.

As we passed through the gates to return to the Mall in the direction of Charing-cross, I fancy he remembered the great time it would take to drive all the way round to Pall-mall by road, when his house was just a few steps away on foot. So, declaring that the day was exceeding fine and he would prefer to use his own legs, he shouted to Spinks to stop and let him down. That left the pair of us to bring the carriage home the longer way, so our bellies would have to groan for a good while yet.

Just before he got down, my master turned back to me and slipped me a shilling, with no explanation, only an instruction not to tell my mistress, and I could see him do the same for Spinks riding up front. Like I say, it is possible to form an opinion of how well an encounter is proceeding without hearing the tidings directly from the parties involved. I deduced that my master had enjoyed his morning with the King and Queen exceeding well. I noticed already, when he painted the King's brother, that he does not hate the business of face-painting so much when the face is royal. He seems to like it even more when the face belongs to the King himself.

So what do you think of that, Ma? I would tell you not to go boasting to all the neighbours about your son mixing in royal circles, but I know there is no point because you will do it any road. Only promise me that you will not tell anyone that I actually met His Majesty, because it is not true, and such a falsehood will only get back to Mrs Dupont and thence to Mr Dupont and my master himself, and I will look a donkey for inventing tall tales about my own importance.

That is all for now, Ma, for I have gone on for far too long, as usual, and poor Dick will be tired from reading it out to you. This letter comes with the greatest affection from a young man who is trying not to acquire too many fancy airs and graces and ideas above his station, viz. your loving son

David

9

Fiammetta reacted as badly as Gemma had expected when she saw her slipping back into the church without Muriel.

'Where is she?' she demanded. She spoke in a hushed tone, lest any spectating punters might overhear, but left little doubt as to her displeasure. 'Don't tell me you couldn't find her?'

'No, I found her,' said Gemma, matching her boss's muted volume. 'But she won't come. She's too upset.'

Fiammetta turned away with a sigh of exasperation, sweeping her hair out of her face and clasping a nervy, heavily ringed hand to her scalp. She closed her eyes and began to knead the top of her head, as if to massage the tension away. Gemma, all too familiar with this body language, knew there was no hope of that happening. These were danger signs.

Now Fiammetta opened her eyes again and turned back to Gemma.

'Didn't you try to persuade her? What did you say to her?'

Gemma took a deep breath. She could either accept the role of punchbag and scapegoat for anything that ever went wrong in the production, because that was what the most junior member of the team was for, or she could give as good as she got. In this instance, fighting back was the only way of avoiding being sent out after Muriel once more.

'Of course I tried.'

It clearly came out with more force than Fiammetta was expecting; the gust of it made her blink in surprise and take half a step backwards.

'I apologised, I pleaded, I said we'd use the footage anyway so coming back was her best chance of salvaging her dignity and recording something better. I did everything I could think of to get her back, but of course she wasn't coming. I mean, would you, after what Kaz said?'

She knew she was laying it on thick about how hard she had tried. The basic point was true, though: Muriel was not coming back, and nothing that Gemma could say would alter that.

Fiammetta closed her eyes again, massaging her temples with a splayed thumb and forefinger. She sighed with profound self-pity.

'What can I do?' she said, as much to herself as Gemma. 'The woman was gold dust – or at least that ghastly piece of grot that she brought with her was gold dust. Now all we have is her pre-interview and some good close-ups of the pictures when she shows it to Kaz.'

'And her storming out.'

Fiammetta shook her head irritably. 'That would only work if we had footage of her coming back so we can all kiss and make up. We can't use it if that's the last we see of her. It will make us look like monsters.'

As if, Gemma wanted to say.

'I'll need to watch it all back,' Fiammetta continued. 'We'll see how much we've got that's usable, without making us look like total bastards. Kaz can re-shoot some close-ups, pretend she's still standing next to him. Oh, it's maddening though.' She opened her eyes again and fixed them on Gemma. 'Are you quite sure you can't persuade…?'

'Quite sure.'

Gemma was impressed at this new-found capacity to stand up to Fiammetta. She hoped it would not get her the sack.

'No, I don't suppose you can. Christ, what the hell was Kaz thinking? Is he still filming?' She craned her neck to see.

'I think so.'

'Send him over for a word when he's done, will you?' She continued to glower in Kaz's direction. 'What was I thinking, hiring a Z-list reality star? They're so up themselves, they've completely forgotten how to talk to ordinary people.'

Gemma sensed that she was supposed to contradict. 'You're not responsible for what comes out of his mouth,' she said, but it sounded lame.

Fiammetta shrugged and turned away.

'Oh, one thing,' she said, wheeling back round with a finger raised to stop Gemma rushing off. 'You don't know where Vivian has got to, do you? He seems to have vanished.'

'I did see him outside in the square. He said, if you asked, to tell you he was nipping out for half an hour. He didn't say why. Maybe the pub, I'm not sure. There was something about a dog too, I think, but I didn't understand. Sorry, I should have mentioned it before.'

'Nipping out? Where does he think he is? This isn't his sleepy little antique shop in Much Widdling-on-the-Wash, or whatever the bloody place is called, where he can close up any time he fancies a pint of stout or an afternoon nap. We've got a schedule here, and a string of punters for him to see. Two or three, anyway. Honestly, where do we find these people?'

In a pool of white lights, Kaz was examining a set of die-cast Dinky cars from the Fifties or Sixties and talking to their proud owner, a well-spoken, elderly gent in a Barbour jacket.

'You've looked after these, haven't you?' he was saying. 'There's not a scratch on any of them. What do you do, polish them with turtle wax and a shammy leather once a week?'

The owner of the cars laughed at the joke but was also visibly pleased with the compliment. If only Kaz would stick to this kind of matey flattery, Gemma thought, life would be so much easier all round.

As the director called 'cut', Gemma moved in to intercept Kaz before anyone else could lure him into conversation.

'Fiammetta wants a word,' she said in his ear.

'Oh, that sounds ominous? Am I in dreadful trouble?'

'Well…' said Gemma, not denying it. It was not her place to pre-empt Fiammetta's reprimand, but there was no point in sugar-coating it either.

'I feel awful about what I said to that sweet little old lady. It just came out. Not that it was wasn't true. That painting was the most grotesque thing I have ever seen in my life, and for her to believe it's a Gainsborough…! But I shouldn't have upset her, I know I shouldn't, and I do feel terrible.'

'Don't tell me, tell Fiammetta.'

He was looking at her with puppy eyes, desperate for a smile of reassurance that everything was going to be all right and he was not a bad person really. She did not see why she should give him that.

Kaz sighed and ran a pudgy hand through his thickly waxed hair.

'Wish me luck, then.'

This time, she gave him a thin smile as he headed off towards the north transept.

From what Gemma could see of Fiammetta's body language, the dressing-down seemed uncompromising, even if it was carried out in hushed tones to thwart any earwigging members of the public.

The pair of them were still in their uncomfortable huddle when Gemma spotted Vivian slipping back into the church. She hurried over to meet him.

'Sorry, Vivian. I did try and cover for you, but Fiammetta noticed you weren't here, and I'm afraid she wasn't happy.'

'Thanks for trying. Actually I need an urgent word with her anyway.'

He too started out in the direction of the north transept.

Gemma grabbed him by the arm and held him back.

'Honestly, Vivian, not now. When I spoke to her, she was spitting feathers because you've got a queue of punters waiting to have their treasures evaluated. Trust me on this: if you go near Fiammetta while they're still waiting, she'll go bananas. We've only got this place for a few more hours, so we're racing against time now to get everything recorded.'

'But that's exactly why I need to speak…'

She cut him off. 'Please, Vivian. Go and see to your punters, then talk to Fiammetta. Whatever you've got to say, she won't want to hear it as long as they're still waiting.'

She was not sure if she had the status to boss an expert around – in fact, she was certain she did not – but there were times when it was worth reminding Vivian that she was the television professional here, while he was the industry outsider.

Vivian turned angrily on his heel, but he was at least heading for the chancel, where his allotted hopefuls were waiting, rather than the north transept.

Now Theo was calling her, so that they could confer on the rest of the shooting schedule for Regina. When she had sorted that out, she was needed in Lavender's corner, where someone had spilt tea and there was a risk of accident if the wet floor was not mopped promptly.

It was not until an hour later that she noticed Vivian in conference with Fiammetta near the doorway. He seemed to be doing most of the talking and a lot of gesturing. Fiammetta looked uncharacteristically passive and was clearly not comfortable. As Gemma watched, she saw her eyes stray from Vivian's face and wander urgently around the interior of the church, as if searching for some kind of rescue. As they fell on Gemma, she visibly brightened. She put her hand on Vivian's arm, to pause his flow, and beckoned Gemma over.

'You should hear this too,' she said, as Gemma approached. 'You were involved with this woman from the beginning and you've spent more time with her than any of the rest of us.'

'What's going on?'

'Vivian, why don't you tell Gemma what you've just told me?'

He turned to face her, breathing heavily, having clearly worked himself into a state. Nothing in his expression said that he had forgiven Gemma for their clash earlier.

'I told you I needed to see a man about a dog, Gemma. Actually I was going to the art gallery round the corner. They specialise in Gainsborough, you know, which is only right, considering he was born here. It means they have a lot of his work to look at. I went there with this picture of Muriel's painting' – he held up his iPhone – 'and compared it with the portraits they have hanging on the walls.'

'And?'

'One of the striking things about Muriel's picture is the difference in finish between the face and the clothing. The face has been carefully done, with plenty of close detail, whereas the clothing was much more hurried, with big, loose brush marks, as if it wasn't finished. Do you agree?'

'Yes, that sounds right.'

'That gallery is full of Gainsborough portraits where the face is very carefully finished and the clothing looks hurried. That's if you're standing very close. But if you move backwards very slowly, you reach a point where the clothes suddenly come into perfect focus and it looks as if he has captured embroidered silk jackets and dresses in perfect detail.'

'What does that prove?'

'It doesn't prove anything. It does, however, suggest that the idea that Muriel's damaged, defaced painting is a Gainsborough may not be as ridiculous as my esteemed colleague Kaz so witheringly pronounced.'

He said 'esteemed' with heavy sarcasm. Gemma has noticed for a while that Vivian was happy to pass the time of day with Lavender, but his distaste for Kaz was barely disguised. She hoped he disliked him for one of the justifiable reasons for finding Kaz too much – he was loud, brash and tacky – rather than because he was gay or Muslim.

'You also said something about the style of the clothes,' prompted Fiammetta.

'Yes I did.' He turned to Gemma again. 'One of the ways you can date an old portrait is by looking at what the sitter is wearing. We may not realise it, but fashions changed from decade to decade in the eighteenth century just as much as they do in our time. A fashion historian could tell us what style goes with each period, but since we don't have one of those to hand, there's an easy way of taking a guess – by looking at other portraits painted at around the same time. From my quick survey of the portraits of men painted by Gainsborough in the seventeen seventies and eighties, I can tell you that fashionable gentlemen were wearing long, coloured jackets with no collars, with fancy brocade around the button-holes and elaborate lacy cravats and shirt cuffs. Can you remember what the chap in Muriel's picture was wearing?'

'Apart from the donkey ears, you mean?'

He did at least smile at that.

'From the neck downwards. Here, let me refresh your memory.' He pulled up the picture on his phone and magnified it for Gemma to see. 'See the cravat? And those button-holes? You can't see the cuffs, because it doesn't go down that far. But you see the top of the jacket?'

'No collar,' Gemma confirmed. 'So what are you saying? You think it's a Gainsborough that someone has defaced and then cut into four pieces? Why would anyone do that? And yet still hang onto it?'

'No, I'm not saying that. I'm not an art historian and I don't have the expertise. I'm saying one very simple thing. The idea that this may be a Gainsborough, which my fellow 'expert' mocked on camera, may not be so daft after all. Granted, the picture has been very badly mistreated, for whatever reason. The lady tells us it has been carefully passed down her family from generation to generation, by people who believe it to be a Gainsborough. Instead of mocking her, we should consider the possibility that she's right. I'm not saying she is right. But she may be. That being the case, the correct thing to do is investigate it further, with the proper experts and proper equipment.'

Gemma felt nauseous as she was hit by a wave of remorse. She was the one who had decided, in a snap judgement, that the painting was a monstrosity. She had introduced Muriel Mudge to Fiammetta as an object of ridicule. She had determined her entire mistreatment with that initial snap judgement.

'You're right,' she said quietly. 'I feel completely awful.'

'Where does it leave us?' said Fiammetta.

'How do you mean?' said Vivian.

'At the moment, the only proper footage we have, apart from a short preview interview, is Kaz trashing the picture and Muriel storming out. If by any chance the picture does turn out to be a Gainsborough, we certainly can't use that.'

'We need to persuade her to come back,' said Vivian.

'Apparently Gemma has already tried until she's blue in the face and Muriel made it clear that wild horses wouldn't drag her back.'

'Yes, I did, that's true,' said Gemma. 'But that was before we thought she might be right about the picture. We could try again. The only thing is, she may not believe us. She'll think we're just telling her what she wants to hear so we can lure her back and ridicule her again. But we can give it a shot.'

'We've got to,' said Vivian. 'If this really is a Gainsborough, it would be a wonderful story for us to uncover. And even if it isn't, we owe it to her to look into it properly.'

Fiammetta looked at her watch.

'OK, you two go and talk her back. Remember, though, we need to be out of here by eight o'clock, and it's half five now. If we don't re-shoot her today, we won't have any footage, so we'll have to go with Plan A, and you can forget about trying to prove it's a Gainsborough.'

Vivian's eyes widened. 'You're not serious? If we can't get

her today, we'll just have to come back another time.'

Fiammetta shook her head, smiling pityingly.

'You don't get the budget thing, do you Vivian? I've got a finite amount to spend on each of these episodes, and it doesn't cover shlepping up and down here with a film crew to satisfy the whims of a mad old bat who couldn't take a bit of banter. And even if I did, you wouldn't have any of the crowd, so it would be obvious it was filmed on a different day. It would stick out a mile, and it's not an option.'

Vivian looked despairingly at Gemma, who decided it was time to take the initiative.

'We're wasting time arguing,' she said. 'Let's go and find her now, while there's still a chance we can get her back today. If we can't do that, we can carry on discussing any further options.'

Fiammetta raised her eyebrows at that. The message was clear: as far as she was concerned, there were no further options.

Gemma ignored her.

'Come on, Vivian. Let's grab her address and get going. I'll check on my phone, but I remember her saying it wasn't far.'

It was cold and dark outside, and most of the parked cars had now left the square. The day clearly finished early in these parts.

Gemma rushed along the pavement, trying to button her coat, wind a scarf round her neck and check Muriel's address on Google Maps, all at the same time. It would be more sensible to stop and work out properly where they were going, but Vivian was striding purposefully ahead.

'Slow down a bit,' she called after him. 'We don't even know where we're going.'

He turned to wait for her, but resumed his brisk pace as

soon as she caught up. 'We know it's in this direction,' he said. 'This is the way we saw her go.'

'I know but… Hang on…'

She pressed the microphone button and spoke with exaggerated diction into her phone.

'*School Lane.*'

Her phone pinged and the red marker popped into place on the correct address. She touched the picture of a stick figure walking, then pressed Directions.

'OK, you're right, it's this way,' she said.

'How far is it?

'It says two minutes. It'll be more like thirty seconds at this pace.' She pointed. 'It's left up there. We should cross the road.'

They followed a narrow alley, with jettied medieval houses looming crookedly towards them on either side, which then opened out into a wider lane, bounded by an ancient red-brick wall leaning into the road at a perilous angle. Only a few steps away from the town centre, it was dead quiet here: the only sound was their own hurrying footsteps.

Muriel's house was one of a terrace of ancient cottages, each just the width of a window and a door, with ginnel passages running through to the back, and each house bearing a large chimney which weighed ominously on sagging tiled roofs. Their rendered fronts were painted in a colourful medley: one pink, one grey, one yellow, one blue, and all looking yellower in the street lighting. One had been recently smartened up, with a pair of box trees trained to spiral up out of sleek slate planters standing sentinel on the narrow pavement, and the woodwork neatly painted a couple of tones darker than the wall shade. Muriel's was the one that let the whole terrace down. A long crack, etched in years of grime, spread the diagonal width of the dirty cream render on the upper storey. Crumbling sills framed windows that were opaque with dirt. At ground level, a square of plywood had been applied as a temporary fix for a patch of render that fallen off completely. Someone had put plastic sheeting at the edges to keep the weather out; the drawing pins that held it in place were caked with rust.

Light seeped through thin curtains drawn across the downstairs window.

'It looks like she's in,' said Gemma.

'Here goes, then,' said Vivian, raising a brass knocker in the shape of a border terrier and bringing it down politely.

They waited. Nothing stirred inside the house.

'Knock a bit louder,' said Gemma.

Vivian rapped the terrier against its brass plate with more force, and the rat-a-tat filled the quiet street.

Gemma took a step backwards and peered up at the first-floor window, looking for any sign of movement.

'I bet she's in there,' she said softly to Vivian.

'She's getting on a bit, so like as not she doesn't answer her door after dark if she ain't expecting anyone.'

'Her and me both. I never answer my door, whatever the time of day. It's only ever chuggers or Jehovah's Witnesses. If it's anyone I want to see, they'll text me when they're outside.'

'I don't think that will work for Muriel. I'm not sure she's the texting sort. Did she even give you a number?'

'Only a landline.'

'Let's try a more old-fashioned approach.'

Stooping in towards the letter-box, Vivian inserted a finger to hold the flap open, and cupped his other hand to make a seal between his mouth and the door.

'Muriel,' he called, his voice muffled through his fingers but louder inside the door. 'It's Vivian Morris from *Britain's Got*

Treasures. I'm here with Gemma, who you met earlier. Can we have a word with you, please?'

He paused and put his ear to the open letter-box.

'Anything?' said Gemma.

He shrugged and shook his head.

Cupping his mouth with his hand again, he resumed, 'I think you may be right about your picture, and it could be a Gainsborough, so we want to look into it properly. If we're going to do that, though, we need to talk to you very urgently. If you're inside, Muriel, could you open the door?'

Again, he pressed his ear to the letter-box.

'Maybe she isn't in after all,' said Gemma, after a minute or so with still no sound of life from within. 'She's drawn the curtains and gone out, leaving the light on. Loads of people do that.'

'Why don't you call that landline anyway? You can at least leave a message, assuming she's actually got a phone with an answering machine. While you're doing that, I'll write her a note.

He pulled a slimline ring-bound notebook from his top pocket, ripped a sheet out, and started to write.

Across the lane, in the flickering light of a television, Muriel sat watching them through the net curtains of her friend Bessie's front room.

'I don't understand what they want from you, Mu,' said Bessie.

They were drinking tea and watching *Pointless Celebrities*, as they often did of an early evening. They usually came up with the same obvious answers as most of the studio audience but, today, Muriel was distracted and not even trying. Bessie had asked what was wrong, but she had not liked to tell her.

She was angry and ashamed. The mockery of her painting had felt like a violation. Those people were not just laughing at the picture, which was unkind enough, but her whole family: those forefathers who had looked after this odd heirloom and carefully passed it on. These blameless ancestors would now be exposed to ridicule, and it was all Muriel's fault for letting it happen. She felt powerless now, but she did at least have the power not to talk to them

'Is it money they're after?' Bessie persisted. 'Are they debt-collectors? Do you want me to go out and tell them to get lost? I don't mind. I can always set my Billy on them.'

Bessie's son Billy, a giant who had to stoop to get through his mother's front door, was always useful to have around in such situations, even if he had never laid a finger on anyone.

Muriel shook her head.

'I owe them nothing,' she said, her face hardening. 'They want to mock me and my family, but I shan't let them. It's my own fault for going to them, but I've learned my lesson.'

'The chap is shouting through the letter-box now. Can you hear what he's saying? I can't make it out.'

'I can't and I don't want to neither,' said Muriel. 'Whatever he's saying, it's lies.'

10

Tom was ushered through the state apartments without hurry. He grasped that he was being encouraged to admire the finery. It was there to impress visitors and he, too, was a visitor, albeit under royal command.

Majestic as the castle's situation was, on its hilltop curl in the river, the interior had seen better days. The plaster was cracked, oak door-frames were studded with wormholes, and such paintings as formed the collection were miserably inferior. Here, for example, was Edward the Third, painted centuries after his death by an artist in Flanders, remote from the sitter in space as well as in time. This face was as flat and wooden as the panelling on which it hung, and what living soul in the painter's time could say if it was like or not? There was a whole gallery of these images, few worth more than a glance. Fortunately there were exceptions. Tom stopped in front of a three-quarter length of Queen Henrietta, by the one true genius from the Low Countries. The incomparable Vandyke had got her face splendidly: a blush of pink in girlish French cheeks, a bonnet of ringlets around her brow. The hands were exceptional too, the pure white of her arms darkening subtly around the knuckles to show that these fingers, however soft, were not always completely idle. Now they gently grasped a fold of her gown, which was a shimmering frenzy of silver silk, brighter than the pearls at her neck where the light caught its folds.

His liveried escort stood at the next doorway, waiting patiently for Tom to catch up. They passed into a smaller room, the ceiling moulded in white and gold, with cabinets full of porcelain. There was just one window, and Tom stopped to look out. Rolling away from the castle mound was the home park, dotted with grazing cattle like gems on a green velvet cushion. In his early days making landscapes, he had shifted a church steeple from here to there to create a more harmonious vision for the eye. Nowadays, creating perfect landscapes on a tray in his studio with his bits of twig, stone, coal and vegetable, he was very used to the idea of improving on nature, and he could see that the architects of the park had done the same thing on nature's own true scale, placing each tree and sculpting each rise and fall of the ground to visual perfection. The sight was better than a whole wall of flat, Flemish pictures.

The footman coughed discreetly into a gloved hand. There was clearly an appointed hour for Tom to arrive, with dawdling-time built in, and now they had reached it.

They passed through one more stateroom – no idling now – and then his usher was knocking at a closed door, opening it when bidden and announcing, with a bow and a flourish, 'Mr Gainsborough'.

A figure in the court uniform of navy blue tailcoat and buff waistcoat and breeches turned to greet him.

'My dear Gainsborough. Very pleasant to see ye again, and welcome to Windsor.'

Tom bowed low.

'Your Majesty.'

'Ye don't mind coming all the way out here, hey? It's your first time here, is it not so? Yes, I thought it was so. We move around eternally, from Buckingham-house to Kew to here. Infernally, as the Queen might say, ha, ha! She hates it, always on the move. But it has to be done, it has to be done, don't it, hey?'

'Indeed, sir.'

It was not Tom's place to ask why the travelling had to be done if the Queen disliked it so much.

'Your first time here, then, hey? I thought it was so, but you might have come as a visitor. Ye can, don't ye know. Pay for a ticket, see the state apartments, hey? People do.'

'So I understand, sir. But I never have.'

'This way is better value, hey? Don't have to pay a farthing. The only snag, ye have to put up with my company for the duration, ha, ha!'

'It is the utmost privilege, for which no sum would be too large to pay.'

'Ha, if ye say so. If ye say so, sir.'

The King wanted to be contradicted, of course, but Tom suspected that his modesty was not entirely false. Having spent three hours in His Majesty's company at their last sitting, he had concluded that this simple, isolated man did not excessively rate his own society. How different, in that respect, from his brother Cumberland, who so clearly thought the world was blessed to have him in it, even though the man who shared that opinion had yet to be found.

'Mark ye, the whole place is a terrible wreck, don't you see, hey?' A sweep of the royal arm invited Tom to contemplate the faded gilding and the dusty wall-hangings. 'Nothing has been done with it for a hundred years. These apartments were laid out by Charles the Second – the carving is all by Grinling Gibbons, do you see, hey? – and he made a capital job of it, 'pon my soul. Sadly none of his successors cared for the place, certainly not my great-grandfather, when he came over from Hanover, nor my grandfather after him. So I fear it has become rather dilapidated, don't ye know. But I am determined to restore it. Refurbishment, that's the thing, hey?'

Anyone who had spent any time in the King's presence made great sport afterwards of imitating his speech, hey-heying for the entertainment of their friends. Tom had always assumed the lampoons were overdone, and had been surprised to find, that first time at Buckingham-house, that the actual version was every bit as pronounced. It was oddly comforting, now, to hear it again.

'It would be a marvellous project to undertake, sir. In the meantime, I trust there is somewhere comfortable for the family while you are all in residence?'

'Oh yes, we have made the Lodge very decent, very decent indeed. Just outside the castle walls. Ye will have passed it, I think? Yes, I knew it was so. It used to belong to Queen Anne. Saved her the bother of coming inside, don't ye know. We have made it exceeding comfortable now, and we are all there, except the Prince of Wales, who has his own apartment here. He is a man now, not a boy any longer, hey? Anyway, enough of my prattle. Mustn't keep ye from your work, hey? Your easel is here, don't you see, and your canvas, and they will close the shutters and light a candle, which is your preferred method of illumination, is it not so, hey? Yes, I knew it was so.'

It had been Tom's first question, upon being summoned here to Windsor, rather than Buckingham-house: would he need to collect his easel and canvas and transport them in his own carriage? No, he was assured – the royal couple and their large family were constantly on the move, in permanent rotation between their three houses, so his apparatus and canvas would be treated as part of the household luggage, to be conveyed wherever their majesties went. Now, the footman who had been standing quietly by the door took his cue to see to the windows and the candle, while Tom opened his box of pigments. A sheet had already been laid over the carpet.

It was the first time he had seen his work in progress, draped ready over the easel, in three weeks. Impractical as it was not to be working in his own studio, there was something to be said for not seeing the painting in all that time. Now he saw it with fresh eyes, as a stranger might. What struck him immediately was the strange shape of the head he had painted. The brow seemed to slope backwards, and the face widened dramatically at the cheeks, an impression heightened by a wig that slicked close to the skull at the top of the head but then curled into a single, woolly scroll over each ear. As yet, the royal body was only sketched out in chalk: left foot pointing forward, the right one behind it at three-o'clock; bicorne hat in the left hand, the right hovering at chest level, gesturing at the Garter star on the breast of the tailcoat. The coat itself cascaded away behind the royal hips, which were notably capacious. The thighs, in this sketch, were also hefty, testament perhaps to His Majesty's enthusiastic horsemanship, but making the royal head look all the smaller. Tom's first reaction was panic: he seemed to have given his sovereign the body of an orchard pear.

As he turned his eyes on the King himself, however, who was

carefully adjusting his feet into the same three-o'clock stance, he saw that his depiction was not inaccurate. Furthermore, His Majesty had had ample opportunity to see it for himself, and had raised no complaint, so there was no cause for alarm.

The court dress had been Tom's own suggestion. All the gentlemen in the household wore the same single-breasted navy-blue tailcoats with scarlet facings over buff waistcoat and breeches. The King's coat had thick stripes of gold braid around the buttonholes, but it was still recognisably part of a uniform, and it made him look like a member of a royal team, rather than the remote, ermined eminence on a throne that Sir Joshua had depicted. It also had the advantage that this was what he would be wearing anyway, so there was no time wasted in robing him up.

He began by applying a little more colour to the royal cheeks. He saw now that the eyes were more tired than he had caught so far. With a dab of brown on his little finger, he traced a line around the right-hand socket, the side that was brightest lit. As usual for this close work, he had the easel very near to his subject and then he himself stood at an angle to it, so that he was no further from the King than from the canvas. It flustered some sitters to have him in such proximity, but the King stood and gazed with the calm of one whose calling it was to stand and be seen. Barely blinking, he might have been made of wax.

'How am I doing, Gainsborough, hey?' he asked after a while. 'Standing still enough for ye?'

'Capital, sir. If only every sitter could hold a pose for so long without a wobble or a fidget.'

Now the waxwork swelled a little at the chest, its lips twitching proudly at the corners. The King was trying so hard to do this well, he wanted the praise.

'I'm only sorry I am obliging you to remain standing for such a period, sir. I believe, though, that you will see the benefit when the picture is done. Standing, you will be a commanding presence. Much more so than…'

'Than sprawled on my perishing throne in a furlong of red velvet, hey?'

Tom had not meant to snipe so obviously at Sir Joshua's painting. He shrugged, in an attempt to seem non-committal.

'Don't want to speak ill of the president, eh, Gainsborough, hey? Aye, aye, ye may not, but I can. Not on my own behalf, don't ye know, but for the Queen. That splendid, kind, clever, selfless woman thinks only of England and never of herself. And what thanks does she receive, eh? To be insulted, by Jove, made to look like… Gah!'

He had lost his composure now. His hand trembled as he groped in his tailcoat pocket for a kerchief to mop his brow.

'I'm sure no slight was intended,' said Tom. Having now viewed Sir Joshua's pictures of the royal couple for himself, he could see that any husband would be displeased. Nevertheless, Sir Joshua was too ambitious to show deliberate discourtesy. If there was any failure, it was of competence.

'It was given, whether intended or not,' said the King, returning the kerchief to his pocket and regaining some of his composure. 'Can't be doing with the man. I wish the Scotch fellow would come back. Ramsay, he is our official painter, don't ye know. Principal Painter in Ordinary, that's his title, and a capital good fellow. We offered him a knighthood, but he wouldn't take it. Frightened of the mob. He said, 'Sir, they hate the Scotch enough already, and I don't want to make it worse.' Dreadful thing is, he may have been right. I gave it to the blackguard Reynolds instead, more fool me. And now we see too much of him, and nothing of Ramsay. Do ye know him, sir, hey? Ramsay, I mean, not the other fellow.'

'We both studied as boys at St Martin's Lane, sir, but he is older than me, and he was gone before I arrived. I lived at Bath for many years, when his career was at its height, so I never saw him then, and now he no longer paints. He cares only for his books, and I believe he spends considerable time in Italy, so our paths have never crossed.'

'Terrible pity that he can no longer paint. An accident, wasn't it? Yes, I thought it was so. He did me as Prince of Wales, ye know, and I enjoyed his company most handsomely. We talked about politics. He knows a good deal about Europe, don't ye know, so it's no surprise that he is always in Italy. Later he did me in my coronation robes. Hey? He made me very handsome, which of course means he has no talent for a likeness – ha, ha! – but he's a fine man nonetheless.'

'I have seen the painting, and, as I recall, it was very like.'

Tom of course knew the picture, which was unforgettable because of the dazzling amount of gold in the coronation coat and trousers. Ramsay had indeed made the King handsome, but there was no flattery needed. The young prince who, twenty years previously, had succeeded his ancient, embittered grandfather George the Second, was known for his rose-cheeked, virginal beauty. That was one reason his betrothal to a duck-billed princess from a tiny German duchy had so confounded his subjects.

'In the past we have had some great men as Principal Painter, hey?' continued the King. 'The German fellow, I forget his name...'

'Kneller, sir?'

'That's the chap. And before him Lely. He was a Dutchman, hey? And before him, the greatest Dutchman of the lot, hey, hey?'

'I have just been admiring his Queen Henrietta in the long gallery. We are all in his debt.'

'And now we have Ramsay, who thinks the mob will hate him for being Scotch. It's high time we had an Englishman, hey?'

Tom leaned close in to his canvas to attend to the fine detail of the royal hairpiece. Was the King teasing him? There was no sign of mischief in his expression. He could hear Mrs Gainsborough's voice, as surely as if she were in the room, urging him to push himself forward, to grasp the moment and vaunt his own keenness. But it would be unseemly, when there was no vacancy. Ramsay might be indisposed, but he was not dead.

'Shackleton was English, sir. And Kent.'

'Aye, aye, Shackleton. Right ye are, he was still there when we arrived. I was thinking it was the Scotch fellow already, but he only had the official appointment later on. Ye have a good memory, Gainsborough, as well as everything else, hey?'

'My wife would not agree on that, sir. By her assessment I am tipping already into my dotage.'

'Pay her no attention! Don't tell her I said so, though, ha! As for Queen Henrietta, she is enchanting, is she not? Not a blood relative, of course. She was married to my great-great-great-grand-uncle, God rest his soul. Poor woman, how she must have suffered.'

Tom's grasp of history was just about strong enough to know who Queen Henrietta was, and therefore to appreciate that the King's great-great-great-grand-uncle was the hapless Charles the First. Of course the King was keen to emphasise that connection, and to assert that his German family did have some blood link to the old kings of England.

'That is the sort of portrait the Queen must have, don't ye

know. Our court painter can't move his painting arm, and the President of the Royal Academy seems to be blind as well as deaf, so I'm counting on ye to make a better a job of it, Gainsborough, hey?'

'I will do my best, sir.'

Tom would need to proceed carefully. While His Majesty had little vanity where his own likeness was concerned, he evidently had higher expectations when it came to his wife.

He worked on, mixing smalt with a spot of black to achieve the dark blue of the tailcoat. The flashes of scarlet at the collar and cuffs offered bright little flashes of excitement for the eye. Sometimes the King made conversation, sometimes he was quiet, and Tom followed his lead, speaking when he was spoken to, not speaking when he was not.

He had been working two hours when his sitter said: 'What of your family, Gainsborough, hey? You have daughters, am I not right? Aye, aye, I knew it. Are they well, sir, hey?'

Tom paused before answering. It was always difficult to know how much to reveal.

'Middling well, sir. The elder, Molly, is beset with a malady of the temperament, and her spirit suffers. The younger, Peggy, is my delight.'

'Daughters are a worry, eh? An agony of worry. I have five of them, don't ye know. Five girls and seven boys, with another on the way. The Queen tells me, as a matter of certainty, that it will be another boy, and she is always right. So, eight of one and five of the other, but the girls are the greater worry. The boys are no trouble. The Prince of Wales will be a fine and brilliant king, if his laziness don't get the better of him. His brother Frederick is the pleasantest, finest fellow you ever met. Young William is making his country proud in the Navy – he's an ordinary midshipman, you know, with no special favours – and the younger boys will all find their way, I have no fear of it. The girls, though… What am I to do with them, hey? Am I to let them be carried to castles in obscure corners of Germany, the kind of place I brought their mother from, by young men whom neither they nor I have met? Hey? 'Pon my soul, I simply can't bring myself to do it. Ye may not know it, Gainsborough, but I come from a devilish unhappy line. My great-grandfather locked away my great-grandmother in a fortress, and he detested my grandfather. My grandfather in turn detested my father. Didn't even go to his funeral, don't ye know.'

Of course Tom knew. The vicious feuding inside this imported royal family had mesmerised England for as long as the Hanoverian house had ruled it.

'I vowed that I would never let that happen to my own family,' continued the King. 'Made a promise to the Good Lord that I would treat my children with kindness and affection; and so I have endeavoured to do. And that means I will not marry my girls off just to build a dynasty and breed more princes and princesses, hey, Gainsborough, hey? What?' He fumbled again in his tailcoat pocket for his kerchief, without once breaking his pose by looking down. 'Ye take it from me, Gainsborough. Be very careful who ye let them marry, hey?'

Tom stood back to contemplate the shaded folds he had been tracing around the silk-clad royal midriff. Had he made it too pronounced?

Daughters were indeed a worry. If only his own girls had a queue of princely suitors waiting to carry them off to German castles. How much sounder he would sleep then. For a moment, he considered whether he might open his own heart to the King, to convey his anguish at the inherited madness that plagued poor, blameless Molly, and to tell him that in her deluded state she imagined herself pursued by fantasy suitors. No, of course he could not reveal that. He might not be able to cure Molly's sickness, but he could at least guard her dignity by preserving the secret of her delusion.

'In my case, sir, the problem is the reverse,' he said. 'Suitors have never banged on our door, and my girls have reached that certain age, I fear, when the knock will never come. I heed what you say, but husbands are the least of my worries.'

'Won't do it,' said the King. 'Confound it, I simply won't, and I won't hear any more about it.'

It took Tom a moment to grasp that His Majesty was still talking about his own daughters and seemed not to have heard anything he himself had said.

He was relieved he had elected not to confide. It would have been galling to be completely ignored.

Pall-mall,
Feb. 21st, 1780

To my dearest Ma

I am writing this downstairs in the kitchen, where the hearth is still smouldering, so it is much warmer than our little attic room. Down here I have the light of one small candle, which I am permitted to use by the generosity of a certain person, as long as I am quiet and Cook does not catch me. I believe I am safe on that score: I can hear her snoring already and there is no danger of my scratchings rousing her.

I was sorry to hear about the cramps in your head, of which Dick acquainted me in his last letter. I hope they have eased. If they have not and you are still ailing, you should carry a small piece of brimstone sewn up in linen and hold it in your hand when you feel any symptom. Cook says she always does this when she is thus afflicted and it brings a rapid benefit. She is fierce at times but she is not a bad sort, with plenty of kindness in her soul, and I told her you would be grateful for her recommendation.

There was much upheaval in this household to-day because Miss Molly was married this morning. Her husband is Mr Fisher, my master's German friend who I have mentioned to you afore. My master and he have many times been in liquor together, but this does not mean my master is content to have him as a son-in-law. I know from all the shouting and raging I have heard in this house that he and my mistress are most displeased, but my master has resolved to feign otherwise for the sake of Miss Molly.

As I acquainted you afore, Mr Fisher was frequently in this house to drink chocolate with my master, only he seemed more keen to cast glances at both Miss Molly and Miss Peggy, which became the cause of much jealousy between the two young ladies. Then Mr Fisher stopped calling, because my master understood his game and made him know he was not willing to let it continue under his roof. The way I see it, Miss Molly and Miss Peggy should both be happy to have a suitor, else they soon become too old for any man to want to bother, so my master ought to have welcomed Mr Fisher. But Perkiss says no sane man would ever want his daughter to marry his own friend, especially if he and that friend have often been a-raking together. When I consider how much gin I can smell on my master's breath whenever he returns home late, I reckon as how Perkiss makes a fair point.

Then, three weeks ago, Mr Fisher came to call. It was I who let him in. I knew he was not welcome in the house, but he implored me with such urgency to ask if my master would see him, I let him into the hall and bade him wait. I know him as a merry gentleman who never talks much because his English is shocking bad, so instead he just laughs, but this day he was not laughing at all. He looked so serious, standing just inside the front door clutching his hat in both hands, that I feared one of my master's other German musick-making friends – Mr Bark, who is very famous, or Mr Able, who is very fat – had perhaps died and Mr Fisher had come to bring the sad tidings.

My master was working in his painting room with Mr Dupont. I told him that Mr Fisher desired to see him most urgent, and when he asked what was the reason, I told him I did not know but Mr Fisher was very grave of countenance. My master said 'd__t the man' (which is a mild form of cursing by his standards) and bade me show Mr Fisher up to the drawing room.

I did this and, as I was escorting him up the stairs, I noticed Miss Molly on the landing of the floor above, looking down at us, with an expression just as grave as Mr Fisher's. Poor fool that I am, I thought perhaps Miss Molly had already heard the same doleful tidings that Mr Fisher had come to tell her father. I did not think to wonder how she could have come by such intelligence without my master knowing.

In any case, there were no bad tidings, not relating to the death of any friend, in any case. It soon turned out that Mr Fisher had come to ask for Miss Molly's hand. It was all agreed between the two of them, but they wanted my master's consent. I did not hear this in person, but I knew it very soon afterwards, because the whole house was in commotion as soon as Mr Fisher had departed. There were raised voices from the drawing room. I was not trying to listen, you understand, but it is my duty to attend quickly when I am bidden, so I stationed myself outside the door to be ready, and I could not help over-hearing, especially if I moved my ear very close to the door.

My mistress was shouting that my master should not give that man his consent, because he is a wastrel, and not even an English one. My master spoke more quietly, so I could not hear his part in the argument, but I heard my mistress respond that it was not true that Miss Molly would end up an old maid else, because she came from a fine line with a very distinguished grandfather. By that, she did not mean my master's father, Mr Gainsborough the shroud-maker of Sepulchre-street, who was always so well known in our town. She was referring rather to her own origins. The talk below stairs is that my mistress is the natural daughter of some eminent personage, a great gentleman, perhaps even a member of the Royal Family. Perkiss reckons it could have been the old Prince of Wales, the King's father. He would have been one-and-twenty years old when my mistress was born, says Perkiss, which makes it possible, but so were ten thousand other young men in England, so I do not see as how it signifies anything. To that, Perkiss would say that my mistress is always dropping hints about how high-born she is, so there must be some substance. That's as mayhap, but the way I see it, there is no point in being the daughter of a noble-born gentleman if that gentleman will not recognise the daughter as his own. I know I am right in this opinion because, in all the time I have worked in this house, I have seen no queue of husbands lining up to woo Miss Molly or Miss Peggy, so even if my mistress is the King's half-sister and the girls are His Majesty's natural nieces, there is not a single gentleman, handsome or ugly, rich or poor, who seems to care, aside of course from Mr Fisher.

While my master and mistress were exchanging their words in the drawing room, a further tumult erupted on the floor above. I head Miss Molly's and Miss Peggy's voices, one of them much louder than the other, and then a lot of caterwauling. At that point, my master opened the drawing-room door and bade me fetch Miss Molly, so I climbed the stairs to the second floor. There I found Miss Molly knocking on the closed door of Miss Peggy's chamber, begging to be admitted so that she could explain herself. I was obliged to interrupt and acquaint her that her father desired an interview on the instant, whereupon she stopped her knocking and began adjusting her bonnet in a most nervous fashion. I have never seen her look so afeared as when she descended those stairs to meet my master.

I did not hear any more loud voices, even though I stationed myself outside the door once more, in case I was required. The unexpected outcome of the interview, as the whole household learned later, was that Miss Molly received her father's consent. We all reckon he feared she would else elope. (You must think we are terrible gossips, Ma, but that is the way of a house like this.) My mistress was not happy with this decision, because she still believed Miss Molly could do better than a foreigner and a musick-maker, and Miss Peggy was not happy because she wanted Mr Fisher for herself. However, their objections were not heeded. My master may not always be master in this household, but on this occasion his wish prevailed.

And so this morning Miss Molly did marry Mr Fisher at a little church near here, in May-fair. There were not many guests, because Miss Molly does not have any friends, and none of my master's kin were present, whether because it was too far to travel or because my master was ashamed to invite them, I do not know. Mr Fisher does not have kin here either, because they are all in Germany, but he did bring his friends Mr Bark and Mr Able, who are my master's friends too. Mr Dupont was a witness, which meant he was obliged to write his name in the register, and I heard from him later that Miss Peggy sobbed through the whole service, quite loudly sometimes. There was no breakfast after, which pleased Cook, because there was no big party to feed, although I reckon we could have made a fine celebration for the happy couple. Poor Annie has returned to her mother in Somerset, which means my master's china is safe from destruction at last, but her position has been filled in a most capable way by… No, I will tell you more of that anon, else I will forget the point of my present story, which is that the new Mr and Mrs Fisher went off alone to their new house, which is also in May-fair, and my master, my mistress, Miss Peggy and Mr Dupont came home.

The mood here has been exceeding gloomy since their return. My master has been trying to console Miss Peggy, whose weeping has barely abated, but with no success. Mr Dupont acquainted me that one of the reasons my master is so vexed with Mr Fisher is that he has caused Miss Peggy such upset. This is puzzling to me. If my master does not think Mr Fisher is suitable to marry Miss Molly, surely that gentleman is no more fitting as a husband for Miss Peggy neither. Mr Dupont says that is not the point, and that Mr Fisher ought never to have made eyes at Miss Peggy, making her think she was the object of his heart's affection, when in truth it was beating for Miss Molly. I told Mr Dupont I understand that reasoning, but I still hold to my own view of the matter: if Mr Fisher is such a bad husband as my master believes, he ought to be congratulating Miss Peggy on her fortunate delivery from the fate that has instead befallen her sister.

Later in the afternoon, when it was quite dark, my master called me into his painting room. There I found him and Mr Dupont standing before the great stack of canvasses that lean against the long wall of the studio. These are pictures that my master has painted but not sold. By the light of his candle, he had been a-searching for a particular painting, which he had now found, and he wanted me and Mr Dupont to pull it out and set it on an easel. This was a complicated task, because the picture was a good deal taller than each of us. It was not so heavy, because it had not yet been given a frame, but it was awkward to lift out of the stack without causing damage to it or to another painting. This was a cause of great fretting for my master, who called us coxcombs and addle-pates, as is always his way when he is nervous, and he said we were in danger of ripping it if we did not take better care. His fears were unfounded, though, and we succeeded in setting the picture safely on an empty easel.

My master bade me stand beside it, holding the candle up so that he could see it properly. From where I stood, I was too close to make the picture out. I could see it was the portrait of a gentleman, but that was all. Then my master fell to complaining that I was holding the candle too close and was like to scorch the paint, which is not true, because I was taking good care what I was doing, and I could tell better how close I was, from where I was standing, than he could from where he was. There was no sense answering back, though, else I would find myself turned onto the street and out of my master's service. So I said I was sorry and I moved the candle further away. My master still found reason to complain about the way I was holding it, so he bade Mr Dupont change places with me and take the candle in my stead. This gave me the opportunity to stand back and see the picture for myself. You will be as surprised as I was, Ma, when I tell you that the gentleman in the picture, leaning on a pianoforte and holding a quill in his hand like he was writing a piece of musick, was none other than Mr Fisher, Miss Molly's new husband.

It seemed from his exceeding smooth countenance in the picture that it was painted some years ago, and Mr Dupont later acquainted me that it was done when my master was living at Bath, a few years before he made his home in London.

Wearing a fine crimson suit, with one white stocking crossed over the other at the ankle, Mr Fisher stood looking up in the air with a most satisfied expression. I have noticed that this is often his expression in real life, because he is the kind of gentleman who always looks very pleased with himself, but anyone looking at this picture who was not acquainted with Mr Fisher would imagine that he was hearing musick notes in his head, which he was about to write down on his paper.

To my mind, this was a very fine picture indeed, although of course I am no proper judge. In this instance, though, I was perchance right, because Mr Dupont said he thought so too. He could not see it well from where he was standing to hold the light, but he had beheld it already from the place where I now stood, and he said to his uncle as how he believed it was a masterpiece, and surely he did not mean to destroy it. I had in my mind the precise same question.

'How, destroy it?' said my master. 'Why the D___l would I do that?' Nay, he said, he meant to send it to the Academy. I was glad to hear him say this, Ma. As I understand it, it will be my master's way of telling the world he means to embrace his new son-in-law, even if in private he considers him a scoundrel. I feared he might break with Miss Molly over this unpopular marriage, but I do not now believe that this is his intent.

You must think me soft in the head, Ma, to take the affairs of this family so much to heart, particularly when my master so often calls me a coxcomb and a numbskull. But he is nearly always kind to me after the vexation has passed and Miss Molly has never raised her voice to me, so I wish her no ill, nor any other member of this family, quite the contrary. 'Tis quite natural for a member of the household to care for the family so. We all say so: not just me, but Perkiss, and Cook, and the other person who is generous in nature, who I have not yet told you about. It is too late to starting telling you now because the candle is burning low and I must get to my bed else I will be too tired for my duties on the morrow.

So that is all from me now, except for the biggest kisses to you and Dick and Jack, from your ever-loving

David

12

Gemma gazed in dismay at her desktop inbox. When they were out on location, she did her best to keep up with her emails, making sure she checked her phone regularly and trying to clear some of the backlog whenever she had a spare moment. Despite her best efforts, they seemed to multiply whenever her back was turned, and she now had three hundred and forty-nine unopened messages.

Not all of them needed opening: there were plenty of the kind that were not quite spam, because it was worth being on such-and-such a mailing list on the off-chance, but they always went straight into the trash as if they were. Over-zealous binning was where mistakes happened, though. It was also easy to click a message out of bold by accident, so that it no longer showed as unread, and then she forgot it was there. With an unforgiving Fiammetta as her boss, that way lay perdition, so it was better to be slow and systematic. The ever-growing backlog was the consequence.

The production office was in a former soap factory in Deptford, now reimagined as a business park for graphics houses and software companies that could not afford Shoreditch or Bermondsey. Their second-floor unit offered a perfect view into the train carriages on the London Bridge viaduct. There was an artisan café with its own DJ, a bike park full of fixed-gear cycles, and modern electronic security on the old wrought-iron factory gates, because the kit in the bare-brick, raw-girdered units was an obvious after-hours temptation for teenagers in the post-war council blocks that ringed the site. Gemma did not ride a fixed-gear bike, nor any other kind; she caught the driverless, elevated train from Lewisham, where she had a room in a characterless semi off the Bromley Road. Fiammetta usually drove from Blackheath – three miles, and a world away – but today there was no sign of her Alfa in the car park and Gemma was alone in the office.

She had already had Kaz on the phone, wanting to know if there was any more news about Muriel. He knew that she and Vivian had raced off to Muriel's house just before the end of filming the previous night. Gemma had already told him their journey was fruitless, and that Muriel was either out or refused to open the door, but now he wanted to know if there was any further update.

'It does put me in a tricky position, you see darling. I said in good faith that picture was a monstrosity. That's what I thought yesterday, and it's what I still think today. If another expert is saying something else behind my back, it's very undermining.'

Gemma knew she must tread carefully.

'Nobody is going behind your back, Kaz, and there is

absolutely no intention to undermine your integrity. You're a hugely valued member of the team. You know that.'

'I'm the only expert with a profile, darling. Who's heard of Lavender Weston-Wotsit or Vivian blimmin' Morris?'

'I know that. You're quite right. And nobody disagrees that Muriel's picture is a monstrosity. But Vivian has a real concern that it may be genuine, as well as a monstrosity, so we have to do what we can to investigate.'

'I don't see why. It was given to me to assess, so Vivian should keep his snout out. That's what I mean about being undermined.'

'But morally, Kaz. We have an obligation.'

'Morally! This is the antiques trade we're talking about!'

'It's also a national television programme where we need to be seen to be fair. Honestly though, Kaz, I don't think you have anything to worry about. The picture will probably turn out to be worthless junk, just as you say. In any case, it doesn't look like Muriel wants any more to do with us. I put my number through her letterbox last night, and she hasn't called back. If she doesn't want to co-operate, we can't take it any further. We either go with the footage we've already got, or we ditch it completely. That's what Fiammetta says.'

'Sounds like I need to have a word with Fiammetta myself.'

'By all means, but she'll only tell you the same as I have.'

'There's no harm in hearing it from her directly. I want her to know I have strong feelings about this.'

'She knows that already, Kaz.'

'And one other thing. If it does turn out to be a priceless work of art, you'll have the footage of me saying it's a load of rubbish and looking like a total wazzock. So here's what I want to know: where's the equivalent footage of Vivian saying it's a Gainsborough, that will make him look like a pillock when it turns out to be a load of old rubbish? Eh?'

It was a relief when he finally rang off. Let him pester Fiammetta instead. She was the one who hired him; let her deal with his fragile ego.

She had reduced her inbox total by twenty when her phone rang again. This time it was Lavender, checking on arrangements for the next location shoot, which was in Kent. She needed to be back in Spitalfields for a friend's gallery opening, so could Gemma arrange for her to finish early? No, Gemma explained, she could not, because it was a filming day, and professional artists were expected to stay for as long as they were needed. She managed to put it a little more politely than that, but the underlying point was clear: Lavender was being paid as a heavy-weight professional, so she should stop behaving like a light-weight amateur. Fortunately, she seemed to get the message and backed off without complaint. Gemma had feared that Lavender, too, might go running to Fiammetta for confirmation, which would not be helpful, coming on top of the Kaz situation. If Gemma was not capable of shielding her boss from the irritating demands of the talent, Fiammetta might legitimately start to wonder what was the point of employing her.

She had cleared another thirty-five emails when her phone rang for a third time. The name that flashed up made it a full house of experts.

'Hello Vivian,' she said, attempting to sound less grumpy than she felt. 'How are you today?'

'I'm on the train,' shouted Vivian.

Gemma moved her phone a little further from her ear.

'I thought you were meant to be back in Norfolk today. Where are you off to?'

'I'm coming to London. Listen, I may get cut off, so I'll

be quick. I want you to meet me on the steps of the National Gallery at half past twelve. I've managed to get an appointment with an eighteenth-century curator, and I want you to be there too.'

'But Vivian, I've got tons to do here. I can't just leave the…'

'Hello…? Hello…? I think I may have lost you. If you can still hear me, that's the steps of the National Gallery, half past twelve. I'll see you there.'

'Vivian…?'

He had cut her off. For all his fogeyish incompetence with technology, Gemma reckoned he knew exactly how to get his way by pretending he could not hear her answer. The thought made her smile, and she realised it was the first time she had done so all morning. Sod it, she thought; she still had a mountain of messages, but she deserved a trip into town. Meeting a National Gallery curator might be fun.

She arrived in Trafalgar Square ten minutes before Vivian's appointed time, but he was there already, standing next to a pull-along cabin bag and smoking one of his liquorice roll-ups. It was a clear day, but cold, and he wore woollen fingerless gloves, which looked incongruous with his tweed jacket and plus-fours, but Gemma had learned by now that incongruity was Vivian's hallmark.

He raised his hand high to show that he had seen her, amid the crowd of hardy February tourists doing selfies in the square.

'I didn't know if you'd come.'

'I shouldn't have,' said Gemma. 'I've got loads of stuff I ought to be doing in the office. I'll just have to stay late tonight to make up for it.'

It was lucky she had no personal life for her work to intrude upon. Staying late at the office was no worse than a whole evening spent watching Netflix in her room.

'It'll be worth it, I hope.' He looked at his watch. 'Let's go inside. He told me to ask for him at the information desk.'

'Who are we seeing?'

'Chap called Richards. He's a specialist on the whole period, rather than Gainsborough himself, but he was very friendly on the phone and he said he was happy to have a look at the photograph I took.'

'You could have just emailed it.'

'Sometimes the old-fashioned way is best. I want him to look at the portrait itself, not the damage or the defacing, and it's easier to make sure he does that if I show it to him personally. Besides, I was coming to London this morning anyway, ready for Kent tomorrow. And it was a nice excuse to come to this place.'

Jolyon Richards, who came to the information desk as promised after they had been through the bag searches on the door, was a tousle-haired blond of about thirty, in chinos and jacket, with a tie slung loose at his neck and a rogue dab of shaving foam behind one ear. He spoke in a lazy drawl, hardly moving his lips. His education had clearly been a good deal more expensive than Gemma's.

He ushered them through a door marked 'private', which led into the behind-the-scenes world of administrators' offices and curators' cubby-holes. His own lair was one half of a small room with a tiny window high in one wall, and books in every available space.

'So,' he said, having offered them his own and his absent colleague's seats, while he perched on the corner of his desk. 'How can I help?'

'As I explained on the phone, we were shown a painting a couple of days ago which looks a complete mess at first sight, but might be worth closer examination,' said Vivian. 'The lady who brought it to us told us it had been passed down her family, generation by generation, in the belief it was painted by Gainsborough. Given that she lives in the town where Gainsborough was born, there's an obvious geographical link. It's possible that has merely fuelled the family myth, but I don't want to dismiss her claim out of hand, even though the picture itself has been both very badly damaged and defaced.'

He pulled out his phone and showed Richards the photograph he had taken in the street of Muriel's picture.

The curator's eyes widened.

'I see what you mean. Someone has tried jolly hard to destroy it. However, as you say, that doesn't mean your lady is wrong about its origins. Let's see if we can have a closer look.' He splayed his thumb and forefinger to maximise the picture on the phone screen. 'Actually, there's a better way. Why don't you email it to me, and I can look at it on my desktop?'

After a couple of false starts, Vivian managed to achieve this. He and Gemma then waited anxiously as their expert – a real one, not the pretend TV version – stared at the image on his screen. They should be filming this, thought Gemma. It was all part of the process of discovery. If the picture turned out to be real, would they have to come back and pretend they were doing it all for the first time?

'Right,' said Jolyon, after poring over the image for several minutes. 'First off, you're not wrong to take this claim seriously. It's very difficult to come to any proper conclusion without seeing the painting itself but, from what I can see, the idea that Gainsborough painted it is not a ridiculous one.'

'Brilliant!' said Gemma, clapping her hands.

'Let's not jump the gun. It's too early for celebration. With questions of attribution, it's much easier to prove that a painting is not by a certain artist than to say for sure that it is. For example, there are tests you can do on the paint itself to try to date a picture, such as by looking for pigments that weren't introduced until known dates. If the artist died before that date, and the pigment is in the painting, the artist can't have painted it. With Gainsborough, it's blue: he used a pigment called smalt, whereas cobalt was much more common later on, but it wasn't around in his lifetime. In your picture, the sitter is wearing a blue coat, and you could test that. If the pigment is cobalt, bad luck: it can't be a Gainsborough. But I'm afraid the reverse doesn't apply. If it isn't cobalt, that won't tell you that Gainsborough painted it, only that he could have. Are you with me?'

Vivian was frowning. 'I thought you could analyse the brush-stroke,' he said.

'Yah, you can, and that would certainly tell you that the work is consistent with a particular artist's style. From what I can see of this picture, I'd say it seems to be, but obviously I'd need to see more than just a photograph. And there are also people far better qualified than me. Do you know Lennie Canham?'

They both shook their heads. Gemma was embarrassed at their ignorance.

'Lennie's your man, as it were. By far the greatest Gainsborough expert, and lives not far from where you found the picture.' He clicked off the photograph and peered at something else on his screen. 'There it is. I'm sending you Lennie's email address,' he said to Vivian. 'That's the best way of getting in touch. Say I sent you, take your picture round, and you should get a much clearer answer.'

'Thank you,' said Vivian, standing up and holding out his hand. 'We really do appreciate it.'

'Hang on a sec,' said Jolyon. 'I haven't got to the most important part. The other thing we can do is look at the historical context. On one level, there's the formal provenance, that's to say, the chain of ownership that brought it into the present lady's hands. We're going back maybe two hundred and fifty years, so there may be records, but I wouldn't count on it.'

'No,' said Vivian.

Gemma could imagine what he was thinking. She could not see Muriel or her ancestors as any great sticklers for clerical detail.

'It's not just about provenance, though. If, for example, we know who the sitter is, we can establish when they were alive, if there's any record in the artist's own papers of his painting them or, failing that, if they were in the same kind of geographical area where their paths could have crossed. And in this case, obviously, we're in luck. It's by far your strongest card.'

Gemma and Vivian looked at each other.

'I don't understand,' Gemma said. 'It's not like we know who the sitter is.'

'Oh my golly,' said Jolyon. 'Sorry, I thought you knew. Forgive me, when you're as immersed in all this stuff as I am, these things seem very obvious, and I forget that...'

'Who do you think the sitter is?' interrupted Vivian.

Instead of answering directly, Jolyon swivelled his chair to face the bookshelf behind him and traced a finger along the second shelf. Finding the volume he wanted, he flicked through the pages and stopped at a full-page colour illustration. He turned the book round so that they could both see it.

'Notice a resemblance?' he said.

Remove the donkey ears from their own portrait, and there was not a shadow of doubt. It was the same man.

13

Mirth swirled in the air along with the smoke of a score of tobacco pipes. Tom was the butt of it, but his friends' teasing caused him no hurt. The subject was musick, the playing thereof – most particularly, his own playing thereof – but he was immune to their ridicule.

He had first attempted to master the violin, spending money that Mrs Gainsborough did not know he had on the finest instrument he could find. Bach had heard him play, then told him the massacre of a herd of cats would sound more melodious. Tom was not put off. Instead, he set about expanding his repertoire of instruments by buying Abel's viola da gamba from him and attempting to learn that, and also taking up the hautboy, in imitation of Fischer. Each instrument made musick of sublime beauty in those men's hands; in Tom's, the result was more feline cacophony, but he had refused to give it up. He knew it exasperated his friends when they were forced to endure his noise; at other times, when they were of more indulgent humour, it caused them great merriment. Their current attitude was the latter, in unbridled expression, after he had announced his intention to take up the harp.

'It is a celestial instrument, to be sure,' said Bach.

'The musick of the angels,' agreed Fischer

Tom had re-admitted his son-in-law as a friend for Molly's sake, and because he liked the society of musicians.

'Indeed it is,' agreed Abel. 'Usually.' He caught his compatriots' eyes and now the three of them began to laugh: Abel shaking silently, his immense belly wobbling under his waistcoat; Bach slapping his own thigh; and Fischer grinning like a cat who had found a whole smoked mackerel as well as a bowl of cream.

Tom sighed, and turned in his chair to wave for more coffee. An aproned boy plucked a tall black pot from its place at the front of the hearth and presented himself at their end of the long, communal table. He proceeded to make theatre of pouring the steaming, bitter liquid into their empty dishes from a great height, without a drop spilt.

If only Tom's friends would understand it, not being good at the instruments was precisely the attraction for him. In the business of pictures, he was always under scrutiny, with the expectations of sitters, the public and the newspapers pushing him to excel. How refreshing it was to have the freedom to be bad at something, completely execrable, and for it not to matter, except to the protesting ears of his musician friends. Let them make as merry as they liked at his expense: he would not desist from his playing.

'It makes my ears to hurt just to think about it, so let us

please stop talking about this,' said Abel. 'Gainsborough, my friend, tell me: how goes the King? I hear you are with him every day.'

'Hardly,' said Tom. 'Every two days, perhaps.'

This was a different kind of ribbing, and he was happy for them to believe, if they wanted, that he spent all his time at court. It was certainly true that his relationship with their majesties had bloomed. He had grown genuinely to like the King. With his slow, earnest ways, His Majesty was not a man of great intellect or fast wit, but he knew it, and he dedicated himself nonetheless to the cause of his own self-improvement, asking Tom all manner of questions about the Italian Masters, which Tom struggled sometimes to answer, having only seen such of those works that hung on the walls of great English houses. The King also fancied himself a farmer, and treated Tom as an expert on the subject, perceiving him as a countryman, however much he protested that he came from a family of merchants and clothiers and knew far more about weaving silk than growing grain or keeping cows.

The King had been pleased with his own picture, when he finally saw it hanging at the Academy, but his far greater rapture was reserved for Tom's portrait of the Queen. Justly so: Tom had been gallant to Her Majesty, although not, he hoped, excessively. He had found beauty in an unexpected quarter, as a number of the notices had observed, but he had not completely invented it. He liked Her Majesty too. She was poised, cultivated, highly intelligent, and had the same clipped, German accent as these, his closest friends. If he had created, as Bate had pronounced in his new paper, the *Morning Herald*, the only happy likeness ever made of her, then he was proud to have done so.

'So, every other day you see him, *ja?*' persisted Abel. 'And how does he do?'

'He does very well. A fine man, who holds his dear wife in the highest esteem. Let that be a lesson to us all.'

Fischer flushed. Tom saw that he had taken it as a jibe, because it had become clear that all was not well between him and Molly. Such meaning was not intended, though: he had meant it as a rebuke to himself.

'She has a fine spirit,' agreed Abel. 'And now you have given her a fine face to go with it.'

That provoked another round of laughter.

'I did not flatter,' Tom protested. 'The likeness is true.'

'Yes, yes, *sicher*,' nodded Bach, trying to maintain the most solemn of faces, but failing in the attempt.

Tom shook his head.

'The three of you are no better than schoolboys. Have you no respect? She is your countrywoman, as well as our Queen.'

Abel made a play of straightening his countenance.

'Quite so. You are right, my friend, and we are wretched men. So, tell us: who are you painting now? The royal children?'

'Not all of them. Have you seen how many there are? Thirteen…fourteen…the King himself tells me he loses count. I have done Prince William Henry…'

'The second boy,' nodded Fischer. 'He is in the Navy now,' he explained to Bach and Abel.

'And the Prince of Wales,' continued Tom.

'*Ach so*, and how does he look?' asked Abel. 'I hear he is as fat as me.'

'Not quite that fat, my friend. He is a handsome boy still, but he lives very well. He is not yet twenty years old. Give him another ten years, and we will see him as fat as you.'

'Good,' said Abel, slapping his own thigh approvingly.

'And this is all you do now, paint pictures of princes and

princesses?' said Bach.

Abel nudged his compatriot, mock-confidentially.

'You know what I think? I think this fellow here is a changeling. Our good friend Gainsborough used to sit in this very coffee-house for hour after hour, telling us how much he hated the cursed business of painting faces, and most especially the highest-born sitters, because they were the greatest pain in the *Arsch* and they made his blood to boil. This fellow before us now, he looks like Tom Gainsborough, and he has the voice of Tom Gainsborough, but where is the complaining? All day he paints the very highest-born people in the land, so he should be in the greatest rage we have ever seen, but this fellow before us is calm! No, my friends, I tell you, this is the work of sorcery. Our friend Gainsborough has been magicked away by devilment, and this fellow here is an imposter, *nicht?*'

The two other Germans had begun to laugh during this speech, and by the end of it, Bach was slapping the table, causing cries of protest from patrons further along, as their dishes of coffee jumped and spilled.

'You are a jackanapes, sir,' said Tom. 'And you, my friend, should take care you do not rupture some blood vessel. You will not think it so comical then.'

That made Bach, who had indeed turned a dangerous shade of puce, laugh even more.

'Not that it is any business of you knaves,' Tom continued, 'but I have many other pictures under way. I am working at another woodland cottage scene, and a fancy-painting that will show a little girl and three...'

He stopped abruptly.

'Three what?' said Abel.

Tom ignored him. 'What is the hour?'

Bach pulled out the pocket watch that was his proudest

possession and squinted myopically at it.

'It is half past three o'clock,' said Fischer, leaning over to read it for him.

Tom slapped his palm against his forehead. How could he have been so stupid? He sprang to his feet, tipped a handful of coins onto the table and picked up his hat.

'My friends, I must take my leave. My apologies. There is no time to explain.'

Leaving the three of them staring up at him in confusion, he ran for the door.

'Three what?' called Abel after him, but Tom barely heard.

He stood in the doorway and looked up and down Bedford-street, which swarmed with chaises, sedans, carts, hawkers and urchins. A small boy in ragged breeches was picking straw from a pile of steaming horse dung. Tom whistled him over.

'I'll give you tuppence to find me a hackney coach, as quick as you can,' he said, and the boy scampered off to fulfil his errand. Tom could barely contain his panic as he waited, attempting to slow his breathing to stop the agitation. How could he have forgotten? It was vital that he be at home this afternoon, yet he had strolled out to the coffee-house without a care for…

''Ere's your 'ackney, sir,' said the boy, looking up at him with his palm outstretched.

There indeed was the coach, much sooner than Tom could have hoped. He pressed a sixpence into the child's hand and climbed aboard, calling to the driver: 'St James's-square, as fast as you can go.'

They clattered down Half-moon-street and into the Strand, past Twining's teashop and the chop houses, taverns and booksellers that lined that street. They swept past the Hungerford-market and the great façade of Northumberlandhouse, then around Charing-cross, into Cockspur-street towards Pall-mall. There they slowed to a halt. There was a blockage at the bottom of the Hay-market where a cart had spilled, and the carriages and coaches were backing up.

Tom leaned forward.

'Take Great Suffolk-street, here, and then Little Suffolk-street, and you can cross the Hay-market towards St James's-square.'

'The passages are too narrow, sir,' the driver shouted back. 'I shall have to go round Piccadilly.'

'Do it, man. We have no time to waste.'

The driver did as he was bidden, cutting around the spilled waggon and the coaches waiting behind it, to go into one of the smaller streets and then a smaller one still, barely squeezing through, and emerging onto the Hay-market, up which he then raced his horses towards Piccadilly.

'Which side of St James's-square, sir?'

'The bottom end, closest to Pall-mall.'

'If you're going to Pall-mall and you're in such a terrible hurry, sir, why don't you let me take you all the way there?'

'No! Just set me down where I tell you, man.'

The driver shrugged.

He was not to know that Tom could only get down from a hackney-coach out of sight of his own windows, otherwise Mrs Gainsborough would give him an ear-bashing for wasting twelve penn'orth of coach hire. It was twelve penn'orth that he himself had earned, from selling face-pictures for fifty guineas, but that counted for little where the finances of the household were concerned.

Pressing an extra sixpence into the coachman's hand, he hastened through the bottom of the square onto Pall-mall. At least the prodigious amount of coffee he had taken had given him energy.

Reaching his own front door, he had to ring the bell twice. The lad David was always loitering around the kitchen these days, making eyes at the new parlour-maid who, it was true, was a good deal comelier than the old one. Now he stammered apologies for making Tom wait.

'Never mind that now, numbskull. Has any person delivered anything for me?'

'Yes, sir. A box.'

'And what was in the box?'

'I don't know, sir. I merely placed it in your painting room. Although…'

'Yes?'

'Some strange noises came from within it, sir.'

'Oh yes? What sort of noises?'

The lad hesitated. 'Squealing, sir.'

'I understand. Anything else?'

'Also a strange odour, sir.'

'What sort of odour?'

The boy squirmed now, pulling nervously at his ear and not looking Tom in the eye.

'Come on, lad. I'm in a hurry. What sort of odour?'

'Well, sir…it smells like the shed at the back of Old Ben Buskett's cottage back home.'

'Does it, indeed? And what does Old Ben Buskett keep in this shed?'

'Pigs, sir.'

'Right you are.'

The lad looked surprised not to be bellowed at.

'Will that be all, sir?'

'Yes. No, wait. Has your mistress seen this box?'

'No, sir.'

'And have you told her about it?'

'No, sir. I've told no one, sir.'

'Good.' Tom pulled out another sixpence and gave it to the lad. The lazy rascal did not deserve it, but needs must. 'That is how we will keep it, do you understand?'

'Yes, sir.'

'All right, that will be all.'

Tom watched him slink back downstairs, and made his own way along the corridor that led to the back of the house, and his painting room. Disaster seemed, for the moment, to have been averted.

To my dearest Ma

I rejoiced to read your last letter, in our Jack's hand, with news of Dick's marriage, although it filled me with sadness that I could not be there to see them wed. I long for the day when I can meet my new sister, who I am glad to hear you love so much already.

You ask if there will ever be a day when you can celebrate the same happy tidings for your eldest son. I too often wonder if that day will ever come. Love does not offer many opportunities to a young man in service, who is at the beck and call of his master and mistress for every hour of daylight and half the hours of darkness besides. Even when hope does arrive, in the form of a kind, generous, beautiful angel, happiness is not always its companion. Just as often, it heralds the torment of a sighing heart that yearns to be noticed but instead is cruelly shunned.

I'm sorry, Ma, to begin on this sad subject, and I will now close the door on it and tell you of lighter matters which I hope will bring a smile to your face, as it has to mine and all of us who dwell in this uncommon household.

I have told you in the past about the noble folk who come to this house to have their faces painted by my master, but they are not all of the highest sort. This afternoon, his sitters – I swear to you this is the truth – were three little piglets. I myself took delivery of the crate containing these animals while my master was at his coffee-house in Covent-garden.

He had forgotten that the creatures were to arrive to-day. When he remembered, he rushed home as fast he could. His face was as red as a soldier-boy's tunic and he was panting like a hound after the chase when I found him on the front step, but his panic abated when I told him I had put the crate in his painting room and I had not said a word to my mistress concerning its contents, which were obvious from the squealing and the stink. He was of much better cheer to hear this. He is sore afraid of my mistress above all other things, and he has no other care but that she must not find him out in whatever scheme he is pursuing.

After I had let him in, he retired to his painting room, which is removed enough from the rest of the house for any squealing and smell to pass unnoticed. Later, though, Mr Dupont hollered for me to attend on him and his uncle. The painting room smelled like a barnyard when I entered, and my master told me that one of the pigs had done its business in the middle of the floor, and it was my job to clean it up. 'Twas not a nice task, as you can imagine, because the mess was sloppy not solid, but this is our life when we are born to the serving classes, and complaining or pitying ourselves will get us nowhere, as you always taught me, Ma.

When I had cleaned up the piglets' mess, I took the chance to look at what my master was painting. On his easel was a half-painted picture, almost finished on the left hand, and not painted at all on the right. The painted side showed a little girl, maybe five years of age, in bare feet and a ragged dress. I do not know where my master found this girl. I have not seen her entering the house, so he must have found her in the street when he goes abroad on his wanderings with his sketchpad and pencil. In the painting, she was sitting on a low step with one bare arm resting on her knee, and the other bent at the elbow so that she could rest her cheek in her hand. She had such a sad look on her face, which was not right for a little girl, who ought to be smiling and laughing without any worldly care. This, I believe, is the power of my master's painting. It makes you wonder what concerns the poor mite to make her so downcast.

In front of her, my master had begun to sketch the outline of the three pigs, gathered around a big basin of milk. Two of them were drinking nicely from it, with the third one waiting his turn at the back, as polite and patient as you like. If he had asked my opinion, I would have told him what I learned from watching Old Ben Buskett handling his litter when I was small, viz. that no pig ever held back when there was food on offer. I also never saw any of Old Ben's pigs eating from earthenware as was fit for the dinner table, but it was not my place to say so. I do not imagine that any of the fine folk who see the finished painting when it hangs at the Royal Academy will know no better, neither, so it makes no odds whether the scene is like life or not.

Any road, my master could see for himself that his sketch was nothing like the scene before him. He directed Mr Dupont to keep the piglets in place so that he could capture their likeness in paint, but Mr Dupont was not discharging this task to his satisfaction. If I were my master, I might have concluded that trying to persuade three hungry piglets to sup nicely from dainty tableware was a fool's game. Unfortunately, my master's way of reasoning is not the same as mine. Instead of allowing Mr Dupont to give up on his folly, he now bade me assist, so now there were two of us running around the painting room trying to tame creatures that were in no mind to be tamed.

My assistance made the matter manageable where two of the piglets were concerned. Mr Dupont grabbed one of them, a plain white animal, and I grabbed another, with black spots on his back. They did not much like being held, so they wriggled and squirmed at first, but they did not object to the direction in which they were being held, viz. with their snouts pointing into a big bowl of whey, which my master was obliged to refill from a great ewer next to his easel, because they had supped so much of it already.

The problem was the third piglet, which took the opportunity to run around to the other side of the dish and sup greedily from there. If it was up to me, I would have left him there, let him sup in peace, and painted the other two in the meanwhile. But that was not what my master wanted. He fell to complaining that he could not see the other two animals properly, because the one at the front was impeding his view of them. In that case, I hear you say, Ma, there was another easy solution, viz. to change the composition so that the piglets were arranged all around the bowl just as they really were, and forget about the nice arrangement my master had already sketched on the canvas. But you, Ma, are not the second-greatest portrait painter in the land, if you please. My master would not consider any change to his plan. Rather, he reckoned he needed a third pair of hands to hold the third piglet in place, so he went to the door and hollered for Perkiss to come and help.

In no time, then, there were three of us crouching on the floor of the studio, each holding a squealing piglet in place. Perkiss had the worst of it, because his own animal, which was white like mine, only dirtier in colour, with a black stripe on his back, was mighty vexed to be held back from the bowl of whey while he watched his brothers a-feasting of it. This made him more determined to escape Perkiss' grip and I cannot say as how I blamed him.

Somehow, we managed to maintain this scene despite the many difficulties, and my master worked at his picture. To record it truly, he would have had to show two young men and one older one squatting on the floor and holding the creatures in place. Of course he did not wish to do that. So, to add to the awkwardness of the task, he told the three of us to place ourselves behind the piglets, and from time to time to change the position of our hands on the pigs' bellies, so that he could paint the area that they had previously covered.

My master paints very fast, so we were not required to hold our positions for too long, which was just as well, because it was harsh on our backs and knees, especially for Perkiss, who suffers much with his rheumaticks. When Mr Dupont began to express his weariness by means of little sighs and groans – which he, as my master's nephew not his servant, is more able to do than me or Perkiss – my master laughed and told us he was grateful for our efforts, but we in turn should be grateful that we were not performing the same duty for Sir Joshua Reynolds, who works much slower and would have us crouching there for two days. Mr Dupont muttered that Sir Joshua is not in the habit of painting pigs, so he would not have us there at all, but he said it very softly and his uncle did not hear this remark.

Despite our discomfort, I am certain that the three of us would have been able to maintain our positions until my master had finished painting the pig. The commotion that prevented us from doing so was none of our making, unless you count Perkiss as responsible for leaving the painting-room door open.

None of us had noticed that the door was ajar, but Fox, my master's dog, has a better nose for such things than we do. He also has a nose for piglets. While we were all engaged in our various offices, he pushed the door open to see what was happening in this room, where often he is allowed to sit and watch my master, but to-day he was forbidden. Just behind him was his friend Tristram, who likes to follow him around. I do not know how long they stood observing the scene, but one of the piglets must have squealed, or wriggled, or both, which made Fox even more curious about these unfamiliar creatures that had arrived in the house. This curiosity was not a general one, but very specific, viz. he was eager to know how they would taste. And so, with a bark very deep in his throat, he pounced, with Tristram pouncing after, taking the three of us so much unawares that we all released our hold on our charges at the same instant.

I have already used the word commotion to describe what happened next, but I fear it may not be strong enough to convey the squealing, barking and shouting that ensued as the dogs chased the pigs around the studio, and the three of us chased both dogs and pigs, while my master guarded his easel to stop it being knocked over while the paint was still wet, and hollered instructions. Perkiss caught one of the pigs and plucked it up in his arms, and Mr Dupont caught another, while I managed to grab Tristram by the scruff of his neck and hold him still. That still left one dog and one pig, and both of them remembered sooner than we did that the door was still open. The little pig – it was Mr Dupont's white one – saw the opportunity first, and Fox went racing after. At this, the colour drained from my master's face so that he was as white as the escaped pig.

'Stop that d____d pig before your mistress sees it,' cried he. This was easier to say than to do, since two of us were holding pigs in our arms, and there was no sense in trying to catch one animal to prevent my mistress seeing it, if in the process we showed her two more. So before we could leave the painting room, we had to put the two captive piglets in their crate. Of course, we had to close the lid very tight so that Tristram, who was about to be shut up in the painting room to prevent him adding to the trouble upstairs, could not get inside. Only when we had done all that could we set off in pursuit of Fox and the escaped creature.

We raced along the corridor to the front of the house. My master sent Perkiss downstairs to the kitchen, in case his dog and its quarry had gone down there, while the rest of us ran upstairs. From the sound of voices – female squeals, to go with those of the piglets and the barking of Fox – it was already clear which direction the fugitive animals had taken.

My master is older than me and Mr Dupont put together, but he leaped up that staircase two steps at a time, leaving the two of us lagging behind. When he reached the front parlour, he stopped, so that Mr Dupont and I near ran right into the back of him. When we had untangled ourselves, we took in the sight that had brought my master up so short. There stood Miss Molly – who is by rights Mrs Fisher now – holding Mr Dupont's white piglet in her arms and making little squealing noises, not in imitation of the pig, but in her own excitement, as she gave it little kisses on the end of its snout. Miss Molly is not always quite right in the head, but on this occasion Miss Peggy was also a-squealing and a-cooing at the piglet, and asking to take a turn at holding him. My mistress had hold of Fox, trying to get him to hush and calm himself, but he paid no heed and was still a-barking because his only desire was a bacon supper.

The most surprising thing in the whole scene was my mistress's face. I know that my master, who is always so afeared of her, expected her to complain to high heaven that he had brought such an animal in to the house. So did Mr Dupont and I, because that is her usual way. We were all mistaken, though. I could hardly believe my own eyes, but there she was, with a big smile on her face that was just as daft as Miss Molly's and Miss Peggy's.

'I bought him as a surprise for you, my dear,' said my master, recovering his wits. 'Only he escaped upstairs before I had the chance to show him to you nicely. I was so afeared that this rascal Fox might harm him.'

This mistress gave him a look that said she knew right well that the pig was his to paint, and he was trying to hide it from her. At that moment, however, Miss Peggy, who had taken her turn of holding the animal, now brought it to her mother to pet, and my mistress fell to smiling and giggling in a manner that I have never witnessed in her before. So my master piped up that he had two more animals downstairs, one for each of the girls.

Miss Molly and Miss Peggy clapped their hands at this, crying 'Oh Papa', and my master beamed from one ear to the other saying they surely did not imagine he would bring them just one to share. So now Mr Dupont and I were dispatched back to the painting room to fetch the other two piglets.

I observed to Mr Dupont that, if his uncle wished my mistress to believe the pigs were a gift for her and Miss Molly and Miss Peggy, he would have to make sure she never set eyes on this picture he was painting. He said as how he had the same thought, but he also did not think his aunt believed his uncle for one instant. 'She simply chuses to forgive him on this occasion because the little pig has won her heart,' said he.

The two little creatures were happy to be released from their cage and conveyed into the arms of the ladies of the house, and the ladies in turn were happier than ever now they each had a pig to kiss and caress. As we returned to the painting room, Mr Dupont fell to laughing. I wondered if he was happy to see how nicely everything had turned out, but he said nay, you numbskull – a word he has picked up from his uncle – he was laughing at the mess his uncle had got himself into with his fibbing. 'Soon he will have to explain to my aunt and cousins that the pigs are hired only for one day and he is obliged to send them back to-morrow,' said he.

I did not say nothing but I was not sorry to hear this news. If those piglets stayed in this house, they would continue to do their business wherever they pleased, and I think you can guess who would have to clear it up.

So that was what happened here to-day, Ma, and sometimes it seems more like a madhouse than a great gentleman's establishment. But it is the kind of madhouse where folk laugh a lot, so fortune has blessed me really by sending me here. Not forgetting Mrs Dupont, of course, because without her kind efforts I would not be here.

Even though my heart is heavy these days, for reasons that I have perchance given you some idea about at the start of this letter, I thank the good Lord for this opportunity he has given

us all to be of good cheer, for what else of value do we possess
in this life? I will finish my account of this day here, and with
it I send you and everyone at home the fondest regards and
kisses of your loving

David

15

Gemma peered through the windscreen at the ramshackle and apparently deserted farmyard. There were various rusting pieces of agricultural machinery parked on the hard area, made of slabs of that kind of ancient concrete where you could see all the individual pebbles, plus a rusting ice-cream van, looking sad and unwanted. None of the weather-beaten sheds looked as if they were still in use, let alone habitable.

'Are you sure this is the place?' she said. 'You didn't give me the wrong postcode?'

'I don't think I did,' said Vivian, squinting down at the sheet of paper on which he had printed his email instructions. 'No, this is definitely the place. "Enter a farmyard that looks like it has seen better days, and continue on the cart track at the far end that leads down the hill.'"

'Over there,' Gemma pointed. 'Where it says "strictly no

entry".'

It was now early summer. Vivian had made contact with Dr Lennie Canham, the world expert on Gainsborough, immediately after their encouraging encounter with Jolyon Richards, the dishevelled young curator at the National Gallery, and had received a friendly reply suggesting that he and Gemma visit when they were next in the area. The address was in Suffolk, the heart of Gainsborough country, and only five or six miles from Muriel's house. Gemma was as keen as Vivian to take up this invitation, but their filming schedule in the next few weeks had taken them to Scotland, Northern Ireland and then the Lake District, making a surreptitious dash to East Anglia out of the question. Only now that all the location episodes had been filmed did they find themselves at the right end of the country, and with enough time to spare to take up Dr Canham's invitation.

Vivian had picked Gemma up at a middle-of-nowhere station on the main line from Liverpool Street and they had taken country roads through a gently rolling landscape of gleaming yellow rapeseed fields, gnarled oak trees on the skyline and vast, ancient willows on the lower ground. Surmounting one long, flat crest, they dipped down into a village straddling a river which marked, according to a faux medieval road sign, the boundary between Essex and Suffolk. Its main street was lined with lime-rendered Tudor houses, twisting alarmingly on their oak frames and leaning towards each other, across the line of slow-moving traffic, on their jettied upper floors.

'Imagine living in a house like that,' said Gemma, peering up at one particularly long, pink-washed frontage, with a complicated floral arrangement picked out in relief on the plaster, and thick-leaded windows in its gables, all pointing at slightly different angles.

'I do live in a house like that,' said Vivian. 'It's what we do in these parts. Round here we think straight lines are for wimps.'

They were following Google Maps on Gemma's phone, clipped to the dashboard, which told them to turn off at the end of the village. They were now on a steep side street which climbed the side of the valley.

'I thought Suffolk was meant to be flat,' said Gemma.

Vivian chuckled. 'Folk come on bicycles expecting it to be like Holland, and they get a shock. Same in Norfolk. Noel Coward had a lot to answer for.'

'Noel Coward?'

'You're too young to know. It's a line from one of his plays. I forget which. "Very flat, Norfolk." It's the only thing anyone thinks they know about the place and, for most of the county, it's not true at all.'

'There are two things, to be fair.'

'What, that we're all in-bred?'

Gemma laughed. 'You said it, not me.'

'Did you notice there was a little railway station in that last village? Lucky for you, because you're walking back from here.'

'Oh, don't be like that.'

They had become quite pally these past few weeks. She liked the fact that she could tease him, and that he took it in good heart.

'It should be just around the next bend,' he said, pointing at the marker on the screen.

They were in open country again, and Vivian's four-by-four filled the width of the narrow lane, which was bounded by steep grass banks and high hedges; they would be in trouble if they met anything coming the other way. Fortunately they did not, and shortly afterwards they arrived at the abandoned farmyard, without any actual farmhouse in sight.

Now they continued past the no entry sign and onto the farm track. The vehicle bumped confidently along the rough, rutted lane, rising up over the top of the valley – again, more of a gentle dome than a ridge – and down into the next one. They passed through a dense little deciduous copse, after which the lane petered out completely. It had delivered them onto a rough lawn, at the far side of which stood a long, low house, with crooked gable windows peeking out of a mossy, thatched roof. The house itself looked freshly painted in a rich shade of mustard, and the grass around it was neatly mown. Two wide beds of purple begonias and lobelias lined the path to a simple brick porch.

'Wow,' said Gemma, as they got out of the car. 'I feel like I've stepped back in time.'

'Not that far back.' Vivian pointed at a ride-on mower that stood beneath a late-blossoming cherry tree.

As they approached the house, a figure appeared from a wooden shed behind the cherry tree. It was a woman with wild, grey hair, wearing a battered poacher's jacket and a shapeless pair of loose trousers, held up at roughly where her waist should be by a belt that had escaped from a couple of its loops. Wearing gardening gloves, she carried a bucket in one hand. She raised the other, which held a trowel, to acknowledge their presence.

'Good morning,' called Vivian. 'We're looking for Dr Canham. He should be expecting us. Is he around?'

'Good afternoon,' corrected the woman, in the kind of voice that Gemma's mother would call plummy. It was true: it was just past twelve. 'He isn't, but I am.' She pulled off one of the gloves to offer a large, red hand. 'Lennie Canham. Very pleased to meet you. Won't you come in?'

Vivian was flustered by his mistake.

'I'm so sorry, Dr Canham. I'm afraid I just assumed…'

'Not to worry, everyone does.' She twinkled when she smiled, Gemma noticed. 'If truth be told, that was part of the point, once upon a time. It's short for Leonarda, in case you were wondering, and who the hell wants to be saddled with that? Please, after you. The door is open. Just give it a good shove.'

Gemma followed Vivian inside. She, too, had assumed that Dr Canham was a man. First calling Muriel 'Mrs', now this… What was happening to her? In her own defence, though, Vivian had talked about their host as a 'he' and Gemma had rashly believed that he was basing this on actual knowledge, not just male assumption.

They were in a small, book-lined hallway with a low, beamed ceiling. Or, perhaps more accurately, an ordinary-sized hallway that had become much smaller as a result of having a layer of books on every available spot of wall space.

'Carry on through,' called Dr Canham from behind them. 'And turn right at the end. We'll go into my study.'

This proved to be another low room, with exposed beams on the ceiling and those parts of the walls that were visible. The floor was tiled with red bricks in a herringbone pattern, with a couple of threadbare Persian rugs thrown on top. There was no desk or other office furniture: such studying as Dr Canham did must be done from the comfort of one of the worn leather armchairs where they were now invited to sit.

'Now, first things first,' she said, when they were settled. 'What refreshment can I offer you after your journey?'

'Do you have any coffee?' ventured Gemma. She had not had time to grab one at Liverpool Street.

'I do, and I can gladly make you some. But wouldn't you

prefer a glass of sherry? I often have one at this time of day.'

Gemma looked to Vivian for a lead, expecting him to decline for both of them.

'That's very handsome of you,' he said instead. 'Just a small one, mind.'

Dr Canham turned to Gemma.

'Do join us, my dear. I find that the young nowadays can be puritanical when it comes to drink. I do hope you're not going to confirm my ageist prejudice.'

Gemma could see that it would be rude to refuse.

'Well, just a very little one. But can I please have a glass of water too?'

Their hostess had disappeared, and Gemma was not confident that she had heard her request. She tried to catch Vivian's eye, but he was rummaging through his briefcase, and now Dr Canham was back with a silver tray, on which stood a bottle sweating with condensation, three enormous, long-stemmed wine glasses, and a tiny dish of cashew nuts and olives. There was no sign of any water.

'I hope you like it very cold and very dry,' Dr Canham said, sloshing an equally generous amount of sherry into the bottom of each glass. 'It's Fino, straight out of the fridge.'

'Wonderful,' said Vivian. 'Your very good health.'

Gemma risked a sip and winced. This was nothing like the sweet, sticky stuff that she had occasionally been given at her grandmother's house. She fished a cashew nut out of the dish in the hope it might take the taste away.

'And yours,' said Dr Canham, raising her own glass. 'And now to business. I understand you have something rather exciting you'd like to show me.'

'We're hoping you can tell us whether we ought to be excited by it or not. Unfortunately, we don't have the painting itself, for reasons we'll come on to, but I've made a full-sized print of the photograph I took.'

He unfolded a large piece of paper that he had taken from his briefcase and passed it over.

Dr Canham pulled out a pair of half-moon reading glasses from her trouser pocket, breathed on them, gave them a quick polish on her jumper and peered at the image spread across her lap.

'Oh my word,' she said softly.

This time, Gemma succeeded in catching Vivian's eye. Was that reaction a good sign, or simply the same exclamation of horror at the defacement and the damage that Kaz had shown?

Their hostess was now poring over every part of the enlarged photograph, variously tutting or saying 'I see' and 'Uh-huh' to herself. She seemed so caught up in her inspection that they might as well not have been in the room.

Finally, she took her glasses off, folded the picture and sat back to look at both of them.

'And where did you say you saw the original?' she asked.

'A lady called Muriel brought it to us,' said Gemma. 'We're making a TV series where the public bring us their treasures, a bit like *Antiques on the Road*, but with more of a competitive twist. We were filming just down the road, which is obviously Gainsborough's birthplace, and when she first said she thought her picture was an actual Gainsborough, everyone laughed because…well…because of the state of it.'

'We should add that Muriel is a very local kind of lady, if you take my meaning,' said Vivian.

'I think I do,' said Dr Canham, winking at him. 'Carry on, my dear.'

'There's not much more, really. She told us it had been passed very carefully down her family, in the belief it was a Gainsborough, and she wanted to know for sure. Unfortunately, one of our colleagues upset her quite badly, by not taking her seriously, and we haven't really had any contact with her since then. But Vivian thought what she said wasn't as daft as our colleague thought, and we both thought we owed it to her to try and find out more. So we took it to Jolyon Richards, who told us who he thought the subject was, and he urged us to bring it to you. So here we are.'

'I'm very glad he did.'

'Really?' said Gemma. 'Do you think Muriel could be right, then?'

'I do. Partly because the picture has the right feel, but also because we know there was an attempt at a portrait of our friend in the picture, whom Jolyon has quite rightly identified, and it was never finished. This could be it, which would really be rather exciting, despite the awful damage, or perhaps even because of it. But I can't offer a more certain opinion until I see the picture itself.'

Vivian sucked air in through his teeth. 'That's where we have a problem, I'm afraid. The lady really was very upset and, despite our best efforts to apologise, she doesn't want to know us. She doesn't trust us, you see, because she thinks the programme wants to mock her.'

'Why on earth does she think that?'

Vivian and Gemma looked at one another awkwardly.

'Because it's true, if our colleague and our producer get their way,' said Gemma.

'Oh dear. That doesn't sound good. Can't you change your producer's mind?'

'We've tried,' said Vivian. 'But if Muriel wasn't prepared to come back and talk to us on camera again, which she apparently wasn't, our boss said there's nothing she can do.'

'Bother,' said their hostess, draining her glass. 'Top-up?'

Vivian said he did not mind if he did; Gemma covered her glass with her hand. Even though she had barely touched a drop, she did not put it past Dr Canham to fill it up even further.

'So it's chicken and egg,' continued Vivian. 'Muriel won't talk to us because she thinks we're setting her up, and our boss won't promise not to set her up unless she talks to us.'

'And Muriel won't budge?'

Vivian smiled grimly. 'Muriel Mudge en't the type to budge.'

'Muriel who?' Their hostess suddenly sat upright and alert.

'Mudge,' said Gemma. 'It's a funny name, isn't it? I guess it's pretty local too.'

'You bet it is. But why on earth didn't you tell me before?'

The second glass of sherry seemed to have gone to Dr Canham's head.

'Tell you what before?'

'That the picture belongs to a Mudge, of course! Tell me, what does your Muriel look like?'

Gemma described the picture's owner as politely as she could.

'Ha!' cried Dr Canham. 'No wonder she says it has been passed down the family. The Mudges have been here for generations.'

'So you know them?'

'Know them? Muriel's brother helped me out in the garden every week for the best part of twenty years, until he passed on.'

'Amazing!'

'That I know the family? Nonsense. Everyone knows everyone round here, in one way or another.' She picked up the corded telephone that sat on a small table beside her chair, thumbing, as she did so, through a battered old address book. 'I'll tell you what really is incredible,' she said, as she began to dial. 'That they had this in the family, and never thought to bring it to me.'

Gemma and Vivian could hear the phone ringing at the other end, and then a disembodied voice answering.

'Muriel? It's Lennie Canham here, up at Belstead St Margaret. You remember, Bob used to come to me...? Exactly. How are you keeping? Are you well?... Very glad to hear that... Oh yes, muddling along, you know. Listen, Muriel. The reason I'm calling out of the blue: did Bob ever mention to you what I do for a living, if you can call it that? He didn't? How strange. Perhaps, come to think of it, he never knew. I suppose we only ever talked about plants. Anyway, the reason I ask is that I'm considered, for my sins, to be an expert on Thomas Gainsborough. Quite well known for it, if truth be told. And I've got a couple of very nice people here who have shown me a photograph of something that belongs to you. I'd very much like to see it for myself. It may be quite important. Would you let me do that? Thank you, Muriel. I'm very grateful... What?... No time like the present, wouldn't you say? You're in School Lane, aren't you? What number? Good, good. We'll be about twenty minutes.'

She put the phone down and stood up, eyes shining.

'Come on then,' she said to Gemma and Vivian, who were both looking up at her in a dazed fashion. 'What are you waiting for?'

They took Dr Canham's car, which seemed a perilous idea to Gemma, given how much sherry their hostess had consumed in front of them, apparently on an empty stomach. However,

Vivian was already slurring alarmingly, so it was perhaps less perilous than letting him drive. At least Dr Canham knew the roads and seemed to have an iron constitution.

Visiting Muriel was less tense than Gemma had feared. The fact that her late brother seemed to have been Lennie Canham's trusty old retainer made most of her previous guardedness fall away, and Dr Canham's effusive reaction to her picture completed the process.

An hour later, they emerged from her cottage with a firm commitment that she would shoot more footage, while Lennie listed the arrangements she would make to run tests on the paint, as well as the string that held the four parts of the picture together. She drove them back to Belstead St Margaret along tiny roads, showing remarkably alert reactions and deftness in squeezing into passing places or onto grass verges whenever they met any oncoming traffic. To Gemma's great relief, Vivian resisted her suggestion to celebrate the progress they had made by opening a bottle of champagne, saying it was high time the pair of them got back on the road. They took their leave with Lennie waving them off from her porch.

'Put it there,' said Gemma, holding her hand up for a high five, as soon as they were out of sight of the house.

Vivian slapped her raised palm inexpertly.

'What a day,' he said. 'Now we just have to let Fiammetta know, so that she can junk that original footage with Kaz once and for all.'

Gemma pulled out her phone. 'Let's do it now.'

'No offence, but I think it might come better from me than you. We've gone behind her back, and I'm harder to sack than you are, so it's only right that I take responsibility for it.'

She conceded that he was right.

He stopped the car in the abandoned farmyard and pulled

out his own phone. He made a face.

'No reception. We'll have to wait till we reach somewhere less isolated.'

It was true: there were no bars on Gemma's phone either. However, they popped up again as the car descended into the village.

'Give me your phone, and I'll dial for you,' she said.

Vivian did not want to talk while he was driving, even on speaker. 'It's distracting, and not very safe.'

Gemma wanted to say that they would also be a lot safer if Vivian had not put away half a bottle of sherry, but she decided to keep that to herself.

They arrived at the mainline station with just five minutes before her train was due, so Gemma gave Vivian a peck on the cheek, which seemed appropriate now that they were comrades-in-arms and not just colleagues, and he promised to call her as soon as he had spoken to Fiammetta.

It was half an hour later, as her train had just stopped at Chelmsford and she was forced to relinquish the spare seat beside her amid an influx of new passengers, that he finally called.

'How did it go?' she said as she picked up, turning her head towards the window to avoid broadcasting to her neighbour and the rest of the carriage. 'Was she pleased?'

'Not really, no,' came the reply down the scratchy line.

'What? How do you mean?'

'I'm afraid it's bad news, Gemma. Couldn't be worse, in fact. Fiammetta has shown Kaz's clip with Muriel to the powers-that-be, and they love it. They want it in the series trailer, and she says there's no way she can scrap it.'

'That's ridiculous. They can't! Wait, though. At least we can do some more filming with Muriel, and show that she turned out to be right in the end, no?'

'We can't do that either. They reckon the episode will only be funny if everyone agrees that Muriel's treasure is a pile of junk.'

'Even if we know it isn't?'

'We have to pretend we don't.'

'You are shitting me. That's insane!' People were looking at her, sensing scandal, and she dropped her voice. 'That's utterly crazy.'

'I know.'

'But…what are we going to do? And what the hell are we going to tell Muriel?'

16

Molly's marriage to Fischer had not been a success. While Tom would have liked to blame his scoundrel of a son-in-law, he knew the cause was more complicated. Molly's malady had begun to express itself in strange and disturbing ways. She fancied herself a much greater lady than she really was – certainly a far greater one than Fischer could afford to keep – and had left a trail of shopping debts all over town which threatened to land her in Newgate. It should be Fischer's responsibility now, but he had been little prepared for the burden, and since he and Molly had carried on in secret, there had been no occasion for Tom to warn him.

He was not displeased when she returned to live under his own roof. He could keep a better eye on her than her foolish husband ever would. As long as the Captain was with her, he was confident that she would stay out of trouble.

Today the pair of them had been to the Academy, and they were full of their visit as they gathered to drink tea and coffee in the drawing room.

'Colonel St Leger is most exceeding handsome, Papa,' said Molly. 'Why did you not alert us to this fact when he was here to sit for you?'

The parlour-maid poured out their tea while the footman, David – always miraculously close at hand when there were parlour-maiding duties nowadays – handed out the cups.

'Because you are a married woman, lest you should forget it, and such things should not concern you, my dearest.'

'I may be, but Peggy is not.'

'Peggy would be well-advised to stay away from that young man. The King blames him for leading the Prince of Wales into dissipation and says that all good men should despise him. Would you have your sister marry such a man, and incur the wrath of her sovereign to boot, just for the sake of his pretty face?'

'It is a very pretty face, Papa,' said the Captain. 'I might be prepared to ignore the King's displeasure.'

'The problem, my darling girl, is that his face is so pretty, he would be busy showing it off all over town, to all manner of other ladies, and you would never see it for yourself. The papers call him Handsome Jack, but I assure you there is nothing handsome about his conduct.'

'Then why did you paint him, Papa? And make him look so fine in his uniform?'

'Because he does look fine in his uniform. He is nothing if not fine-looking. Would you have me paint his face ugly, just because his soul is so?'

'And he would not pay for it else,' said their mother, entering the room and taking the chair next to Tom. 'Your papa does not paint their faces for the love of the art.' She glanced at Tom as she stirred sugar into her tea. 'Has he paid for it yet?'

'He has not.' Tom let the remark sit for a moment before adding, 'He has not, because the Prince of Wales commissioned it. For his own portrait and this one, he has promised to pay five hundred guineas apiece.'

It was rare to see Mrs Gainsborough look so impressed.

Molly was impressed too.

'So, Papa, you exhibited eleven pictures this year. I counted. If they are each worth five hundred guineas, eleven must be worth...' She began to compute the sum.

'Five thousand five hundred guineas!' said the Captain, getting there first.

'Oh Papa! What will we buy with such riches?'

'If we did have such riches, they would go to meet the considerable expenses of keeping you, with your own carriage and servants, in this house. Sadly, those pictures are worth nothing of the kind. The Prince of Wales has said he will pay five hundred guineas apiece for two full-lengths because he likes spending money, or being seen to spend money. I cannot charge that for half-lengths, let alone landscapes. And I cannot charge Colonel Tarleton, for example, five hundred guineas for his full-length, because that is not my rate and it is not what we agreed.'

'Colonel Tarleton must be quite rich, Papa. There are two portraits of him in the exhibition. Did you see?'

Tom had seen. Another young roué in the St Leger mould, Colonel Tarleton had come back from the American war boasting that he had butchered more men and lain with more women than any person alive. He was precisely the kind of fashionable figure the public expected Tom to paint, whether he wanted to or not, if he were to maintain his reputation. Sir

Joshua was under the same pressure, and the pair of them had found themselves in the absurd position of painting rival portraits not just of this swaggering popinjay, but also of his mistress, Mrs Robinson. The prints had loved it, just as they had loved pointing out that Sir Joshua's version of the young braggart was a good deal better than his own.

'Sir Joshua's is very fine, Papa,' said Molly. 'Did you see it? The colonel is standing on a fallen cannon, after conquering the enemy, and his horse is rearing behind him, with the smoke of battle all around. I could have fainted with the danger of it all.'

Tom had examined the painting closely before the exhibition opened to the public. The composition had the obligatory classical reference – all Sir Joshua's subjects had to assume the pose of some Grecian or Roman statue that the President had observed on his travels in Rome or Paris – but the picture undoubtedly had an energy and a thrill, and he had no doubt that Molly's reaction was far from unusual. His own composition was a good deal less successful. Tarleton had wanted to be shown on horseback and, against his better judgement, Tom had agreed, but he had got the motion all wrong. Some whoresbird of a critic had written that the front legs seemed to be galloping while the back ones stood still, and while Tom could have licked the fellow handsomely for saying so, he could not deny there was truth in it.

'I think I remember it.'

'We also saw – didn't we, Peggy? – Sir Joshua's portrait of Mrs Robinson. He has painted her against a scarlet curtain. Did you see it, Papa? That is very clever, is it not, as a comment on her way of life. We did not linger in front of it because we did not think it proper, and in any case there was scarcely any room, so large was the crowd of men who were peering at the

very great expanse of flesh which Sir Joshua has left visible…'
She fluttered her hand vaguely over her own breast, to indicate
the area which the President had so lovingly rendered in
gleaming white. 'It is such a pity that your own portrait of Mrs
Robinson could not be hung, Papa.'

Again, this was not a subject on which Tom had any wish
to dwell. Mrs Robinson, discarded by the Prince of Wales
and now picked up by Tarleton, had been a ravishing sitter, of
course. She was also newly rich, having persuaded the Prince
of Wales to pay her a large amount of money not to publish
his letters. Word of this arrangement had leaked out, and Tom
had withdrawn his portrait of the lady at the eleventh hour.
The scribblers had interpreted this as a mark of his respect for
Royal sensibilities, which Tom was happy for them to believe.
The truth was more prosaic: his likeness had ended up nothing
like, which was an embarrassment, considering that this was
usually his proudest boast. While she was in his painting room,
Mrs Robinson had mentioned that Sir Joshua had required no
fewer than eleven sittings of her, a ridiculous number even by
the President's over-fussy standards. This had spurred Tom to
work even faster than usual, to show off his own agility. Pride
had been his undoing. By rushing, he had not captured her at
all. Sir Joshua's attempt was no masterpiece, but at least it was
like her. Tom had taken the opportunity to withdraw his own
work because he had no wish for it to be lampooned in public.

'You seem to have seen a great deal of Sir Joshua's work,' the
girls' mother intervened, 'but rather less of your papa's.'

'Oh no,' cried the Captain. 'We loved the little boy with the
long golden hair, in the historic costume, didn't we, Molly?'

'Yes! And Lord Camden with his fat belly, although he was
difficult to see because they placed him so high up. Of course,
we could not stand in front of your dancing Italian with her

face covered in rouge. It would not be respectable for us to view the picture of a woman whom we would not acknowledge in real life... Is it true that she is the mistress of a duke?'

'She is the mistress of a duke's house, which is a much finer claim. She lives in a palace in Kent. Would you really refuse to know her?'

Their mother, who would also refuse to know Madame Bacelli, attempted to steer the discussion back to a more wholesome subject.

'And what of your papa's Prince of Wales? Did you admire it?'

'Oh yes!' said the Captain. 'There was quite a crowd around it. The Prince of Wales is not so handsome as Colonel St Leger, of course, but he seems such a fine figure. So elegant, with his arm resting on his horse. He has a narrower waist than we expected. We heard other people say so, too. Is he really so thin, Papa?'

'The artist never lies.'

Unless, Tom might have added, he wishes to be invited back to Windsor to paint the King's other fourteen children.

'Of course not,' said the Captain. 'But sometimes he may fib a little, may he not? Like he did with Mr Abel?'

Tom winked at her, enjoying her teasing. He had found the Prince an amiable young man, with refined tastes and an agile mind, much quicker than his father's. Their conversation had touched on many subjects, not all of them suitable for female ears, but including the unlikely topic of morality, to which the heir to the throne had given more thought than his reputation implied. Tom was inclined to believe the King's view, that the Prince had been led astray by the smart young blades in his circle. In his picture, he had played down the physical effects of this errant course, reducing the bloating of the Prince's face and the swelling of his hips; he had presented the young man that he wished the public could know.

'In any case, Mama, there is no doubt that Papa's star shines the brightest in the show,' said Molly. 'The biggest crowd of all was in front of his work, not Sir Joshua's.'

'Which? The Prince?'

'No, Mama, not he. A portrait of the three most handsome subjects in the entire exhibition. More handsome than Colonel St Leger and Colonel Tarleton and the Prince of Wales put together. And I know that you, Mama, will agree with us.'

Their mother looked bewildered, but Tom knew what was coming.

The Captain could not hold back the joke any longer.

'The pigs, Mama! Theirs is the portrait that every visitor to the exhibition wants to see. Molly and I stood watching them all, so tempted to tell them how Fortune had smiled on us by allowing us to caress these very creatures in our own home. How they would have envied us! Instead we decided to keep it as our nice little secret, our memory to treasure, and we left the crowd to sigh and squeal to their heart's content.'

'And we walked with our heads held high, knowing that our papa had painted the most popular painting in the entire show.'

Tom felt himself blushing. It was true, his pigs were this year's triumph. Everyone had said it: his friends, and all the press notices. To have his own daughters take such pleasure in it was an additional, unexpected joy.

'Perhaps the Prince of Wales will buy that one too, for another five hundred guineas,' said Molly.

'Oh yes! And our pigs will hang at Windsor, or Buckingham-house!'

Tom shook his head.

'Even for the Prince of Wales, such prices are only for the faces of his friends. A face is a valuable item. A man wants his own face on the wall, not to remind himself how he looks – a looking-glass would serve just as well for that – but to tell the world that he is the kind of man who has his face painted, and his wife's face, and his children's. Once they are on the wall, he can rest in the knowledge that he is that sort of fellow, and the world knows it, and the world will also remember him and his wife and his children when their physical bodies are long departed. For that, he will pay handsomely. By contrast, a picture of a cottage in a wood or some cattle at a stream may gladden the heart, because it speaks of a more innocent age, of simpler needs and pleasures, but it will not gladden a rich man's heart sufficiently to make him pay more than fifty guineas for it. The same is true, I fear, of your poor pigs. The crowd at the Academy may squeal and swoon with joy, but will they reach for their pocket-books? Your mother knows the answer to that one, don't ye, madam?'

His wife was about to speak but he cut her off. He had been holding this news back too, and he proposed to enjoy its impact.

'Except in this instance.' He pulled from his pocket the letter that had arrived this morning. 'I received today a communication from a certain gentleman, expressing the wish to buy my pigs. The asking price, he has heard, is sixty guineas. He proposes to give me…'

He held up the letter theatrically, enjoying the expectant looks on their faces.

'Fifty?' said Molly. 'Do not accept, Papa. Hold fast, tell the miserly gentleman you require the full price or you will not part with our pigs.'

'He proposes to give me…one hundred guineas, and he has

also sent me half as many elegant compliments! What do you say about that?'

'One hundred guineas!'

'Papa, how wonderful!'

'Congratulations, husband. A fine achievement indeed!'

'And who is this gentleman, Papa? Do we know him?'

'I do not believe you have yet had the pleasure of his acquaintance, but his name is known to you.'

Now, at last, he held the letter close enough for them to reach, whereupon Molly snatched it from him. She unfolded the paper, examined the address at the top, and then the signature.

'Leicester Fields… Sir Josh… No! Papa? Can it be true?'

It was true: an offer from his greatest rival to buy the painting hailed as the greatest in the Academy exhibition, and to pay nearly twice the asking price. Sir Joshua was known as a collector, but he had never bought any work of Tom's before. It was a magnanimous gesture.

That was his immediate thought, at any rate. A little afterwards, the doubts had come. Why the ostentatious over-payment? Was it designed to remind him that Sir Joshua's means were still so much greater than his own? And why a picture of pigs? The two of them were rivals in portraiture, and the President had pointedly chosen not to bestow his favour on one of Tom's face-pictures, as if to say they were still unworthy of his attention. Instead he wanted to buy a composition involving farmyard animals. Was that an insult? Would Tom be a laughing-stock if he accepted?

Eventually, though, wiser counsel had prevailed. Even if it were intended as a slight, where was the sense in refusing? That would make Tom seem the petty one, the party who could not accept a compliment from his rival. If Sir Joshua could not bring himself to admire any of Tom's full-lengths, so be it, but his admiration for the pigs was welcome, because they were indeed admirable. And one hundred guineas in the hand from Sir Joshua was a surer prospect than the promise of a thousand guineas from the Prince of Wales.

'One hundred guineas!' said Mrs Gainsborough, breaking into his thoughts. 'I hope you have already accepted?'

Later, when he sat down to write his reply to Sir Joshua, he fell to thinking about their rivalry. Was it real, or a confection of the scribblers? On his own side, Bate had certainly not helped by cheering so devotedly for Tom, and the public seemed to enjoy the idea of the two greatest painters of the realm as warring pugilists.

Was there really any quarrel between them, though? Sir Joshua's style was certainly not Tom's. Tom did not give tuppence whether Lady So-and-so held her arm in the same position as the goddess Diana, and he was certain that Lady So-and-so did not either; she only cared to look beautiful. Nor had he ever felt the need to heed Sir Joshua's lectures at the Academy on the right colour clothing for sitters to wear or the correct angle at which to place their feet. The President was a terrible bore on such subjects, but that was no reason to despise the fellow. Aside from that one unpleasantness over the hanging of Tom's work, which was long enough ago to be near forgotten, there had never been rancour between them. They were never likely to be close friends, and Tom could not imagine shouting confidences into Sir Joshua's ear cone. Nevertheless, having painted – or endured – so many of the same sitters, they had a good deal in common.

It was time, therefore, to accept the President's generosity of spirit and purse with matching grace. He dipped his pen and wrote:

'Sir Joshua, I think myself highly honoured and much obliged to you for this singular mark of your favour. I may truly say I have brought my pigs to a fine market.'

It was short but sincere, which was all that was required. Signing himself 'your ever obliged and obedient servant', he sprinkled pounce on the wet ink, shook it a moment to prevent it sticking, then up-ended the paper to tip the powder off when the letter was dry.

As he folded the paper, it occurred to him that he might usefully ask the President to sit for him, as a bold and friendly reciprocal gesture. Not today, perhaps; it was not worth ripping up the letter and writing a fresh one. Nevertheless, it was not half a decent scheme, and he would think on it.

Pall-mall,
Nov. 15th, 1782

To my dearest Ma

I am so happy to hear that Dick's wife has been safely delivered of a healthy infant. Once again, while I rejoice at your good news, it pains me that I have missed so much of all your lives by being so far away here in London.

However, in this letter I am at last in the happy position to bring you some glad tidings of my own. For some time now, as I have given you to understand already, my heart has belonged to another, a kind and generous person of rare beauty, who is also a member of this household. Until now I have not told you that person's name, but it is Nelly, and she is the parlour-maid here.

For many moons now, I have sighed in despair of this angelic creature ever noticing me, even though I have made it my business to spend as much of my time as possible in the kitchen. Luckily I am not so afeared as I used to be of Cook, who threatened to turn my insides into sausages when I first came to this house, but I have learned that her growl is worse than her bite and, any road, these past months she has treated me with more pity than suspicion. I reckon as how my lovelorn countenance has made itself obvious to the whole household – not just to Cook but also to Mr Dupont, who has lent his ear to my confidences on this matter, and to Perkiss, who has teased me on the subject for months, and even to my master, who makes merry at my expense and comments in a satirickal manner about the amount of time I have spent below stairs. He feigns to believe that I am in love with Cook, who is old enough to be my granddam, but I am sure he knows the real object of my sighs.

I never believed that lovely Nelly paid me any heed, and I thought perchance her heart was already given to another. It was only when Perkiss told me that I was a blockhead and she was simply shy, that I realised she had been waiting all these months for me to declare myself. This I have now done and I own I am the happiest man in the world. I hope I will have the honour of introducing Nelly to you afore long, but as always it depends on whether my master will ever stir himself to go to Suffolk. If not, you will have to take my word that the beauty of her face is matched only by the beauty of her soul.

Alongside this news, which I hope it gladdens you to hear as much as it gladdens me to tell it to you, I have more tidings of the affairs of this household which I'll wager may bring a smile to your lips.

Do you remember when I told you about the Duke of Cumberland, the King's brother, coming to this house? It was close after I arrived here, which is now nearly six years since. It was such a special day, to have genuine royalty in the house, even if it was not the kind of royalty that the King himself is prepared to entertain in his own home. Since that day, as you know, my master has been to paint the King and Queen at Buckingham-house and at Windsor, he has painted the Prince of Wales, and he has lately been painting all the royal children. So we are not so overcome by royalty in this house as once we were.

This morning, however, we had a visitor more important than the King himself, if the fuss aforehand was any measure. Perkiss and me, and Nelly of course, were bid to clean and polish the house, and we could see how nervous my master was. When he is in an anxious mood he curses, and this morning he was cursing fit to shock a jack tar. He took his cup of chocolate, but would consume nothing else for his breakfast, and when I came to attend him later in his painting room, he was a-pacing up and down like a man with hornets in his breeches. At this time, I was still ignorant of who was coming to visit, but it was clear it must be a very fine personage indeed.

We were instructed to be ready inside the front entrance at eleven o'clock sharp. It came as no surprise to any of us that this guest was too important to be punctual, and we stood a full twenty minutes in our places, with my mistress and the Misses Molly and Peggy running out of their rooms to look down from the top landing every five minutes, and my master striding up and down the corridor, pocket watch in hand, the entire while.

When the knock finally came, I had the task of opening the door, and I found myself looking down at a red-faced gentleman with a nose that look like it had been smashed with a fist, and a matching red cone in his hand. I knew who he was, even afore he said good morning and bade me tell my master that Sir Joshua Reynolds had arrived for his appointment.

I naturally invited him to step inside, where I expected to

find my master himself, ready to greet his visitor, but there was no sign of him. After driving us all half-mad with his pacing up and down and inspecting his timepiece, he had now repaired to his painting room in pretence that he was very busy and not at all fussed about Sir Joshua coming to call. So I had to go and fetch him, which meant I had to go through a pretence of my own, of telling him that Sir Joshua Reynolds had come to call, as if I did not know that my master knew exactly who it was a-knocking at his door.

'Sir Joshua?' said he. 'Ah yes, I do recall he is to sit for me to-day for his portrait.' Trying to keep my face straight, I followed my master as he strolled to the front of the house, as cool as you like, to greet his visitor, bowing low and saying 'My dear Sir Joshua'.

Sir Joshua told him 'My dear Gainsborough' and bowed even lower, although he had the advantage in that game because he was starting from a much lower position. Then my master called upstairs to my mistress to come and meet Sir Joshua Reynolds, who had come to sit for his portrait. My mistress came down the stairs in the same pantomime of not knowing who was coming. Sir Joshua kissed her hand and told her what an honour it was, and now the Misses Molly and Peggy appeared, and my master presented them – Mrs Fisher and Miss Gainsborough, he called them – for Sir Joshua to kiss their hands too. He held on to their fingers longer than he had with my mistress, telling them how charmed he was. While Sir Joshua is a strange old gentleman with the complexion of a boiled beetroot, who has little conversation because he is stone deaf, he is also a ladies' man. I have heard tell that, while there is officially no Lady Reynolds, there are several unofficial ones, and his behaviour suggested he would fain add Miss Molly and Miss Peggy to their number.

After all that greeting was done, my master and Sir Joshua disappeared into the painting room: the greatest portrait painter in the land, and the second-greatest, although of course my master would dispute the order in which those titles are bestowed. Naturally the entire household was keen to know what would pass between these two gentlemen as the one painted the other, because they have been reckoned to be such enemies in the past. Mr Dupont and I lingered in the corridor outside, which was not improper because it was possible that my master would need our services. He never called us, but we waited ready for him any road.

As we stood there, Mr Dupont acquainted me with the history of this encounter. He told me my master had asked Sir Joshua to sit for him after that gentleman bought his picture of the pigs at the Royal Academy six months ago. My master wanted to show that he appreciated the great honour Sir Joshua had shown him by buying that painting, and at a much higher price than he expected. Asking if he could paint Sir Joshua's picture was a great compliment in return, and also a cheaper one than buying one of Sir Joshua's own pictures, which my master would not like to do, because he does not buy many paintings, and if he does, Mr Dupont says there is nothing by Sir Joshua that he would want to hang on his wall.

He expects Sir Joshua to come once or twice more, which is all that my master will require, and after that no doubt Sir Joshua will return this compliment and ask if he may paint my master. My master will of course be pleased to grant this request, even though it will mean going to Sir Joshua's house eight or nine times, because that gentleman paints so slow. My master will complain and curse every time, but he will be pleased to go all the same. Mr Dupont thinks this will be a good development, because it is better to be friends not enemies, and in any case, there were never proper enemies, not really, and their fight was only in the eyes of the press.

While he was telling me all this at a discreet volume, we heard a great row from the painting room. It was my master shouting at the top of his voice, and Mr Dupont and me looked at each other most afeared. In spite of what I have just said about their hostility being a confection of the press, it sounded like warfare had broken out behind that door after not half an hour of those gentleman being in each other's company. Then we listened harder and we heard my master laughing, and we remembered that Sir Joshua is as deaf as an oak bedstead, and my master was not raising his voice in dispute, but only to make himself understood. This was a great relief, and we laughed about it, taking care to do so silently. Sir Joshua may be deaf, but my master is not.

They were in the room together for nearly two hours, and then the door opened. I heard my master asking Sir Joshua if he was sure he did not want to stop to dinner, because there were a couple of boiled rabbits with onion sauce, some beef steaks and a knuckle of veal. Sir Joshua would not be pressed. He said he had an engagement with the Duke of Somewhere and the Earl of Somewhere-else, but his mood was cheerful and he promised to make time to dine when he next came to sit.

While my master was seeing Sir Joshua out, Mr Dupont and I went into his painting room to see what the portrait looked like. The canvas was hanging loose over the easel. As you know, this is my master's way when he is painting a portrait as large as the sitter himself. Even though Sir Joshua is not very large, my master must be planning to fill the rest of the canvas with furniture, or painting apparatus, because it seemed to measure about seven feet in length. The outline of

Sir Joshua's body was sketched out in thin brown paint, but to-day my master had been working on the face, which he had positioned at the edge of his easel, as is his custom.

The likeness he can create, Ma, is something amazing to see. I had seen this gentleman walk past me, close enough to touch, just a few minutes earlier, and now here he was again, looking out at us in oil paint. You would think it a form of magic, Ma, if you saw it. How I wish you could! I yearn to show you something of my master's work, these marvels of art that I have the good fortune to live amongst. One day, I swear to you, I will do it.

Mr Dupont noticed that he had not included the trumpet. I said mayhap that would come later, and Mr Dupont knew what I meant. 'Tis often his job to help with the clothing and the scenery in my master's paintings, so if the trumpet is to go in the picture, it will likely fall to him to add it. In truth, though, I do not think my master means to include it, because Sir Joshua might take it as a slight. Now that they are becoming friends, I do not believe my master will do anything to upset that peaceful state. That is my prediction, any road.

And on that tranquil note, I will end yet another long letter to you, Ma, by sending my sincerest affection to Dick and his wife and their little one, and to Jack, and I hope you will all have the pleasure of meeting my lovely Nelly soon. The place she occupies in my heart does nothing to reduce my love for you, Ma, as your son

David

18

Gemma fell into step with the procession of homeward-bound commuters leaving the train. She shivered in her short sleeves. There was a breeze in the September afternoon air and she wished she had worn a jacket. She climbed the steps off the platform and filed through the electronic barriers. Everyone else knew where they were going, but Gemma stopped to check directions on her phone.

She had never been to Blackheath before, this dinky little village with its butcher, baker, greengrocer and florist clustering around the station. It was so different from the grimy parade of takeaways, rental agencies and betting shops that characterised her own part of southeast London, only a short train ride away.

With the first two episodes of *Britain's Got Treasures* already broadcast, there was not a great amount for Gemma to do in the office. The edit had been long and arduous. Fiammetta had spent several weeks on it, emerging for a few hours' sleep every night, but little else. Now it was finished, she was demob-happy and running around London, glad-handing commissioners and talking up programme deals all over town. Gemma spoke to her on the phone several times a day, but seeing her face to face was a rarer event. Today, however, halfway through the afternoon, she had blown through the office like a tornado in Fendi, flinging out instructions as she went. One of these was for Gemma to pick up her dry-cleaning, because Fiammetta simply had not time to do it herself, and to deliver it to her home, ready for a breakfast meeting first thing. It was tedious and demeaning, the kind of instruction a male boss would never dare give a female employee nowadays, but Gemma was in no position to argue. Not having enough to do was an invitation not to renew her contract.

Not that she had been idle these past few weeks. She had worked almost as long hours as Fiammetta during the edit, and there had been little time to think about Muriel and her painting. Gemma was still appalled by Fiammetta's attitude in refusing to acknowledge that they might have a genuine find on their hands, simply because some suit had already decided on the clips for the series trailer. However, she knew enough about this industry to realise that it was a waste of time and energy to lobby any further on Muriel's behalf: a decision was a decision, however ridiculous. In any case, those trailers had started to go out weeks ago.

Vivian was less willing to let it go. He had remained in close contact with Lennie and Muriel, keeping Gemma abreast of some of what had been going on while she was locked away in the edit suite.

Now that Muriel was willing to co-operate, the painting

had been put to as many tests as Lennie could devise, and had sailed through all of them.

First, the canvas itself had been inspected. It proved to be plainly woven linen of medium weight, with a weave count of sixteen picks per centimetre in both directions. Gemma had no idea what that actually meant, and she suspected Vivian did not either. What mattered was that this weight was standard for the period, and consistent with Gainsborough's known work. Once again, it did not prove that the artist had painted the picture, but it did mean he could have.

Next, the background colour – the bottom layer of paint, some of which showed through in shadows and tones on the face – was russet pink. This did not need any kind of scientific test: Lennie could see it with the naked eye. It was another good sign. Most artists of the period, apparently, started with a pale grey or fawn ground, whereas Gainsborough experimented, first with orange, then with pink and sometimes even brick red. In this case, because the sitter had a florid complexion, pink was an appropriate colour for the background. It was another nod in the right direction.

Finally, the pigment mixtures in the face, hair and upper clothing were complex, which was also good, because it was characteristic. They included siennas, umbers, Cologne earth, translucent bone black, opaque red, vermilion and lead white. All these were typical, and nothing was out of character or out of period. There was also a trace of expensive ultramarine in the sitter's eyes. If it were Gainsborough, he would have to have painted it late in his career, because that pigment was not available earlier on, but that was indeed when this subject was known to have sat for him. Likewise, some of the cracking in the picture was a sign that the artist had used asphaltum, a tarry substance that made dark colours translucent, but which darkened and cracked over time. Gainsborough had begun to use it in his last years and did not live long enough to discover how badly it aged.

So the news for Muriel was all excellent. There was no way of proving beyond any doubt who had painted the picture, but the outcome of every test and examination reinforced Lennie's conviction that the portrait really was what Muriel thought it was. The fact that Gainsborough was known to have painted this particular sitter was a major plus point, she said, which would be capped only by 'provenance': if Muriel could show some chain of ownership that traced a clear line back to the painter himself, there would be no doubt. Unfortunately, no one had any expectation that Muriel could provide that. The Mudges had never written much down for as long as she had known them, said Lennie, and she had no reason to suppose that previous generations of the family were any different.

The way Vivian told it, Muriel's mood had improved with each of these findings. That mood would plummet if she knew that none of these results would be included in the programme that went out, but Vivian had yet to get round to breaking this news. Gemma had impressed upon him that he would have to do it sooner or later, and he was already on borrowed time, given that the trailer had been airing for several weeks already. It was the one time when they were both relieved to be working for a channel that hardly anyone watched. How else to explain Muriel's continued state of blissful ignorance?

In their last conversation, Gemma had asked Vivian why he was doing all this, since none of it had a chance of inclusion in the programme.

'We owe it to her,' he said. 'And if it really is a Gainsborough, then the programme itself won't matter too much.'

'Won't matter as much, maybe. So, basically, you're doing

all this on your own time? Like a kind of freelance effort to make it up to her, completely separate from *Britain's Got Treasures?*'

'You could say that.'

'Good for you. It's great that you're doing it.'

He was a kind-hearted man, she thought to herself again now, in the smart little Blackheath village street, as she followed her phone's directions to the dry-cleaner's. There it was, across the road, next door to the wholefood shop. Quality Cleaning, prop: M. Zahra.

'You've just caught me. I was about to close,' said the elderly Asian man behind the counter – presumably Mr Zahra. His voice was soft and his accent genteel. Even the dry-cleaners in Blackheath were posh.

'Really? You don't stay open late?'

'I used to, but at my time of life I want a shorter working day, and my regular customers all told me they could manage. The ones who work long hours all seem to have someone they can send to pick up their stuff.'

As did Fiammetta, of course.

Gemma fumbled in her bag for the ticket for the clothes. It was only after she had taken everything out that she remembered she had tucked it in the side pocket for safe-keeping.

As Mr Zahra went off into the back of the shop to fetch Fiammetta's items, her phone rang, flashing up the caller's name.

'Hey, Vivian, how are you?'

'Not so bad, thanks. And yourself?'

'I'm good, but can I call you back in five minutes?'

Mr Zahra was back now with what appeared to be two suits and a dress, all on thin wire hangers and swathed in plastic so thin that it floated up with any movement of air.

'Yes, no problem. It's just that Muriel's programme goes out tomorrow night, and I wanted to have a quick word about…'

'Trust me, I haven't forgotten.' She had been dreading this transmission for weeks. 'It's just that I'm tied up doing an errand for Fiammetta at the minute, and this nice man is about to close…'

'No problem at all. You take your time, and call me when you're free.'

'Thanks Vivian. Talk to you in five.'

She hung up and reached for her purse.

'Can you make sure you give me the receipt?'

Fiammetta always blithely assumed that Gemma could pay for these personal expenses without difficulty, no matter which end of the month it was. Gemma had learned to her cost that it was vital to hang on to each and every receipt.

When the payment had gone through, she put her bank card back in her bag along with all the other stuff she had removed from it, picked up the dry-cleaning haul and allowed Mr Zahra to hold the door open for her. She wished him good night and heard him locking up behind her. She reached in her bag for the page of notebook on which Fiammetta had scrawled her address. There it was, crumpled but perfectly legible. Now to find the place. She put her hand back in her bag, fumbling for her phone. As she did so, a gust of wind caught the floaty plastic, blowing it up in her face. Cursing herself for not checking the directions while she was still in the shop, she stepped into a side-alley to get out of the breeze. The floaty plastic settled down and she carried on rummaging, but there was no sign of her phone in her bag – not in the outer pocket, and not in the inner, zip-up one. No wonder, she realised with that familiar, sinking feeling that came with lost keys, phone or purse: she had no memory of putting it back after speaking to Vivian. She must have left it on the counter, and now Mr Zahra had… She ran back out into the street and along the short stretch of pavement to Quality Cleaning. The door was locked, the lights were off and there was no sign of the proprietor. Surely he had not left the premises completely? She rattled the door and then banged on it, once, then again, harder. She waited for a minute, and then two, before banging again. Another two minutes went by. There was no sign of life.

Swearing under her breath, she fought to tame the billowing plastic as she tried to gather her thoughts. At least she had the address: she could find Fiammetta's place the old-fashioned way, by asking for directions. She would just have to drop the dry-cleaning, go home, spend a peaceful, phone-free few hours and come back and pick it up in the morning. Having to come back was tedious, but she had only herself to blame. Or maybe Fiammetta; she could blame Fiammetta for making her do stupid errands. Not to her face, mind. Anyhow, there was nothing else to be done.

It was only when she was halfway home that she remembered she was meant to call Vivian back. Rats. There was nothing she could do about it now. There was no landline at home and even if there were, her only record of his number was stored in her phone. She would just have to call him back in the morning. She was sure he would understand.

It was strangely liberating spending a night without her phone. She checked her emails on her laptop in case there was anything urgent from Fiammetta, but all was quiet. One of her housemates was also in and at a loose end, so they ordered a pizza and a large bottle of Diet Coke, and watched a romcom.

It was weird not being able to double-screen during the slower parts, but by the end she had almost forgotten her phone existed. Not being able to check her apps last thing at night felt wrong, like going to bed without cleaning her teeth, but she consoled herself that she would have the phone back in less than twelve hours.

She woke at seven, as usual, and googled Quality Cleaners on her laptop to see what time it opened. Mr Zahra did at least make up for his early closing with a prompt start in the morning. He was open from eight.

Travelling against the rush-hour flow, she arrived in Blackheath at five minutes past.

'Ah yes, I was expecting to see you today,' said Mr Zahra. 'I'm afraid I had to turn it off. It's been ringing rather a lot.'

'Really?'

Panic suddenly knotted her stomach and she felt her heart beat faster.

'I'm afraid so. Someone seems to want to speak to you rather badly.'

She turned her phone back on once she was on the pavement. It was not just one person who wanted to speak to her badly. She had eight missed calls: one from Vivian, two from Kaz, four from Fiammetta, and one from a number she did not recognise. She also had five voicemails.

Ducking into the side-alley, to get away from the traffic noise this time, she touched her voicemail button, feeling sick with worry. What the hell had happened to bring everyone heavily onto her case?

The first message was from the previous evening.

'Hello, Gemma. Vivian here. I've been waiting for you to ring me back. I hope everything is all right. The thing is, I do need to speak to you before tomorrow morning, just to fill you in on what's about to happen. I couldn't tell you before, because it was best you didn't know. So do please ring me back tonight. You've got my number, haven't you? Just in case you haven't, I'll give it you again…'

He read his number out twice, even slower the second time than the first.

The next one was from the unknown caller. It had been left just after Vivian's message, early yesterday evening.

'Hello, Gemma. My name's Frances Carter, and I'm the arts correspondent at the *Times* newspaper. We're doing a story in tomorrow's paper, and I was hoping that you or someone else in your production company might be able to give me a comment. Could you call me back as soon as you get this? I'll leave you my number…'

The Times? A story? What the hell had Vivian done?

The next one was from Fiammetta, who was much more brisk.

'Call me as soon as you get this, Gemma. I've just had a very disturbing message from a journalist, and I want to speak to you urgently before I call her back.'

The fourth message had been left at seven o'clock this morning.

'Hi Gemma, it's me, Kaz. I've just seen this news story. I'm sure you've seen it too. I don't know if you knew about it. I assume you must of. I won't lie to you, Gemma, I'm literally speechless. I feel completely undermined, and the fact that nobody told me it was coming… I can't even begin to tell you how furious I am. I don't know who's responsible for this but, trust me, I can guess. I've tried to call Fiammetta just now, but her phone's busy. Honestly, this is worse than my wildest nightmares. I just want you all to know I'm calling my agent now, and I've also put in a call to my lawyer. Can you please call me back, literally as soon as you get this, and if I'm on the phone, leave me a voicemail. I expect to hear from you very soon, OK? Thank you.'

The last one was from Fiammetta.

'Gemma, why the hell haven't you called me? I need to know exactly what you knew about this and when. Get back to me immediately, OK?'

Gemma was trembling now as she searched for the number. Fiammetta picked up after half a ring.

'Where in God's name have you been? I've been trying to get hold of you half of last night and all this morning.'

'I'm sorry, Fiammetta. I left my phone in the dry-cleaner's last night, and I've only just picked it up.'

'You left your phone to be dry-cleaned? That makes no sense to me.'

'No, no, I just left it there by accident, and the guy closed really early, so I couldn't go back and get it last night.'

There was an impatient sigh from the other end.

'I take it you've seen this appalling story in *The Times?*'

'No, I haven't, Fiammetta. I'm sorry. Like I say, I've only just got my phone back. I had a message from a journalist last night, and then a hysterical one from Kaz this morning talking about a news story, saying he's speaking to his agent and his solicitor. So I know there is a story, but I don't know what it's about.'

There was a long silence, and she thought she had been cut off.

'Hello? Are you still there?'

'Gemma, I'm going to ask you this once, and once only, and I want the truth, OK?'

'OK...'

'Did you know anything about this, anything at all, in

advance?'

It depended what 'this' was. It was best she did not know, Vivian had said.

'No, Fiammetta, I keep telling you, I don't even know what you're talking about.'

'Check your emails. I'm sending you the story now. Call me back when you've read it.'

'OK, I will, but can you just…'

She was talking to herself.

She checked the bars on her phone. There was not much internet reception in the alley, so she headed for the nearest café, where she could use the wifi. A hit of very strong coffee would not go amiss either.

By the time she got the password sorted and had logged in, Fiammetta's email was in her inbox. It was a link to the online, subscriber-only edition of the *Times*. She winced as she read the headline:

'Long-lost Gainsborough portrait of Joshua Reynolds makes an ass of TV experts.'

No, Vivian, surely not…

She carried on reading the story.

By Frances Carter
Arts correspondent

A half-finished portrait by Thomas Gainsborough, painted in 1782 and previously thought to have been destroyed or over-painted, has come to light in Sudbury, the Suffolk town where the celebrated painter was born.

The picture is believed to show his rival Sir Joshua Reynolds, the President of the Royal Academy, who was regarded by the artists' contemporaries as the finest portrait-painter of the day. Reynolds is known to have sat for Gainsborough, but until now there have been no reports of any resulting picture.

The head-and-shoulders portrait, which is in private ownership, is thought to have gone undetected for more than two centuries because it has been badly vandalised as well as damaged. Sir Joshua is depicted with a pair of giant asses' ears, and the canvas has been cut into quarters, before being crudely stitched back together.

Serious as the damage is, art historians now believe that the ears were painted at the same time as the portrait, and may even have been added by Gainsborough himself, although the precise circumstances remain shrouded in mystery.

The painting came to light when its owner, retired supermarket cashier Muriel Mudge, took it to be assessed by experts on the new daytime antiques show *Britain's Got Treasures*. In an episode to be screened tonight, former *Big Brother* contestant Kaz Kareem, now rebranded as an antiques expert, is shown ridiculing the picture. A distressed Ms Mudge then removes her painting and storms out of the filming venue.

However, *The Times* understands that another of the programme's experts, Norfolk antiques trader Vivian Morris, considered the painting worthy of closer examination. Thanks to his efforts, the painting has now been authenticated by the world's top Gainsborough scholar, Dr Leonarda Canham.

'This truly is an astonishing find,' Dr Canham told *The Times*. 'Between them, Gainsborough and Reynolds painted all the great figures of their time, including Royals, aristocrats, courtesans, military heroes and all the celebrities of the day, but until now, no portrait has existed of one by the other.

'Reynolds is known to have sat for Gainsborough, but the project was never completed and it was always assumed that the work in progress never survived. I am confident that this painting, which has remained in the same family in the town of Gainsborough's birth for two centuries, is that very work in progress.

'It has been very badly defaced and damaged, which naturally affects its quality as a work of art, and no doubt its potential value too. But it also presents us with a fascinating historical puzzle: who damaged it, and why?'

Mr Morris was not available for comment, but sources close to *Britain's Got Treasures* claim that the programme's producer, Fiammetta Moore, was made aware of the authentication but chose not to include any details in tonight's episodes. Neither the programme's host channel nor Ms Moore's production company, Little Flame, were available for comment as *The Times* went to press.

It is not known whether Ms Mudge proposes to sell the portrait at auction or keep it in her own family. However, Dr Jolyon Richards of the National Gallery predicted there would be a strong public desire to view the painting as soon as possible.

'It will need restoring, because it's very dirty, and it will never be an object of beauty, because of the vandalism,' he said. 'Nevertheless, it's an object of immense historical curiosity. Whoever eventually owns it, be it Ms Mudge or a new buyer, I hope that they will give the public the opportunity to see it.'

Gemma put her head in her hands and groaned.

However much she been dreading this day, this was far, far worse than anything she could have imagined. Had Vivian taken leave of his senses? No wonder he did not want to tell her earlier what he had done.

She sat there without moving, as her coffee went cold beside her, before remembering with a start that Fiammetta was waiting for her call.

She picked up her phone, wondering if she would still have a job when the conversation was over.

19

Was any man in the world so blessed? In his own estimation, Tom would always be the son of a debt-ridden shroud-maker from Suffolk, yet here he was, in the noblest castle in the land – which was looking smarter every time he visited, as the King's refurbishment gathered pace – in the company of three models of angelic perfection. Granted, the eldest was plain and spoke with a stammer, and the youngest was plump. However, the middle sister was a beauty, and all of them embodied a kind of virtue that humbled a man of his own deficiencies. More than once he had turned away from this canvas to dab a tear from his cheek.

They had been sitting for him individually as he worked on one face at a time, but now that most of that detail was finished, they were back as a group, in the way that he had first assembled them. The eldest stood in the centre, wearing a primrose silk gown trimmed with blonde lace. Her next sister, the beauty, wore peach to match her cheeks. She stood at the left, sideways on, with her face turned towards Tom; the pair held their arms entwined in the most endearing way. The third sister, the youngest of the group, although by no means the youngest of the family, was on the right, dressed in forget-me-not blue, and seated in a chair. What a delightful trio they were, these three graces made flesh. What a privilege to...

'I'm hungry,' said the youngest.

'You're always hungry,' said her eldest sister. 'You'll just have to wait. Can't you see that Mr Gainsborough is working?'

'Thank you, ma'am,' said Tom, adding to Princess Elizabeth, the youngest, 'If I could but entreat your forbearance for a further hour, ma'am. No longer than that.'

'An hour? I'll die!'

'You will not die,' said Princess Augusta, the peach. 'It will do your jaws good to rest them.'

'You're horrid. She's horrid. Tell her, Royal.'

This spat was conducted with perfect physical discipline, none of them moving their heads even the fraction of an inch, so that they looked like bickering waxworks. Now, however, the eldest – the Princess Royal – permitted herself a half-smile, before restoring her face to the posed expression on which she concentrated so diligently.

'I will do n-nothing of the sort. I am devoting all my energy to remaining still for Mr Gainsborough, otherwise he will never be able to get us right. Is that not so, Mr Gainsborough?'

'Movement and conversation are permitted in moderation, ma'am. The experience is not intended to be an ordeal.'

'Do you remember how poor Octavius sat?' continued the Princess Royal. 'He was just three years old, and he could sit n-nicely without the need to fidget or to constantly seek refreshment. So ought you, Elizabeth.'

Princess Elizabeth flushed at the rebuke which was, in Tom's judgement, much harsher than she deserved.

Painting little Prince Octavius had been the highlight of the most entrancing engagement of Tom's career. The Queen had commissioned fifteen heads: her husband and herself, and all their children. Tom had completed the assignment in six weeks, with the King, Queen, princes and princesses sitting one by one. The only one left out was the Duke of York, who was in Germany. Prince William was away at sea, but Tom had based his likeness on an earlier portrait, and he had even managed to include poor Prince Alfred, dead a month earlier, just short of his second birthday; he had done it from memory. Octavius, who, with that loss, had once again become the baby of the family, was in robust health when his turn came to sit: a truly angelic child, with bright blue eyes, apple-red cheeks and silky golden hair tumbling around his tiny shoulders. He had indeed sat perfectly, just as the Princess Royal recalled.

How abruptly the poor mite's fate had turned, just a few short weeks later. Barely had the pictures gone on display at the Academy – clustered in a tight block, according to Tom's strictest instructions – when Octavius suddenly took ill and died. Thanks to a misguided attempt to ward off smallpox, he passed from the peak of health to death in forty-eight hours. Nobody who witnessed it would forget the sight of the Queen and her elder daughters, attempting to put aside their grief and visit the exhibition, suddenly overcome with emotion as they saw this dear boy, so bright and bonny, looking out at them from the wall.

Again, Tom had to turn away to dab a tear.

'Let us not quarrel,' said Augusta. 'Otherwise Mr Gainsborough will make us look cross, which would not do at all. Our dear brother will complain.'

'We cannot have that,' said the Princess Royal.

This commission had come not from the King or Queen, but from the Prince of Wales. Proposing to pay five hundred guineas, he wanted his sisters' picture for his late grandmother's house, just over Tom's garden wall, which he was presently refurbishing in order to set up his own court.

Allowing the Prince to run his own household, and on such a scale, was a bold venture. Tom suspected that, if the King had greater powers of imagination, he would not permit it, but His Majesty was a simple, innocent soul, and so it had been allowed. The rest of London, being much less simple and far from innocent, had put a great deal of energy into imagining what life would be like behind the colonnaded façade of Carlton House. Some of these projections owed more to the character of those imagining them than to the behaviour of the Prince himself, but it was fair to say that these lovely princesses in their gilded frame would set a purer example of womanly virtue than most of the flesh-and-blood ladies who were likely to frequent the establishment.

Before that, however, the picture was to be shown in a place of better repute.

'Don't forget, ma'am, that you will also be displayed at the Royal Academy, where I am certain that Your Royal Highnesses will be chief among all the attractions.'

'Did you hear that, Elizabeth? You had best not fidget, or the p-public will not love you.'

Elizabeth pulled a face to make it clear she did not care if the public loved her or not. Tom, who alone was in a position to see it, leaned in close to his canvas, feigning to do some very near work on the Princess Royal's eyebrows, so that none of his sitters could see him smile.

'Gainsborough!' bellowed a voice behind him, making him start. 'How de do, sir?'

Laying his palette down, Tom turned and bowed. 'Your Majesty.'

The King, wearing the same Windsor uniform in which Tom had painted him, was standing in the doorway.

'Ye don't mind me coming to see how you're getting on, hey? Don't want to get in your way, don't ye know. How de do, girls? I hope you're staying still for Mr Gainsborough.'

'Quite still, Papa. All of us,' said the Princess Royal, sisterly loyalty taking precedence over any irritation with Elizabeth. 'Forgive us, Papa, if we do not curtsey. It will ruin the arrangement.'

'Ye must not do that, no indeed. I should hate to be the instrument of ruining anything of Gainsborough's. He's a very fine fellow, ye know, and don't ye ever forget it.'

Tom inclined his head to acknowledge the compliment.

'Ye carry on, sir. Paint away, don't mind me.'

To his surprise, Tom did not mind. It usually caused him intense irritation to have a spectator at his shoulder. Now, however, it brought him joy to have his sovereign take such pleasure at his dear eldest girls coming to life on the flat canvas before him.

'You're making them very light, I see. I notice that, ye know. I have an eye for these things. It is not dark, like most of these paintings ye see, all terrible gloom, as if the fellow painting them doesn't want ye to see the blessed picture. This has a brighter quality, is that not so? Yes, I knew it was so.'

'You are perceptive, sir. I have used a much lighter ground than usual, and I am using pastel shades, because I want to achieve a delicate, gentle tone, which suits the simple goodness of their royal highnesses.'

Did Tom spot young Elizabeth rolling her eyes?

'It does, by Jove! A capital idea, capital. Tell me, though: are ye not worried that it will fade from view, high up on the wall at the Academy? That it will be too delicate to be seen, I mean to say?'

With his eccentricities of manner and ponderous speech, the King did not present himself as a man of brilliant intellect, but his understanding of practical matters was impressive. The painting was indeed too pale to go in the usual place, above the line of the tops of the doors.

'Exactly right, sir. It will be invisible if they hang it too high up. I will send them instructions to put it lower down.'

'Don't he have rules, though, the President fellow? I've heard he's very fond of his rules, and he don't like to break them. That's the way I've heard it. Am I not right? I think I am.'

'He does like his rules, sir. And not just for the exhibition. He gives lectures about his rules on painting, and he has published them in a book.'

'I know it, sir. I know it. The book is dedicated to oneself, and he sent me an inscribed copy. Haven't opened it, mind ye, except to write the inscription. Hey?'

'That is much the best course, sir. However, regarding the hanging of the present picture, I am optimistic that the committee will see the sense if I explain my requirements. I was very firm with them last year, you know, when I sent my fifteen portraits of your dear family. The committee's rule is that any painting larger than a three-quarter length must go above the line. Each of my pictures was smaller than three-quarters, but I instructed them to be placed together, with the frames touching, and I envisaged Sir Joshua deciding that, together, they made one large painting and must go up in the sky. So I swore to them that, if they failed to comply with my instruction, as I breathed, I would never send another picture to the exhibition. I am happy to say that they were most compliant.'

'Ha! Good man! Of course, ye and the President fellow are good friends now, are ye not? And this is a benefit, is it not? He will do as ye ask, accommodate ye, and so on.'

'I would not quite say good friends, sir.'

'Didn't ye say ye were painting each other? That's the way to get to know a fellow, sit for him while he paints your face. Worked capital well with oneself, wouldn't ye say?'

'Indeed, sir. Exceeding well. And the honour was of course mine. However, in Sir Joshua's case, I am sorry to say that our appointments did not continue beyond his first sitting.'

'Ye don't say? Why was that? Was there a reason given, hey?'

'As I recall, Sir Joshua was unwell, so he delayed arranging another appointment. After that, I was occupied with other commissions as, I have no doubt, was he, and we neither of us bestirred ourselves to agree another day for him to sit. Perhaps we will resume after this year's exhibition is hung. We shall both be exceeding busy until then. Unless, of course, he has decided we are enemies after all, without acquainting me, and he does not wish to come.'

'Ye do not really think so?'

'No, sir, not really. He has given me no offence and I cannot think that I have given him any.'

There was a cough from the other side of the easel. Princess Elizabeth, making up in boldness for what she lacked in years, was evidently tiring of too much talk and too little industry.

'Ha! My daughter is sending me a message that I am impeding your work,' said the King. 'I am not too proud to be told. I will withdraw. I wish ye good fortune in your labours, and I promise I will not disturb again.' He had already reached the door, and Tom turned to bow. 'My dears, I will take no further interest in this picture until it is finished. I swear to ye I will not attempt to view it again until it hangs in pride of place on the wall of the Royal Academy, 'pon my life. Does that satisfy ye, hey? Good day to ye, Gainsborough!'

The flunkey standing at attention opened the door, and the King swept out, humming to himself.

Princess Elizabeth giggled.

'Elizabeth, that was most d-discourteous,' said the Princess Royal.

'I know, but it worked.'

Again, half-smiles briefly appeared on the faces of the two elder waxworks.

'Do carry on, Mr Gainsborough,' said Royal. 'My poor young sister is so d-desperate for her dinner. Let us not let my father's interruption delay that happy event too much longer.'

Pall-mall,
April 11th, 1784

To my dearest Ma

Words can scarce describe my joy to have seen you all this last month gone by – to meet Dick's wife and little ones and to see Jack so big and strong. We must all give thanks to Mr Pitt for calling a general election, which brought my master back home at last to cast his vote – although Mr Pitt has nothing to thank my master for, because Mr Dupont tells me he cast it for Mr Fox. My only regret was that our whole household did not come, so you were denied the chance to meet Nelly, my betrothed. She bids me send you her best love and hopes to make your acquaintance soon, when I am confident you will share my highest regard for this fairest of creatures.

Now we are back in London, and I'm sorry to tell you that my master has been in the worst rage I have ever seen in all my time here. This makes life difficult for all of us in the household, as we have to tread exceeding delicate around him else he will call us knaves and numbskulls.

As you know, the annual exhibition at the Royal Academy is a very important event for him. Each year he spends months pondering which pictures he will send. This choice is important, because the publick and the newspapers are very fickle, and if they do not like a painting, they like to say so very loud. You may ask why does he bother, and I have asked Mr Dupont the same question: if Lord So-and-so wants his face painted, and he has paid my master handsomely to do it, why should my master bother showing it to the publick and the press, who may be exceeding critical of it, when he will not receive a farthing from them? Ah, says Mr Dupont, you have to understand that all the best painters must show their pictures at the Academy in order to maintain their fame, else the finest folk will no longer come wanting their faces painted. He explained that if that happened to my master, he would no longer be able to keep a carriage and live in style in Pall-mall, and I would most likely be sent home to you.

'Tis not just the quality of the paintings that matters, but also the quality of the person being painted. You must understand that I use that word 'quality' in a loose sense, because several of the ladies my master has painted are of a loose persuasion themselves, if you take my meaning; but if a particular lady is the talk of London for her strumpet ways, that same London wants to see her face in the Academy exhibition. And if London wants to see the face, then the most important painters always think they should be the ones to paint it.

The two most important of all are my master and Sir Joshua Reynolds. Do you recall the excitement in this house when Sir Joshua came to sit for his portrait? We thought it was the start of a friendship between the two of them, after all these years of grousing at one another from a distance. I know my master thought so too, because he was exceeding cheerful in the days just after. I am sorry to say, that friendship never happened, because Sir Joshua did not ever come back, which meant my master never finished his portrait, and Sir Joshua never asked if he could paint my master's face, which would have been the gentlemanly thing. In consequence, the two of them are back to grousing. At any rate, my master grouses about Sir Joshua, because I hear him do it. I cannot say for sure whether Sir Joshua grouses about my master, but in my estimation they are each as bad as the other, so I wager that he does.

Sometimes they are so keen to paint the same faces that they both submit the same subjects to the exhibition, and the pictures are displayed in the same room so the publick can decide which one is better. This should be to my master's benefit, because he is skilled at making the faces very like, and Sir Joshua is not, only the publick will never know that, because they are not acquainted with the sitters, so they do not know if the paintings are like or not. Also, sometimes my master rushes his work, particularly the scenery and the silks, which means the publick will favour Sir Joshua, who takes great care over these details. So my master does not always emerge well from the comparison and he frets a great deal before the exhibition, not just about which paintings he should send himself, but also about which ones Sir Joshua will send.

This year, Mr Dupont tells me, Sir Joshua has sent his likeness of the Prince of Wales, which everyone wants to see, not just because he will be King one day, but because at present he is keeping all the tongues in London busy with his bawdy behaviour. Sir Joshua has also sent Mrs Siddons, who is a very famous actress. They say that, if she is playing a role where she has to die on the stage, which she very often does, her agonies seem so real that gentlemen have tried to come to her rescue from the audience. He has also sent Fanny Kemble, who is another actress, not so good as Mrs Siddons, but she is Mrs Siddons' sister, so she is famous too. He has also sent a picture of Emma Hart, who is the most famous strumpet in London at the moment, because she has risen from the serving classes to become the mistress of divers fine gentlemen, who do not care about her low birth because she is exceeding beautiful. I am telling you this, not because I wish to alarm you about the loose morals of this great city where I am living (although they are indeed exceeding loose), but to show you that everyone wants to see Sir Joshua's pictures this year.

I cannot say the same for my master's work. He has sent an old admiral who is lately a hero from beating the French in the West Indies; an old vice-admiral, same; an old army commander, same, only on land not sea; an old Earl of somewhere I cannot spell; his wife, the Countess of that place; and some other persons who are rich, but there is nothing more to say about them. I know we must honour those brave officers who fight for the King in every corner of the Earth. Without them, we might all be talking French by now, and for that I give thanks from the bottom of my heart. However, I do not have any great curiosity to know what their faces are like, and I do not imagine many of the publick have either. They are very keen to see the handsomest young heroes from these wars, especially the womenfolk, because they like to swoon over them. But nobody is going to swoon over these gray old officers.

Only one of my master's pictures is expected to inspire any great interest. It shows three of the Royal princesses. I am not sure of their names, because the King has so many daughters, but they are the eldest ones. As you know, my master is willing to relax his objection to painting faces when the faces are royal.

That was never more true than when the royalty happen to be children. We had great mirth in this household at my master's expense a year or so since, when the Queen asked him to paint all the princes and princesses, and he came back every day with tears rolling down his face, speaking of angels in human form. My mistress warned him that, if he did not stop, she would have him removed to the asylum. He did stop in the end, but only because he finished painting the last child and there were no more angels to make rapture about.

This year, the Prince of Wales asked him to paint three of his sisters, which sent my master back to his rapturous ways. I heard from Mr Dupont that he never stopped talking about the beauty of Princess This and the spirit of Princess That, until the Misses Molly and Peggy grew quite jealous, and complained that their Papa loved the princess more than his own daughters. He said it was not true, and chid them for even thinking such a thing, but I would think it too, the way he was going on.

Now that picture is finished, my master is exceeding proud of it, and not just because he has lost his head over the King's daughters. Mr Dupont says the painting itself is very well done, and I believe him. It is painted in a most delicate way, using very pale colours, as if the princesses were heavenly will-o'-the-wisps, not living creatures. This may be a further sign of my master losing his head over these ladies, but Mr Dupont says the effect is very bold and modern, and it will make the style of Sir Joshua look ancient in comparison.

You may be wondering why I am telling you about the manner of the painting, as if I have taken ideas above my station and fancy myself a great judge of these matters, but it is important, as you will shortly see. All these long explanations are necessary to understand what has happened in this house to-day.

Because his picture is painted very faint, my master thought the publick might not see it properly if the Academy hung it in the usual place for large paintings, which is very high on the wall. This Royal Academy is a very grand room, as high as a church, with a great window where you would expect the roof to be. It is made like this so that a large multitude can gather in the room to look at a great number of paintings. There are strict rules for displaying the pictures, viz. the large ones go very high up, and the smaller ones lower down. My master's picture of the princesses is very big, because it is done at life-size, and there are three princesses, so it is the size of three ladies, with a lot of scenery around them, and that means it should go very high on the wall, to obey the rules of the Academy.

My master has already sent all his pictures, but he has been fretting about the way his princesses should be hung. So, last evening just before his supper, he wrote a letter to the Academy committee. I know this because I was sent to deliver it. When I returned to the house, he was eating. He had taken both wine and beer with his meal, as is his custom, and afterwards he was sitting in the drawing room smoking a pipe with Mr Able, who had come to sup with him. That was when the boy arrived from the Academy, with the committee's reply. I had not expected a reply so soon, else I would have waited for it, but I supposed that my master would wish to see it straightway, so I took it upstairs to him and waited while he read it, in case he had an answer for me to send back.

Reading it did not take him long, because the letter seemed to be very short. We could see that the words displeased him greatly, because he jumped up from his chair and threw the paper down on the floor.

'Coxcombs!' shouted he. 'Snivelling whoresons! They have done this to spite me. No, not 'they'. *He* has done it! This is what he has always wanted, to have rid of me from the exhibition, because he fears me. He fears the comparison, I tell you. D__n and blast the man. D__n his eyes and d__n his ears.' Excuse me for repeating my master's bad language, Ma, but I want to convey to you the colour of his rage (although I have left out the worst of his cursing).

Mr Able was thrown into confusion by this explosion. 'Voteffer is the matter, Gainsborrow?' said he, whereupon my master bade him read the letter for himself. It was still lying on the floor, and Mr Able is too fat to pick anything up, so I picked it up for him. There were only two or three lines of writing and, as I passed it over to him, I could see what they said.

The letter read: 'Sir. In compliance with your request, the council have ordered your Pictures to be taken down, to be delivered to your order, whenever you send for them.'

I did not understand what this meant. Why had my master asked all his pictures to be taken down? Now Mr Able fell to reading it, and he did not understand it neither, for he said to my master: 'But vot are they talking about, Gainsborrow? Vy did you ask for your pictures to be taken down?'

My master said he had done no such thing, shouting so loud that Fox and Tristram, who had been taking their ease in their customary places next to the chimney-piece, got up and fled the room. He said he simply sent a letter saying as how he could not consent to his picture of the princesses being placed higher than five feet and a half, because it was painted in so tender a light that the likenesses and work of the picture would not be seen.

Mr Able still did not look convinced. 'And for this they haff ordered all your pictures to be taken down?' said he, whereupon my master owned that he had been emphatic in his manner of expressing himself, which might have made the gentlemen of the Academy take umbrage. Mr Able asked him in what way he had been emphatic, and now my master explained what he had actually written to the gentlemen of the committee, viz. if they did not comply with his request, he begged them to send the rest of his pictures back.

At this, Mr Able fell silent, and I could see he was thinking that it was all my master's foolish fault for giving such an instruction. He did not say this, though, because he could see, just as well as I could, that my master had gone purple in the face, and the vein on his forehead that always pops up when he is upset was throbbing fit to burst open.

By now my mistress had arrived to see why my master was raging, and he explained it all over again, saying 'he has done it to spite me' (by which he meant Sir Joshua). While Mr Able was too nervous of my master's rage to tell him it was his own fault for inviting this rejection, my mistress is not Mr Able, and she came right out and asked him what he expected, if he begged them to send the rest of his pictures back not three hours previous. If he did not mean them to take him at his word, he should not have told them that. Now it had all gone wrong, and the person to blame was himself.

My master would never dare strike my mistress, because there is every chance my mistress would strike him back even harder. The look he gave her, though, suggested he would dearly like to strike something, and for a moment I feared for my own safety, because I was standing closer at hand than anyone else, especially since the dogs had now departed. I was trying to step further away from him, but suddenly my master moved too. Happily, 'twas not to attack me. Instead he stormed out of the drawing room, abandoning his guest, and when I followed after, I heard a great hullabaloo from his painting room, where it sounded like he was kicking the walls and all manner of other things. After that he went out, and I believe he drank a lot of gin, because he could barely find his way up the stairs when I let him in at two o'clock in the morning.

To-day his mood was no better. In fact it was worse, because he had a splitting head from the gin as well as his rage at Sir Joshua and the Academy still. When he beheld the mess he had made in his own painting room, overturning his easel, smashing a jar, and much other disorder besides, he instructed Mr Dupont to clear it up, and Mr Dupont asked me to help him.

I entered the room very nervously, because it felt like my master's rage was still present there, even though my master himself was not. However, Mr Dupont had already begun picking up the mess from the floor, and he bade me set to and help him. When we picked up my master's fallen easel, we saw there was a canvas on it, so we raised it carefully, not to damage it. The sight we saw took us completely by surprise, Ma. I have lived in a painter's house these six years, and I tell you have never seen the like.

The painting, which was not even halfway finished, was the likeness of Sir Joshua, or as much of it as my master had painted in that single sitting more than twelve months since. The finished part was the face, which did look just like Sir Joshua, but he had not painted any of the body or the scenery. 'Twas now very clear what my master had been doing last night after he had stopped kicking the walls and throwing his jars about the room. For on Sir Joshua's head, as nicely painted as the rest of his face, with the skill of the great artist such as my master truly is, were a pair of ears. Not human ears in the normal position on the side of his face, mind. I am speaking of an animal's ears, pointing straight upwards.

At first I fancied they were the ears of a hare, and I said so to Mr Dupont. 'What are you saying?' said he. 'You come from the same country place as me. Surely you have seen a donkey's ears before?' And then I saw it was true: my master had attached a pair of asses' ears to Sir Joshua's head, as if they were growing naturally there, to make him into a jackass. Would you ever believe that such a fine gentleman as my master, in his fancy house next to the Prince of Wales, would do such a trick?

Do not tell anyone this, Ma, not Mrs Dupont for certain, because I am still afeared of my master's rage, and if this story gets abroad, he will want to know who in his household is spying on him and telling his secrets. So I implore you to keep silent, as I have not been able to keep silent with you, because I have no secrets from you, Ma.

Now my hand is very tired so I will finish this long letter. I will write to you very soon with more news from this strange household, where no day is ever dull. Until then, my love to you all, from your

David

21

It remained a source of amazement to Gemma that she still had a job. When Vivian dropped his newspaper bombshell, on the day that Muriel's episode was due to go out, she fully expected to be unemployed by nightfall. That she was not, she reluctantly conceded when she looked back, was testament to the care that Vivian had taken to keep her in the dark about his plans.

Fiammetta had cancelled her breakfast meeting and was already in the office when Gemma arrived. It was always a bad sign when the rush of angry air from her nose was audible. Today it was gale-force.

'Gemma, I'm going to ask you a question,' she said. 'I'm only going to ask it once, and I want you to answer truthfully. If you are not truthful, I will find out. Understood?'

This was actually the second time she had said she was only

going to ask once, but Gemma thought it best not to point this out. She could hear her heart pounding. Could Fiammetta hear it too?

'Did you know that Vivian was planning to go to the media?'

There was a copy of *The Times*, folded to the offending news story, on the desk between them.

Gemma swallowed, which must look like a sure-fire tell.

'No, I swear to you. The last time I had any involvement in this was the day we saw Lennie – Dr Canham, the Gainsborough expert quoted in that story. Since then, Vivian hasn't told me anything. I had no idea that he was planning to go to a newspaper, and I was as shocked as you when I read that story.'

She liked the way that had come out. It had the added virtue of being completely true.

Fiammetta held her gaze for an unnervingly long time.

'All right,' she said finally. 'I believe you. So, damage limitation. We need to make a statement.'

'Do we have to? Can't we just try and ride it out? Because, if we do make a statement, then…'

Gemma stopped.

'Then, what?'

The snorting had stopped, but Fiammetta still looked fierce.

'It's just that…I mean…'

'For pity's sake, spit it out.'

'OK. Anything we say has got to be true, right, otherwise we'll be found out, and we'll get in all kinds of trouble with the channel.'

'Of course. Why wouldn't it be true?'

'Well, one obvious response might be that we didn't know Muriel's painting really was a Gainsborough until this morning.'

'And the problem with that is…?'

'The problem is that we did know. You knew. Vivian told you, right after we'd seen Lennie Canham. Sorry, I don't mean to come over all 'I told you so', but…'

'You're failing on that score.'

'Yes, I know. Sorry. I'm only trying to think what's the best way forward.'

The nostrils flared dangerously again.

'When Vivian called me, it was already too late to change the programme. I had orders from on high.'

'Let's use that, then. When we became aware that one of our experts might have got his assessment wrong, it was too late to change the programme. That's nice and unspecific. It could mean we only found out about it this week.'

'It's a start, but it sounds callous, like we only care about the programme, and we're not bothered about the truth. Don't roll your eyes like that at me, young lady. You're not out of the woods yet, by any means, and don't you forget that.'

'Sorry, but…well…it is kind of true, isn't it? Unless we make it clear we're going to do right by Muriel later in the series.'

'How?' snapped her boss. 'We can't just schedule another episode on a whim, even if we had the budget.'

'We do have a programme slot, though. The auction show is live, isn't it? Why don't we bring Muriel back then? We'd look magnanimous, like we're prepared to admit we got it wrong, and nobody loses face.'

'Apart from Kaz.'

Gemma shrugged. It was true, but there was no honest way through this that did not involve Kaz losing face.

Fiammetta narrowed her eyes, thinking the options through.

'All right,' she said. 'Here's what we'll do. We'll put out the first part, as you said: mortified when we found out, but too late to change, blah, blah, blah. However, this *Times* journalist was quite wrong to assume we were just leaving the matter there, as we would have told her, if we'd had proper warning of the story, rather than a message left at the eleventh hour. We already had plans in place to acknowledge the authenticity of this item later in the series, and it's quite wrong, a grave injustice, to state or imply otherwise.'

Gemma nodded. It was a cynical lie, but this was television, and lying went with the territory.

'That'll work.'

Fiammetta stood up. 'OK, you type it, and we'll get it out as soon as possible, before the damage gets any worse.'

Gemma had passed her first test, by finding a public relations solution that would also benefit Muriel.

She did not watch the episode itself: she could not face it. However, the situation took a dramatic turn for the better the next day, when the overnight viewing figures came in. Nobody had ever entertained high expectations for a daytime show on a channel that most people, as a badge of pride, never watched. Even by this modest yardstick, the ratings for the first few episodes had been a disappointment. The only positive aspect of such a small share was that a minor improvement in actual numbers would constitute a major percentage boost. That was precisely what happened now. The interest generated by Vivian's media leak was necessarily limited by the audience's availability to tune in at four o'clock in the afternoon. However, once catch-up figures were added, the boost was dramatic, and certainly significant enough to transform the mood of the suits. That, in turn, brought a turnaround in Fiammetta's demeanour. She began asking concerned questions about Muriel and talking about 'our discovery', as if she had played a part in it too.

The entire media seemed to want to follow up the *Times* story. Some just copied it out and repackaged it as their own. Other publications contacted the office to ask for a comment. Gemma fielded the calls, pinging Fiammetta's statement over to them, and referring them to the channel press office if they wanted more. Within an hour of the first of these calls, the line about acknowledging the authenticity of Muriel's picture later in the series was live on the internet. That felt like a significant step forward: there was no going back on the commitment now.

Vivian and Lennie took it upon themselves to look after Muriel. She was predictably upset when she saw the episode itself, but the blow had been softened in the hours leading up to the broadcast, when Vivian took her a copy of *The Times*, and she was even more impressed when the story appeared in *The Sun* and the *Mirror* the following day. She did not need Vivian to tell her that these stories all presented her and her picture in a very favourable light. *The Sun* emphasised the point with its headline KAMP KAZ DOESN'T KNOW HIS ASS FROM HIS GAINSBRO. Amid this kind of vindication, it was easier for Muriel to surmount her earlier humiliation.

She began to receive requests for interviews. She was asked to appear on *This Morning* and *Lorraine*. The *Mail on Sunday* sent a feature writer, and the *Daily Mail* sent two, neither of whom knew about the other. Vivian had his work cut out trying to shield Muriel from intrusion. He and Fiammetta had reached a fragile, unspoken truce: she had neither formally forgiven him, nor conceded that he had done them all a favour by leaking the story of the picture to the media, but she had allowed him an ongoing role by conferring with him on their future media strategy, namely that Muriel should do one short television interview now, and save any further coverage until the run-up to the auction. Since Muriel's nervousness of film cameras had, if anything, increased, persuading her to turn invitations down was not difficult. The hard part was getting her to accept a carefully vetted one, but eventually she was coaxed into appearing on *Look East*, in a pre-recorded interview with a nice young reporter who was used to putting elderly Suffolk ladies at their ease.

Kaz remained a marginal figure, nursing a badly bruised ego. In her guiltier moments, Gemma was conscious that she had made the exact same judgement call as he had, when she first saw Muriel's picture. She was the one who had presented it to the rest of the team as the perfect object of ridicule. It was Kaz's ill fortune that he had expressed his reaction on camera, whereas she had not. Doing so had established him as the villain of the affair and demolished his pretensions to expertise. Had Gemma been the on-camera expert in his place, would she have done any different?

Actually, she hoped she would. The more she thought about it, she was sure she would not have been so rude to Muriel's face. And Kaz's subsequent behaviour, she reminded herself, had done little to dispel the impression that he cared only about the impact on himself. Once his snap verdict had come into doubt, he could have joined the quest to investigate the painting, or at least taken some interest in it. As it was, he still seemed to regard any suggestion that it might be of artistic or historical value as a personal slight. Gemma had tried to explain that nobody cared about his initial verdict, and it would all be forgotten if he could only find it within himself to be happy for Muriel and make some sort of gesture to show it. Kaz merely repeated that he was being undermined, and Gemma decided she was wasting her breath.

This was confirmed when Kaz gave an interview to *Pink*

Times. Had the programme been edited to make him look bad, the paper asked. Kaz did not like to say, but he was confident that any *Pink Times* readers who had seen the clip of Muriel showing him her picture – by now a minor sensation on YouTube – would draw their own conclusions. So if he had deliberately been made to look ridiculous, was that motivated by homophobia? Again, Kaz did not want to comment, because he was not a mind-reader; but he could not help noticing that the rival 'expert' who had emerged as the hero of Muriel's story came from a generation that was much less accepting of difference, and lived in a notoriously backward part of the country. Besides, the *Sun* had called him Kamp Kaz, and that was certainly prejudiced. That gave *Pink Times* the headline it was angling for: 'I'm the victim of homophobia in lost Gainsborough row says Big Brother's Kaz.'

It did not go down well with Fiammetta.

'Homophobic?' she shouted. 'I've been a flipping fag-hag since before Kaz was born. I barely know any straight men, and I've got the non-existent sex life to prove it!'

Gemma decided against showing the article to Vivian, because it would be needlessly hurtful, but he found it anyway. To her surprise, he thought it was hilarious.

'I may be getting on, but if I had a problem with gays, I honestly wouldn't have spent my life in the antiques trade,' he told Gemma, laughing so much down the phone that it triggered a smoker's coughing fit.

'Thank you for taking it in such good heart,' she said. 'He really shouldn't have said it, though. Aside from being completely unfair to you, it's very unprofessional.'

'Well, let's be honest, I'm in no position to judge anyone for tattling to the media, am I? I understand the lad is hurt, because he's made a pillock of himself on national television, so he needs to lash out at someone. I only hope he hasn't burnt his boats with Fiammetta. She won't renew his contract if he's not careful. He may not care about that at the moment, but I imagine he will do once all the fuss has died down.'

Gemma wondered if she ought to have another word with Kaz, urging caution in any further dealings with the media, for his own benefit. He was unlikely to listen, though, and she was angry with him, so she decided against it. She had no great inclination to put herself out for him, particularly now that preparation for the live auction episode was beginning to take up all her time.

This would be her first experience of live television. To her mind, it was an absurdly stressful and risky venture. They could easily pre-record a programme centred on the auction, with all the same thrills and tension, and none of the terror that doing it live entailed. True, there was serious media interest in the fate of Muriel's picture, and it would be important not to let the result of the auction leak in advance of broadcast. The tried-and-tested way of doing that was to impose a strict embargo on any news stories, and make sure nobody broke it. However, the suits were dead set on the idea of doing it live. It had been part of the concept for the show all along, and now that the media was genuinely interested in the outcome, they were keener on the idea than ever, and the press office was talking it up as a historic television event. Normally, the only time the word 'historic' was used in connection with the channel was to describe record lows in viewer share, so their enthusiasm was understandable. It was all very well for them, though: they were not the ones who had to make the broadcast happen.

Fiammetta, who had spent part of her early career on breakfast television, kept telling Gemma not to worry: it was a piece of cake, provided all the proper preparations had been done and everyone knew exactly what they were meant to be doing. For Gemma, that was precisely the point. On breakfast television, everyone involved did a live show in the same format every day of the week, so it came as second nature; they were also based in a nice, safe, purpose-built studio, not some draughty auction room in Southeast London. However, several other members of the production and camera crew said they were comfortable with a live broadcast, so she forced herself to trust their judgement.

Regina was dispatched to make a film about the lost Gainsborough, which would be slotted into the live programme. Gemma heard from Vivian that Muriel finally relaxed at the eighth or ninth take, and ended up telling the story of her picture concisely and engagingly. She showed Regina where it was usually kept – under the bed, not on the wall – which made it clear that she was under no illusions about what it looked like. She told how it had come down the male line of her family over two centuries, ending up at her brother, and since his death it had come to her. She had not yet decided what would happen to it when she was gone.

'That also depends on what happens in the live auction, doesn't it, Muviel?' said Regina.

Muriel just shrugged.

After completing that interview, Regina went on to speak to Lennie Canham and Jolyon Richards. The latter said that if Lennie Canham thought the picture was a Gainsborough, that was good enough for him. For her part, Lennie said there were still unsolved mysteries surrounding the painting, such as who had overpainted the ears onto Sir Joshua Reynolds' head, why it had been cut into four pieces, and how it had come into the possession of the Mudge family. Nevertheless, she stood by her verdict. Muriel was distressed because she now remembered that her brother had some old family papers which might shed more light on those mysteries. She had searched her cottage high and low, however, and could not find them. Vivian had done his best to reassure her that the papers did not really matter: with Lennie Canham's endorsement, her painting was officially the real deal.

The auction was to take place at a sale-room a mile or so down the Thames from the production office. Its normal trade was house clearances. From what Gemma had seen in a couple of preparatory visits, the clientele were unshaven men in anoraks scrawling notes on the back of envelopes, not the sharp-suited agents of the super-rich who might bid for a lost work by one of England's greatest painters. However, there was no budget for Sotheby's, and the cameras did not have to show the shabby foyer and the Styrofoam coffee bar. Once the room was packed with those members of the public who had applied for tickets, the media, members of the antiques trade whom Vivian had talked into coming and any genuinely deep-pocketed bidders interested in Muriel's picture, it ought to look much more the part. And any real interest in the lost Gainsborough would come via the internet, or the phone banks that were to be installed for the occasion.

In the original plan for the series, each of the experts was to choose a trove of three treasures from the series to champion, and the one who ended up with the highest total bids would be crowned the winner. Regina had done her best throughout the run to make this competition sound exciting, but no amount of pretence could change the fact that the concept was lame. The genuine excitement over the lost Gainsborough had made it much easier, for production team and viewers alike, to overlook the flimsiness of the central conceit. Nevertheless, this format was still technically in place, and the experts were obliged to corral the owners of their treasures into teams. On the day of the broadcast, at just before four o'clock, these people were all standing ready, in allotted corners of the sale-room, as the director began the countdown. Then, finally, after all the weeks of preparation, the programme was on air.

Amid the continuing chatter of the sale-room – it was important to maintain a buzz – Regina delivered her introductory piece to camera, then toured the groups one by one, reminding viewers of the treasures in each trove. Lavender's was first, with a haul that indulged her own collecting obsession: a Victorian amethyst pendant, a nineteenth-century Limoges coffee set hand-painted with purple violets, and a mauve decanter in vintage Murano glass.

'So, Lavender,' said Regina. 'I can't help noticing that everything is purple. Might we say you're Lavender by name, lavender by taste?'

'I wouldn't say that,' said Lavender, her fixed beam betraying a touch of irritation. Until now, nobody had mentioned her purple mania in public. 'I simply like beautiful things and these are the ones I chose.'

Amid all the other tensions of the show, this was a potential area of difficulty that Gemma had not anticipated. But the moment passed. After a token chat with each of the owners – all three confirming that they were excited, proud and hopeful that their treasure would attract high bids – Regina moved on to Kaz's group.

From her vantage point beside the camera crew, Gemma was shocked to see the change in Kaz. At the beginning of the series, what he lacked in expertise he had made up for in enthusiasm; while his patter was cliché-ridden, he radiated delight at being in front of a television camera. That easy confidence now seemed a distant memory, and Kaz now looked as if this sale-room was the last place on earth he wanted to be. He remembered in the nick of time to smile as he came into shot, but there was conspicuously little warmth in it.

His treasures were less thematic than Lavender's. He had chosen a Victorian rocking-horse, a silver cutlery service which appeared to be Georgian, and a pair of pug figurines in Staffordshire porcelain, which appealed to him on the grounds that pugs were currently all the rage as pets in Shoreditch, ergo there was bound to be a lively market for pug kitsch.

Regina went to the three owners first – eliciting the obligatory excitement, pride and hope – and then came to their team leader at the end.

'So, Kaz. Which of your tveasures do you think will fare the best in this afternoon's bidding?'

Kaz sighed.

'I'm confident in my silver cutlery. I think that's my best prospect. But whaddo I know? I'm just a fat poof from Essex.'

There it was again, the grating catchphrase that was normally so jauntily delivered. This time, though, Gemma noticed him shoot a dark look in Vivian's direction, and his smile was less convincing than ever.

Regina clearly sensed the bitterness too, and attempted to redress the balance with a peal of laughter. This encouraged Kaz's treasure-owners to laugh too, which drew the focus away from Kaz himself, as the supremely professional Regina no doubt knew it would. Taking a step back from the group and spinning around to face the camera directly, with Kaz no longer in shot, she invited viewers to join her in the final corner, with Vivian and his hopefuls.

As the filming moved away, Gemma noticed Kaz turn his back and take something from the inside pocket of his jacket, raising it to his lips and tilting his head back. Gemma was genuinely shocked. She had never seen Kaz drink alcohol and had assumed that, as a Muslim, he might be teetotal. There was no reason he should be, of course, but drinking on set during a live broadcast was seriously reckless. She ought to tell him so, but there was no time to linger, in case she was needed by the crew, so she had no choice but to follow Regina and her entourage. She would decide after the show was over whether to talk to Kaz discreetly, or rat on him to Fiammetta. That would depend on how he behaved with Muriel.

Regina's pre-auction routine had been carefully choreographed to circle around, and then build up to, the main event of the programme. Now, finally, she was talking to Vivian – but only about two of the objects he had chosen to champion, a shooting stick with an interesting crest on its silver top, and a brass barograph in a walnut case. The respective owners were allowed a quick word about their feelings – excitement! pride! hope! – while the third owner stood to one side, deliberately out of shot.

After talking briefly to Vivian about the reasons for those two selections, Regina turned back to the camera.

'You may have noticed that Vivian only mentioned two tveasures just now. He does have a third one, and the identity of that object may come as a surpvise if you were watching the fourth episode of our sevies, filmed in a market town in Suffolk. Let's remind ourselves what happened.'

This was the cue to run the pre-recorded package, which began with the notorious footage from the programme itself. Watching on a monitor, Gemma could hardly bear to look at that, and she hoped Muriel could not see it from where she was standing. Then it cut to Vivian, who related his own discomfort with the outright dismissal of Muriel's picture.

This was followed by clips from Regina's interviews with Lennie, Jolyon Richards and Muriel herself, and finally a montage of the press coverage, now deftly reclaimed as an investigative triumph for *Britain's Got Treasures*.

'So, Vivian,' said Regina, live once more. 'Tell us, as if we haven't guessed, which is the third tveasure that you've chosen to champion here at the *Bvitain's Got Tveasures* Super Salevoom Slugout!'

Vivian beamed at her, as the camera moved into close-up. He had risked a lot for this, thought Gemma, and he deserved to enjoy it.

'Well, Regina, you won't be surprised to hear that I'll be championing the lost Gainsborough portrait of Sir Joshua Reynolds, brought to us damaged and defaced, but still very much the real deal, by a lady who it's been my honour to get to know, Muriel Mudge.'

'And here is Muviel Mudge, together with her lost Gainsbvough painting!' cried Regina. 'Welcome back, Muviel! Tell me, how does it feel to see your painting vecognised as the genuine article, making headlines in every newspaper in the countvy, and now going under the hammer, with bidders from all over the world logging in on the internet this afternoon?'

'Well...' said Muriel slowly.

Gemma closed her eyes. If anyone was likely to dry on live television, it was Muriel. It would be tragic if, in what should be her hour of vindication, she ended up looking like a bumbling bumpkin all over again.

But no, it was all right. She was still talking.

'It certainly feels better than being made to feel like you're stoopid on national television, with the whole country having a good laugh at you,' she said.

Way to go, Muriel! Gemma could have punched the air.

That pause had not been nervous hesitation: on the contrary, Muriel was savouring her victory. Gemma glanced over to see how Kaz was reacting to all this, but he had his back to her, so she could not see his expression. He was too far away to have heard directly. He might be watching a live monitor, though. She hoped not.

'I can well imagine, Muviel.'

Regina was good, Gemma had to acknowledge. The knack was to seem to be entirely on Muriel's side, without ever going so far as to admit the programme's total responsibility for her humiliation, still less to apologise for it.

'And what are you hoping for this afternoon? What sort of selling pvice would make you very happy?'

'I shouldn't like to say.'

'Any ballpark figure in your head? Pick a number!'

'No, I have no idea. I really can't say.'

'And in fact, nor can any of the vest of us, because that's the joy of an auction. So we'll just have to wait and see, won't we? Not long now, though. In fact, I'm getting a message…' She put a finger to her earpiece. 'Yes, I'm being told we're veady to begin and the auction is just about to start. So let's move over into the main sale-room and meet our auctioneer, whose name is…'

The items had been lined up for sale in ascending order of how much they were likely to fetch. First was the Murano decanter. After a shaky start, with the auctioneer struggling to coax the price above fifty pounds, bidding rallied on the internet and the piece ended up achieving nearly two hundred. At this point, the owner was formally invited to decide whether she wanted to take the money or keep the treasure. It was meant to be a moment of tension, but she jumped in to say she was opting for the cash before Regina had a chance to string the decision out.

'Very wise, madam,' commented the auctioneer, over his half-moon glasses. The implication was clear: if someone was daft enough to pay that kind of money, grabbing it was the only rational option.

The Staffordshire pugs fared less well, selling for just seventy-five pounds. Either *le tout* Shoreditch was occupied elsewhere at this time on a Wednesday afternoon, or Kaz's assessment of the dogs' popularity was flawed. Nevertheless, cash once again trumped sentiment for the owner. And so the trend continued: despite Regina's best efforts to generate keep-or-sell excitement, each of the owners elected to part with their treasure without a moment's hesitation. Even the owner of the rocking-horse, who said it was a much-loved family heirloom and had given the impression that he would never let it go, had a rapid change of heart when offered more than five hundred pounds.

Gemma was keeping a running total of the hammer price for each of the three teams, which she handed to Regina at convenient, off-camera interludes. Once more, Regina displayed her professional mettle by trying to wring competitive excitement out of the tally. She was hindered by the experts themselves who, far from biting their nails with the thrill of it all, seemed hardly to be paying attention. Lavender was scrolling through her Twitter feed when Regina and the camera approached, and had to pretend she was searching for previous selling-prices for Limoges porcelain. Kaz was in the lead after the first six items had been sold, but it was beyond Regina's best abilities to persuade him to look pleased about it. Trailing in third place, Vivian expressed confidence that everything would change once Muriel's picture reached its turn, but then he spoiled everything by saying it was not the price that mattered, but the authentication.

'It does matter a little bit, though, when you're in competition with Lavender and Kaz,' prompted Regina.

'I suppose so, if you care about that sort of thing.'

'It is the whole pvemise of the sevies.' Regina's smile had by now acquired a wintry froideur.

The sale wore on. Lot seven, Lavender's amethyst pendant, went for six hundred and twenty pounds. The owner opted to take the money. As the auctioneer introduced lot eight, the atmosphere shifted a gear. Bidding for Kaz's cutlery, now officially dated to the late eighteenth century, opened at one thousand pounds, shooting quickly upwards, with three online buyers vying against each other. The soaring price caused genuine gasps from the sale-room spectators, and the elderly owner was genuinely speechless – Regina had to take the microphone away after getting nothing – when the hammer fell at six thousand two hundred pounds. Would the owner sell? She frantically nodded, not needing a voice for that.

At last, it was time for the main event.

'And so, ladies and gentlemen, we come to the final lot in this short but enthralling sale,' said the auctioneer, as all the people who had been standing at the back of the room now pressed forward. 'Lot nine, which has received a good deal of media attention, is a lost portrait by Thomas Gainsborough, showing Sir Joshua Reynolds. It's believed to have been painted in late 1782. It's unfinished, and has been subjected to some unusual and extreme vandalism, by hand or hands unknown, and thereafter crudely repaired. Ladies and gentlemen, this is an object of considerable art historical interest. Ordinarily it would have been cleaned and restored before being brought to market, but *Britain's Got Treasures* is working to a strict broadcasting schedule, so there has not been time. The buyer will have the chance to restore it, thereby enhancing its value greatly. There has been a lot of advance interest, so I'm going to open the bidding at twenty thousand pounds. Twenty. Who'll give me twenty-five? On the internet. Thirty? Thirty thousand pounds, on the internet again. Thirty-five? Thirty-five on the telephone, thank you very much. Forty?'

It was extraordinary how quickly these vast sums were advanced. The dynamic was bewildering at first, but Gemma grasped that all the key participants were bidding remotely, rather than from the sale-room: either online, or on the phone, via three assistants. Each with a receiver to their ear, they relayed the progress of the bidding to interested parties at the other end of the line, occasionally calling out a figure to the auctioneer.

The price continued to rise.

'Seventy-five? Seventy-five on the internet. Am I bid eighty? Eighty thousand pounds? Yes, on the telephone, thank you. Eighty-five?'

Gradually, the pace slowed. There were longer pauses as the remaining contenders weighted up their options. Gemma willed the bidding up, partly for Muriel's sake, but also for the kudos: an item fetching six figures would be an amazing achievement for a debut show on a no-hope channel. It was not to be, however. Despite the auctioneer's best efforts, the bidding would not go above ninety-five thousand.

'Calling it once, calling it twice... Sold for ninety-five thousand pounds, on the telephone.'

The gavel rapped decisively down.

On the phone, the assistant congratulated the buyer. There was no time to wonder who that might be, though. Regina was ready to cut to Muriel and Vivian, who had been watching from the back and were both giggling excitedly.

'So, Muviel. Ninety-five thousand pounds! Is that more or less than you expected?'

'I honestly didn't know what to expect. But ninety-five thousand pounds sounds a lot of money to me.'

Regina nodded happily.

'And so, Muviel, you know what I'm going to ask, and I suspect I know what the answer will be. But I'll ask you anyway: what are you going to do, keep the picture, or take the cash?'

Muriel glanced at Vivian by her side, all camera-shyness banished now.

'Oh, that's easy.'

'I thought it would be. But go on, tell us.'

'I'm keeping it.'

'Sovvy? Do you mean, keeping the cash?'

'No, I'm keeping the painting. I wouldn't ever part with it, not after my ancestors passed it down so carefully. It wouldn't be right.'

Regina looked stunned.

'Are you sure, Muviel? It's a very big decision.'

'Course I'm sure. I feel bad for whoever wanted it so much, but them's the rules of the show, aren't they? I had to put it up for auction, but I was always going to keep it.'

'That tvuly is an amazing turn of events,' said Regina, putting her finger to her ear as she received a message from the director. 'We haven't got much time left, but let's quickly go to our expert. Vivian, it was your hard work that bvought us to this point. Are you surpvised by Muviel's decision?'

'Not in the least,' said Vivian. 'Muriel's a woman of honour and integrity, and she's doing what is right for her. I'm sorry, too, for the winning bidder, who hasn't actually won. However, as Muriel says, those are the rules, and she's quite within her rights to turn the money down.'

A crowd had gathered around them: spectators from the sale-room, the production team, and the other two experts. As Kaz pushed past Gemma, she smelled gin on his breath. He began edging close to Vivian. Had he finally found the Dutch courage to make that long-overdue magnanimous gesture? Gemma hoped that Regina had seen him, so that she could bring him into the group if necessary.

'The main thing,' continued Vivian, 'is that Muriel has been vindicated. She believed in her painting, she trusted us to tell her what it was, and we have now shown ourselves worthy of that trust.'

Gemma was watching the clock. There were now just thirty seconds to go until they needed to cut to the credits. Both Regina and the camera-operator would be getting wind-up messages through their earpieces. Would Regina have time to say that Vivian had won the battle of the treasure troves?

Vivian himself was still talking.

'It wasn't nice when some people laughed at her at the start of this process, but I'm glad we can now draw a line under all that.'

He was straying into dangerous territory. If Kaz had come to bury the hatchet, that kind of talk would not help. As Gemma looked at Kaz's face, however, she realised with alarm that peace-making was the last thing on his mind. Suddenly she knew she must get to him, and hold him back, just for twenty more seconds, but even as she tried to push through the crowd of onlookers, she saw him draw his arm back. His eyes were bloodshot, and he looked seriously drunk now.

'Bastard!' he shouted.

The punch landed on Vivian's left cheek. The force of it, and the surprise, knocked him off balance, and he toppled into

Muriel, who yelped as she fell to the floor.

The last thing viewers saw before the live broadcast came to an abrupt end was Regina, Gemma and Fiammetta attempting to pull Kaz off the prone figure of Vivian.

22

'Ramsay is dead. I heard the news late last evening, and I wanted you to know as soon as possible.'

It was August. The air was close, the streets reeked worse than ever and all right-thinking folk had left town. Tom had been obliged to remain, having thrown his house open to display the paintings that the Academy would not show. It was a return to the days of his previous exile from the exhibition, and it had been a dispiriting business, not least because the hastily conceived venture had taken some weeks to organise, and now all the most likely patrons had departed London. Next year (for he would surely never go back to the Academy) he would open his doors in the spring. For the moment, however, he had little choice but to remain at home to play host to those few visitors who deigned to come.

Bate was still in town too, because his readers wanted the

news, no matter what month it was. He had banged on Tom's door at ten o'clock in the morning, and now they were in the parlour, taking chocolate and discussing the fate of poor Ramsay.

'I understand he had been in Italy for more than a year,' said Bate. 'The climate helped his rheumaticks, and he has been writing a book, something about the poet Horace, which has been his obsession since putting down his paintbrush. He moved from Rome to Florence to pass the winter, and now he was returning to England to see his daughter before she sails to Madras, where her husband is newly appointed governor. Sadly it seems that he was weaker than he knew. Even though he was attempting the journey in short stages, the jolting of the carriage was too much for his nervous system. He had a high fever by the time he reached Paris.'

'Dear, dear. How he must have suffered! And so he died in France?'

'No, he managed to reach Calais and cross the Channel, but that last effort was too much for him, and he died at Dover yesterday.'

'So very tragic. Was the poor man travelling all alone?'

'I believe his son was with him.'

'That, at least, will have been a comfort to him. May God have mercy on his soul. You know I never met Ramsay in all these years, but he was a good fellow, by all accounts. The King liked him very well. He told me they used to talk about European political affairs – a subject about which I myself am unable to join together two words. What age was he, do you know?'

'I am told he was in his seventy-second year.'

'So he completed his three-score years and ten. We should be thankful for that.'

Bate sighed, and they both fell silent. Tom waited. He knew what was coming, and he would not be the first to raise it.

'While it is undoubtedly very sad,' began his friend, 'it does mean that there is now a...'

Tom feigned innocence.

'A...?'

'A vacancy.'

Tom let him flounder a little longer.

'Vacancy?'

'Ramsay was still the court painter, was he not?'

'Ah! Now I understand you. But fie, my friend, it is too soon to talk of such things.'

'Much too soon, of course. I should not have said it.'

They each reached for their cup, Bate blowing to cool his chocolate, Tom slurping noisily.

After a few moments, he decided he had made his friend suffer long enough. He did, after all, wish to discuss the subject just as much as Bate did.

'I dare say you will write about this very sad news?'

'Indeed I will.'

'When will your report appear?'

'Tomorrow.'

Tom nodded pensively, as if weighing up the propriety of the matter.

'While it is of course far too early to speak of any vacancy today, tomorrow it may not be. In any discussion of poor Ramsay's life, you will of course say that he was the King's official painter. And your readers will naturally wonder who his successor might be. So I imagine it would not be too indecent to suggest the identity of...'

'Not too indecent at all. Well said, sir. I shall write something straightway, for publication tomorrow, and I shall make mention of the only possible candidate. Consider it done.'

'Consider what done, Mr Bate?'

Molly swept into the parlour and allowed Bate to take her hand. She was evidently in one of her livelier moods, which often boded ill. Lately, her delusions had been bad. She had become convinced that the Prince of Wales was wooing her from his new residence over the garden wall, an advance which she was determined to resist. To outsiders, even close friends such as Bate, she appeared quite normal, but Tom could always detect the warning signs. Exuberance was one of them. He hoped any conversation could be prevented from touching on their royal neighbour.

'How de do, Mrs Fischer?' said Bate. 'I have been giving your dear papa the very sad news that poor Mr Ramsay, the painter, is dead.'

'Mr Ramsay, the court painter?' Molly clapped her hands. 'So the position is vacant, and Papa shall fill it!'

'Molly!' said Tom sharply. 'For shame! The man is dead less than four-and-twenty hours. It is not the time to speak of such matters.'

Ignoring him, Molly ran back to the doorway and called up to the second floor.

'Peggy, come quickly. Mr Bate has brought such news.'

'Molly, I insist that you…'

She was not listening. Tom sighed. At least she was not talking about the Prince of Wales.

'What news?' said the Captain, hurrying in. 'How de do, Mr Bate? What has happened?'

Molly told her before Bate had the chance, speaking not just of Ramsay's death, but also the implication, and now Tom was obliged to rebuke the pair of them.

'Forgive us, Papa,' said the Captain. 'Of course it is not nice to speak of such things so early, but how can we help it? The King is bound to give it to you, because he adores you, as you are always telling us, and you surely cannot blame us for being excited about it.'

'You have painted the entire Royal Family,' added Molly. 'All those princes and princesses. Not just the Prince of Wales' – she whispered his name, as if not wanting to attract his attention – 'but all his brothers and sisters too.'

'Except the Duke of York,' said the Captain.

'Except the Duke of York. But all the rest of them, and they are so many! You are the court painter already, in all but name.'

'Stop now, both of you. I forbid any more of this talk!' said Tom. 'Poor Ramsay is not yet cold. Even if he were, I care nothing about these fripperies. You should know me better than that.'

The girls had their eyes down, but he could see them giggling behind their hands. They knew him well, and they knew when he was dissembling.

Bate cleared his throat.

'Not entirely a frippery. Ramsay received two hundred guineas a year, you know, and a payment in addition for every portrait painted, even those by another hand. And of course there is a knighthood in it, by rights.'

'Is there?' Molly's eyes widened. 'But Mr Ramsay did not have one.'

'He turned it down. Is that not so, Gainsborough? You told me so yourself, and you had it from the King.'

Tom nodded reluctantly.

However much he had dissembled with Bate, his dislike of his daughters' indecorous conduct was genuine. On the other hand, Bate made a good point, that Tom himself had not considered. 'Sir Thomas Gainsborough' did indeed sound well. How proud it would have made his father, who had suffered the humiliation of being the failure of the family, to see what he had made of himself. And it would be so nice for the girls' mother to be Lady Gainsborough. She took it so ill that she was never received in the royal and other grand houses that he visited. A title would transform her social standing.

'What is all this commotion?'

Here was the future Lady Gainsborough, as yet ignorant of her impending good fortune.

'Good morning, Mr Bate. How de do? To what do we owe this unexpected honour?'

And off they went again, Molly and the Captain babbling excitedly about the glories certain to come, their mother torn between her normal instinct to scold them and excitement at the prospect that had now been put before them all. Concluding that indignation was futile, Tom let them get on with it.

Bate finished his chocolate and hastened back to his office, where he promised to write some words in the *Morning Herald* that would encourage the King in Tom's direction.

Tom returned to his painting room, threatening dire consequences if the subject was mentioned in his hearing for the rest of the day. The girls seemed to take him at his word, for it was not raised in front of him again. He had little doubt that they made up for that when he was out of earshot.

The next day, the debate entered the public realm. As good as his word, Bate declared in the *Morning Herald* that no artist living had such originality, or so strong a claim on the now vacant position of court painter, as Mr Gainsborough.

'Have you seen what Mr Bate has written, Papa?' asked Molly, when he came upstairs at one o'clock for his dinner. She had a copy of the paper in her hand.

Tom had sent the lad David out very early, and another copy

of the same paper lay downstairs in his painting room, open at just the place. However, he saw no reason to admit that to the womenfolk. Raising an eyebrow to affect mild curiosity, he went through the motions of looking the article over, grunting non-committally at suitable intervals, as he picked at the food on his plate. After such time as he thought had sufficed to reach the end, he put the newspaper down and sighed.

'It is very generous of Bate, and he will make my head swell, as he always does. However, I repeat: let us not excite ourselves about this bauble job, with poor Ramsay not yet laid in the ground.'

'Your papa is right, girls,' said their mother, spearing a piece of mutton on her fork. 'We should also remember that Mr Bate is just one voice, and there will be other, just as powerful voices urging the King to choose Sir Joshua.'

Tom choked as a mouthful of meat went down the wrong way.

'Take care, husband. You always chew so fast, it is no wonder the meat takes a wrong turn and chokes. Yes, take some beer. There, the moment has now passed, and all is well.'

He had recovered from the digestive mishap, but not from his wife's slight. Sir Joshua? The King loathed Sir Joshua! He said so all the time. Yes, Sir Joshua was president of the Academy that bore the King's name, and was therefore the senior painter in the realm. That did not mean that the King could tolerate his presence.

He forced a smile, for the benefit of Molly and the Captain.

'Thank you, my dear. Girls, you should heed your mother. As she says, Sir Joshua has a better claim than I to this frippery appointment, so let us show some respect to Ramsay and hear no more.'

He seethed in silence as he ate. Her disloyalty was

horrifying. How did she ever expect to become Lady Gainsborough if she were forever the champion of Sir Joshua? Perhaps she would prefer to be Lady Reynolds.

He took another swig of beer and wondered if he ought to try to call and see the King.

The *Herald* still lay on the table in front of him, folded to Bate's article, and his eye returned to that very complimentary line.

'No artist living has so much originality or so strong a claim, as far as genius is concerned, on the King.'

It soothed him to read it. Good for Bate. Thank heaven for Bate. Bate, at least, was a loyal friend.

To my dearest Ma

If you are listening to these words, that means this letter has arrived safely from Mrs Dupont. I expect you were surprised to see a parcel. I will explain presently what is inside: it may seem a puzzling gift at first, but I assure you it is most precious, and I hope you will treasure it. That is why I would not entrust it to any thieving post-boy, and I waited all these weeks until Mr Dupont was next returning home to see his good mother. Be patient a while, and I will explain everything to you. Only, before I say anything else, it is very important that you do not show the contents of the parcel to anyone, which not even my beloved Nelly knows about. Our Dick and Jack can see it, because one of them is reading this letter to you and they will know about it any road, but no one outside the family must see it, and especially not Mrs Dupont, else I will get in trouble with my master.

(As I write these words, I have a sudden fear that perhaps it is Mrs Dupont reading this letter to you now. If that is so, I implore you to be patient, Mrs Dupont, and you will see I have done nothing wrong. I swear it on my life, else my name is not David Mudge.)

I have told you often, Ma, that my master is forever painting the King and Queen or the princes and princesses at Buckingham-house, or their other houses. He is now well known in those places and I have myself have been at Buckingham-house too, as you know. After all this time, the King is exceeding fond of my master, and he is not at all fond of Sir Joshua Reynolds, even though it was the King himself who gave him the 'Sir' to put afore his name.

In spite of the great favour in which my master is held, he is not the King's official painter. That title belongs to a man named Ramsay, who is said to be a very decent gentleman, even though he is Scotch. Many folk in this town do not like the Scotch, because they control the banks and live in the finest houses, and it is said that they have grown rich off the labour of poor, honest Englishmen. In fact I have learned from my master, who is for the most part a kind and trusting man, that this is not true and most Scotchmen are good fellows, with none better than Ramsay himself, or so my master heard tell, because he never had the pleasure of making his personal acquaintance.

Nor will he now neither, for this Mr Ramsay passed into the next world three months back. This news caused great turmoil in our household, not in a grieving way, I am sorry to say, but an excited one, because everyone knew that the King would have to chuse a new court painter. The Misses Molly and Peggy were straightway certain that my master would be chosen, and they were so delighted by this prospect that they quite forgot to show any sadness over the poor departed Mr Ramsay. My master chid them for their unchristian attitude, but I could tell by his good humour in the next few days that he was right excited himself. I heard him whistling merry airs while he was at his painting, which is not a sound we often hear in this house, and twice in one week he slipped me a shilling when my mistress was not there to see.

All of us in this house know that my master's good humours do not last forever, and I noticed after that first week that the whistling had gone quiet. He replaced his cheerful attitude with a nervous one, and he was quick to anger if his chocolate was too cold or I was slow to answer his summons, or anyone else displeased him in any other way. I reckoned as how I knew the reason right enough, and Mr Dupont confirmed that it was as I supposed: my master had not yet heard from the King, and was fretting that it was not so certain after all that he would step into Mr Ramsay's boots.

My mistress said he should go and ask the King directly, since he is always saying as how His Majesty is his good friend. My master said this would not be seemly and, besides, nobody pays visits to the King uninvited, as if he were an ordinary neighbour and you could knock on his door whenever you fancied. He said it showed how little my mistress knew about such things, even if she gives herself airs about her descent from nobility. I had never heard my master talk so sharp to my mistress before, and I do not believe he would have done so if his nerves had not been so strained.

I know also from Mr Dupont that my master was frustrated at not having the right friends to call on, who might whisper words in his favour into the King's ear. His friend Mr Bate wrote about the matter in the *Morning Herald*, which he owns, but Mr Dupont said Mr Bate always takes my master's side in that paper, so it was no more than anyone expected. Otherwise, Mr Fisher knows the Queen well, because he plays in her musick band, but my master's relations with him have not been good since Miss Molly returned to live at home, and his other friends are actors and carousers who do not mix at court.

Miss Molly told my master she would have been happy to have a word on his behalf with the Prince of Wales, only the King does not welcome advice from that quarter and would more likely do the opposite and, besides, she feared it would only encourage the Prince in his quest for her heart. (If it surprises you, Ma, that the Prince of Wales should hold amorous feelings towards Miss Molly, believe me, it would surprise the Prince of Wales even more. Poor Miss Molly's malady is getting worse.)

In the third week my master was not so nervous in his disposition, but instead he was morose. On the Monday night he stayed out very late with Mr Able, who is his main friend now that Mr Bark has passed on and Mr Fisher is estranged again. He came back very late and very intoxicated, and the next day he stayed abed until the middle of the morning. He only rose when Mr Bate came to call. The visit did not portend well, because Mr Bate's expression was very solemn, and the tidings were indeed bad: he had come to tell my master that Sir Joshua Reynolds is the King's new court painter.

By that time, I think my master was expecting this outcome, but to hear it confirmed was nonetheless a heavy blow. It was either a betrayal by his friend the King, or the King was never his friend in the way he thought. My master is a proud man, so it was very hard for him, and also, of course, to be beaten by his old enemy Sir Joshua.

In former days, if Sir Joshua was described like that, my

master would insist, no, no, he is not my enemy, I bear him no ill-will, it is all got up by the newspapers. He would not say so now. I heard him shouting at my mistress that Sir Joshua conducted a shameless campaign, asking all the dukes and lords of his acquaintance to entreat the King in his favour. He also said he had heard that Sir Joshua had threatened to resign as president of the Royal Academy if the King did not appoint him.

It was difficult to have all this shouting and hollering happening because, in those weeks, the house was open to the publick, who were invited to pay sixpence to see the paintings that the Academy sent back after my master quarrelled with them. My mistress was anxious lest my master start raging about the perfidy of Sir Joshua Reynolds in the hearing of this publick, who would surely run and tattle to the press, which would then mock my master for his jealousy. So it fell to Perkiss and me, and also to Mr Dupont, to accompany the visitors and make certain my master could not be heard. Luckily there were not many of them, because it was August, when the stench of this city is always even more foul than usual, and all folk of means depart for the country.

The day after Mr Bate called with the bad tidings, I had just seen a small party of visitors out of the door when my master called me to his painting room. I do not mind admitting I was afeared, because it was most likely he would tell me I were a blockhead or a coxcomb, for what reason I know not, but he does not ever need one. I need not have fretted, though, because he only wanted me to help him fetch a particular canvas which was stored among the stacks of pictures and frames at the back of the room. I had to lean the frames forward so as he could pull it out. As he did so, I saw what it was. It was the unfinished portrait of Sir Joshua Reynolds, with the asses' ears added on his head. I wondered what on earth my master was planning to do with the picture now. Did he mean to put Sir Joshua's head on a mule's body? It seemed to me a foolish enterprise, but if the task soaked up his rage and stopped him shouting at everyone in the house, it would have my approval. I did wonder how he meant to paint the ass itself, when there was none to copy. Perhaps he meant to bring one from the same source where he found those little piglets, although I could not imagine what my mistress would say about a full-size donkey coming into the house and doing its business anywhere it pleased.

Afore I could wonder any further, however, my master bade me take myself away and leave him in peace. Then, after not half an hour, he summoned me back again. I expected to see the picture of Sir Joshua on his easel, but I could see from the doorway that it was not there. Instead of letting me into the room, my master came over to me and pressed a sacking parcel into my hands. 'Run to the kitchen and put these pieces to burn on the cook's hearth,' said he.

So I turned around and he shut the door behind me. Now, if I were a truly obedient servant, I would have gone directly to the kitchen to discharge my master's order. However, as I suppose you have already guessed, I did not do that. The corridor from the painting room at the back of the house to the staircase at the front of the house is a long one, and while I was walking this passage, I took the opportunity to peep inside the sacking to see what I was being asked to destroy. It was just as I thought: the package contained the face of Sir Joshua, complete with the ears of an ass, which had been cut from the rest of the large canvas and then slashed into four pieces. At that moment, I resolved to disobey my master's order, which is the first time I have ever done so. The picture is half destroyed, first with the ears, and then with the slicing in four pieces, but it is still a precious thing, showing my master's great skill at capturing a perfect likeness, and it would be sinful, as I see it, to destroy it. I also thought to myself, how often have I wished I could show Ma the beautiful paintings that my master creates? Now I had the opportunity, and if you open the parcel, you will find those four pieces, which I have kept carefully with my own things these past two months. You are so good with a needle, I hope you can stitch them together, for canvas is nothing more than heavy cloth, which just happens to dry flat when it is stretched inside a frame and has oil paint upon it.

Everything I have told you in this letter is God's honest truth, so you need have no fear that I thieved this painting to send to you. It is not thievery to save something from the flames when its owner had already cast it out. The only way I have done wrong is to disobey my master by not destroying the pieces when I was bidden to, and that is why you must never say that you have this painting by the great artist Mr Thomas Gainsborough, nor show it to no one that is not our blood.

And now I have to end this letter, Ma, because it is nearly time for Mr Dupont to depart for the stagecoach, and he is hollering that if my parcel is not ready now, he will not take it. I have told him it contains a suit of clothing for our Dick's littlest one, and I hope he believes me. I send you and all the rest my fondest love, and also the dearest regards of my Nelly who does not have people of her own and looks forward to the day when she can call you her Ma too. Until that happy time, and also long after it, I hope you will treasure this secret gift as a Mudge family heirloom entrusted to you by your loving son
   David

24

Against her better judgement, Gemma was on a train to Suffolk. At first she had resisted Vivian's entreaties to meet him at Muriel's cottage. Since losing her job, she could not afford the fare, aside from anything else. The rail ticket he sent her in the post had finally worn her down. If he was that keen for her to go and meet him, she might as well find out what he wanted. It was not as if she had anything better to do.

The punch-up at the end of the sale-room broadcast had signed the death warrant of *Britain's Got Treasures*. Until that point, the channel executives had been so pleased with the unexpected ratings and the media coverage for the series that they had been more than happy to overlook the eccentric way it had arrived at that point. However, the chaos of those last few seconds of the live broadcast was unambiguous: the programme was a national, if not international, laughing-stock, with that moment doomed to dominate compilations of top TV cock-ups for the rest of time. The only possible response was to pull the plug and try to forget the programme had ever existed.

This had been a major setback for Fiammetta, whose professional reputation had been dealt a serious blow, and it came as little surprise to Gemma when her own contract was not renewed. She sent her CV to everyone she could think of, but *Britain's Got Treasures* was her principal credit, and who was ever going to hire anyone with that employment history? She spent most of her time at home off the Bromley Road, feeding herself on sell-by-date reductions from her local Co-op, and wondering about retraining as a primary school teacher.

And now here she was, heading back to Gainsborough country.

All Vivian had said, once she eventually agreed to make the trip, was that Muriel had something to show them both, and that he also had a proposition of his own that he wanted Gemma to hear. The former, she imagined, was the properly restored painting, thanks to the conservators at the local gallery. What the latter might be, she had no idea.

The day was cloudless, and the Essex landscape glistened under the wintry, pale blue sky as they emerged from the East London suburbs. At the country station where Vivian had picked her up the previous summer to visit Lennie, she changed onto the single-track branch line that served Muriel's town. The train was standing waiting as she and a handful of other passengers walked across the platform. It felt two or three degrees colder here than it had in London.

The connecting train led up the river valley, so Lennie's home at Belstead St Margaret must be round here somewhere.

She had pleasant memories of that day, but the same could not be said of filming in the town, so it brought her no satisfaction when the train finally arrived at its destination. The road from the station took her across the bottom of the square. At the top end, in front of the church where they had set out their stall almost a year ago to the day, the bronze form of Thomas Gainsborough gazed over the town, oblivious to the battles fought in his name over the past twelve months. They might have ended well as far as Muriel was concerned, but the fiasco that had begun here had cost Gemma her job and perhaps her whole career. This place had been bad karma for her.

To her surprise, it was Lennie who opened the door of Muriel's cottage.

'Hello, Gemma, my dear, I'm so pleased you could come. How was your journey? Do come in. Let me take your coat and scarf. There's tea in the pot, and some rather good iced buns.'

The door opened directly into Muriel's tiny front room. The low ceiling was striped with rough-hewn wooden beams, painted black. Vivian and Muriel were sitting on either side of a large brick fireplace which took up all of one wall. Vivian stood up as Gemma came in, and they hugged. She bent to kiss Muriel on the cheek.

'Don't get up. How are you doing? I expect you're pleased to see the back of all those TV cameras.'

Muriel gave a girlish little laugh – Gemma was not sure she had heard it before – but it was Vivian who answered.

'Thereby hangs a tale,' he said. 'It's why we were so keen for you to come. But, first things first, Muriel has something to show us. We've been waiting till you arrived.'

'She hasn't had her tea yet,' said Muriel. 'Give the girl a chance to catch her breath.'

So Gemma was required to drink tea, which was served on a tray, with cups and saucers and a proper milk jug, and a giant woolly tea cosy to go over the pot. Lennie was right, the buns were good.

When Muriel was satisfied that Gemma was refreshed, she pushed herself up from her chair, with a helping hand from Vivian at her elbow, and shuffled off into the back of the cottage.

Gemma licked the last bits of sugar from her fingers.

'I assume she's getting the painting?'

'Oh good gracious no,' said Lennie. 'It's still being restored, which will take a while longer yet, and when it's done, it will be far too valuable to keep here. Muriel doesn't have the security. She's going to hand it over into more suitable safe-keeping. Aren't you, Muriel?'

'En't I what?'

Muriel had reappeared with an ancient-looking Clarks shoe-box in her hands.

'I was just saying, you're lending the picture to the town gallery. It's not very safe to keep it in the cottage.'

'Oh yes, that's right. It would be too much of a worry to have it here, after all that publicity. It will go very nicely in the gallery, which is just over the road, and they're giving me life membership, so I can go in and see it whenever I please.'

Gemma was getting impatient.

'So what have you got to show us?'

Muriel held out the shoe-box for her to take. The lid was held down with a large elastic band, looped twice round. This Gemma removed, and she gingerly opened the box. Inside was a thick bundle of yellowed envelopes, tied with white ribbon. The top one bore an address in faded ink, in an antique, copper-plate hand. It was to a Mrs Martha Mudge, of

Sudbury. There was no stamp. Gently, because these envelopes looked so fragile, she untied the ribbon. Vivian reached across and picked up the top one.

'There's no stamp on it, because it's long before the penny post was invented,' he said.

'Open it,' said Muriel. 'Don't be shy.'

He pulled three or four sheets of folded paper from the envelope. Gemma noticed that his hand was trembling.

'You remember that Muriel kept telling us she thought there were some family papers with her brother's things?' said Lennie. 'Well, she was right. That's what you're looking at.'

'*Pall-mall, London, February 2nd, 1777,*' read Vivian.

Lennie winked at Gemma.

'*To my dearest Ma,*' continued Vivian slowly, as he tried to decipher the Georgian handwriting. '*I know you cannot make out my scratchings on the page, because you never learned how. But I trust our Richard to read this out to you. It shall be one of his duties now he is become the man of the house in my absence. He is good with his school learning and 'twill be no trouble for him.*'

'Who is it from?' said Gemma. 'Not…Gainsborough himself?'

'No, that really would be a find,' said Lennie. 'It's a little further down. Can you see, Vivian?'

'Hang on. Yes, here's something. *My master – that's the brother of Mrs Dupont, although he seems so much finer than her – is a great gentleman…I sleep in the top attic which I share with Mr Perkiss, the groom…*'

'It's my great-great-great-great-great-grandfather,' said Muriel. 'I think that's right. Maybe one more great, maybe one less. He was in service with Gainsborough, along with my great-great-great-great-great-grandmother. He wrote a lot of letters to his mother, and they have all been kept and passed down, along with the picture. I knew I'd find them if I carried on looking hard enough. They were up in the attic, and I couldn't get up there myself, but my neighbour's son Billy went up there for me, and he found them. My brother Bob had stashed them in an old chest.'

Suddenly, Gemma was very glad that Vivian had persuaded her to make this trip.

'Have you read them all?'

'No, but Lennie has, and she's made a transcript, haven't you Lennie?'

'I have indeed, and I've shown it to Vivian.'

'But I haven't held the letters themselves in my hand until today,' said Vivian. 'Call me daft, but it brings tears to my eyes, just to handle this piece of paper. We should be wearing gloves, by rights.'

Gemma scarcely dared ask. 'And…is there anything about our – I mean Muriel's – painting?'

Lennie's eyes gleamed.

'Is there? I should cocoa! You can read it all in the transcript. But first, I think Vivian should tell you our other piece of news.'

Gemma looked at him.

'Well? Come on, you can't keep me in suspense! What is it?'

Vivian cleared his throat.

'This is the first time I've held these letters in my hands but, as Lennie says, I've read the transcript. David explains everything about the ears and the cutting-up. You can read it for yourself, so I won't spoil it. He also gives us a window into the life of Gainsborough and his family over a period of about ten years. It's a remarkable find, and we thought it deserved a much wider audience. So we've been talking to a publisher, and we've also had discussions with the BBC. Fruitful discussions.

So fruitful, in fact, that they want to make a documentary about everything that has brought us to this point. It will set the record properly straight for Muriel. And, if it goes well, they're thinking of a follow-up series, with Lennie and me as art detectives.'

'That's brilliant!' said Gemma. 'I'm so pleased for you, really I am. And you're happy about going back in front of the cameras, Muriel?'

'She's a past mistress at it now, aren't you, Muriel?' said Lennie.

Muriel shrugged, but she was smiling. Clearly the prospect held no fear for her.

'And you'll never guess who the presenter's going to be!'

Gemma's eyes widened.

'Don't tell me it's Kaz!'

Vivian rubbed his left jaw, where Kaz's fist had collided with it.

'I think not. No, it's much more exciting than that. We've got Fenella Bryan!'

Fenella Bryan was the household-name presenter of *Antiques on the Road*.

'No! But isn't she technically our competitor?'

'That doesn't matter. She's the face of antiques on the Beeb. Which is fine by us.'

'Certainly is,' agreed Muriel.

'Anyhow,' continued Vivian, 'we had one stipulation when we agreed the terms.'

Muriel and Lennie both nodded. Whatever it was, they were all in on it.

'Go on.'

'We said we'd only do it if we could bring you with us as part of the team. They went away and thought about it. And then they came back and agreed. Done deal.'

Gemma had begun to suspect something of the sort, but hearing the actual words made her well up.

'I...I don't know what to say...'

'Ta very much will do,' said Vivian.

She laughed.

'Thanks so much. I mean, obviously. So much.'

She leaned over and gave Vivian a kiss on the cheek, and then hugged Lennie and Muriel in turn.

'So when do we start?'

'Soon. We need to work out dates for the auction.'

'Auction?'

'Don't worry, not a live one this time.'

'But...I don't understand.' Gemma turned to Muriel. 'You just said you were loaning the picture indefinitely to the gallery here in the town. Or have I missed something?'

'The auction isn't for the painting. It's for these.' Muriel held up the box of letters. 'We're going to sell them at Sotheby's, and the BBC's going to film it.'

'You don't want to keep them as a family treasure?'

'Do I heck! I never knew I had 'em until a few weeks back. I don't think my ancestor would mind. In fact, I think he might be quite pleased. I fancy a new bathroom, one that isn't freezing cold in the winter. It will be his gift to me, across the centuries.'

'Quite so,' said Lennie. 'It's the least you deserve, my dear.'

Walking back to the station a couple of hours later, Gemma regretted her earlier negative reaction to the town.

This morning, it had seemed as if this place had jinxed her life. Now, a short time later, the same chain of events had put her in a far better place than she had started a year ago. This new venture would be the kind of programme she would be proud to have a hand in, and her mother would be even more proud on her behalf. She would love the idea of her daughter working with Fenella Bryan.

So the saga of the lost Gainsborough had served nearly everyone well. Not Fiammetta, but she would bounce back somehow; however much face she had lost, she had connections all over the industry. Anyway, she had pots of money, so she did not even need to work again, if the worst came to the worst. Of the others, Regina had her news-reading role, and Lavender had always been a distracted, semi-detached member of the *Britain's Got Treasures* team, so she would surely take the collapse of the programme in her mauve-trousered stride.

The real casualty, Gemma thought, as she cut into a newsagents to buy a bottle of fizzy water for the journey, was Kaz. He had been a graceless buffoon, and throwing a punch on the set of a live broadcast was unpardonable, so he had only himself to blame for the catastrophic nose-dive in his fortunes. Nevertheless, she could still not shake the thought that she had made exactly the same initial judgement call on Muriel's painting as Kaz, and that he had simply had the misfortune to make his on camera, which meant its consequences had been much harder to avoid. It was not that she felt sympathy, exactly: Kaz had made himself too unpleasant to everyone for that. It was more a case of 'there but for the grace of God...'

As she was leaving the shop, she thought she saw a picture of Kaz from the corner of her eye. It must have been a trick of the mind, she told herself. She was thinking about him, so some similar-looking face must have jumped out at her from the rack of newspapers and magazines on display near the door, and drawn her attention. To prove the trick false, as much as anything else, she stopped to check. No, she was mistaken.

There was no sign of anything with Kaz's face…no wait! There it was, and she had not made a mistake! On the front of the *Daily Star*, in a teaser box above the main headline, was a headshot of her former colleague, with the words alongside it: 'KO KAZ OKs TV PUNCH-UP SHOW – P7'.

Checking her watch to make sure she had enough time, she quickly flicked to the right place. And there indeed it was, covering the entire page: as the thrower of Britain's most celebrated on-screen punch, Kaz had been the obvious choice for a new show, on some channel even more obscure than her own previous one, about celebrities learning how to box in the ring.

She ran back to pay for the paper, so that she could read the whole article properly on the train.

She was deeply grateful to have seen it, and to have done so on this, of all days. Now, she could finally let go of her guilt. Unlikely as it had seemed even half an hour ago, everything really was going to be all right, for everyone. For the time being, at least.

To my dearest Ma

I was exceeding relieved to hear from Jack that Mr Dupont delivered the parcel to his mother, and that she gave it into your hands but you did not open it before her eyes. That means Mr Dupont is still ignorant of the contents, so our little secret is safe. I do not have much time to spare, for my master requires me to pick up an order of pigments from his colour-man, but I have two pieces of news that I am sure you would like to hear.

The first is that my Nelly and I took your advice, and we went to speak to my master and mistress together about our plans to be wed. We asked if they would give us the morning off so that we can make our love official in the eyes of the good Lord. My mistress was most friendly to our request, as you said she would be, and she said of course it would be no trouble to her if we had a morning off, as long as we came straight back in the afternoon with no dawdling. While she was saying this, my master was a-nodding and a-smiling, and when she had finished he said, you are right, as always, my dear wife, but let us do a little more for these young lovebirds who have been a-billing and a-cooing under our roof these past two years and more. Let us give them three full days' holiday and, as my wedding gift, I will pay their stage back home so they can be wed in the presence of this lad's dear mother and his brothers. He is a numbskull and a fool, as you hear me tell him most every day, but he is our numbskull and fool, and we must do right by him and his bride, as they have always done right by serving us very nicely in this house.

As he said this, I had to wipe a tear from my eye, and I could see that my Nelly was so grateful, she near threw her arms around my master's neck to thank him, only I fancy she saw the look in my mistress's eye, which told her not to do that if she knew what was good for her. My mistress was already looking peevish at my master's bounty towards us, and I feared she might contradict him and tell him not to throw away his money on his servants. But then my master shed a tear in response to the water in my own eyes, and I saw my mistress's countenance soften, and she finished up by telling my master that this was a most noble gesture he had made and she was proud to call him her husband. I know this news will fill you with joy, Ma, just as it has done for me and Nelly. Perchance you can ask the parson at All Saints if he will marry us one day next month and then we can be man and wife as we do sincerely yearn to be.

The other piece of news concerns my master himself. Jack told me you were distressed, in your kind-hearted way, at my master's unhappiness after being passed over by the King. Some information reached this house to-day which made him much happier, and I hope it will have the same effect on you, so I will scribble it hastily in these few lines.

My master's latest subject is Mrs Siddons, the most famous actress in all England. When Sir Joshua Reynolds painted her portrait last year, my master pretended not to care, but he was exceeding jealous, and since then he has been wooing that lady to sit for him too. I know not what inducement he used, but at last she has consented, and to-day this most celebrated lady sat for him a full three hours. I had the honour of opening the door to her, and I can tell you that Mrs Siddons is not a beauty, by any means. I mean no harm by saying that. The fact that she is plain makes it all the more remarkable, to my mind, that she brings grown men to tears in the great scenes she plays upon the stage. I know that my master was also a-fretting about how to make her likeness in oil paint without being ungallant. In the middle of the morning he came out of his painting room and told Mr Dupont that the problem was her nose. 'There is no end to it,' said he, and I have seen that feature myself, so I know what he meant.

He did not say any such thing to her face, of course, and they spent the whole morning conversing like they were old friends. I know this because Mr Dupont was in and out of the room assisting my master, and he heard a deal of their talk. One part in particular he heard was when they fell to discussing Sir Joshua.

Now, Sir Joshua painted Mrs Siddons sitting on a throne and dressed as the Muse of Tragedy, so Mr Dupont tells me, although I cannot rightly imagine what sort of costume the Muse of Tragedy would wear, and my Nelly says she has no idea neither. The portrait pleased everyone who saw it at the Royal Academy, which does not include anyone in this house, of course, but the newspapers said nobody could talk about anything but how wonderful this picture was. Because of this, Mrs Siddons is very nicely disposed towards Sir Joshua, and my master was obliged to take care what he said to her about that gentleman. Luckily, he did not need to say very much at all, because Mrs Siddons did all the talking on the matter.

'Poor Sir Joshua,' said she, as Mr Dupont told me. 'He is exceeding unhappy in the role of court painter. Did you know, Mr Gainsborough, that the late Mr Ramsay received two hundred guineas per annum for the office, but the King has reduced this to thirty-eight pounds, not even guineas, for Sir Joshua. The poor man has taken it as a terrible slight. He always suspected that the King disliked him, and now he is sure of it. He told the Bishop of St Asaph, who told the Duke of Bridgewater, who told Sir William Hamilton, who told me, that the role of the King's Rat-Catcher would command greater respect.'

Mr Dupont observed my master's face as Mrs Siddons was saying this. She could not see him, because she was arranged to look towards the window, but Mr Dupont could, and he told me my master turned as red as a raspberry through the effort not to laugh. He was afeared that his uncle might burst. So you see, Ma, Sir Joshua wanted this role of court painter so very bad, and now he has got it, he does not like it. You had a saying that you used to tell us when we were small, Ma, didn't you? You told us a person should always take care what they wish for, for fear it may turn out to happen. I never understood that correctly afore, but Sir Joshua is the living proof of your adage.

I need to finish this letter now, Ma, because my master is calling me, and if I do not come promptly he will call me a blockhead. I will give this to the post-boy on my way to the colour-shop. I only thought you would want to know that, after this period of recent despond, my master is cheerful again, for now, which means the whole household will likely be the same. It does not help my mistress become Lady Gainsborough but, as you also used to tell us when we were little children, we cannot have everything that we want.

With all my fondest love

Your son

David

Afterword

Fairly soon after I started living in the Stour valley, on the border between Suffolk and Essex, I realised that the experience would be more rewarding if I developed a deeper interest in the work of the area's most famous son, Thomas Gainsborough.

As a frequent gallery-goer, I already had an affection for his work. I had played that game in front of his portraits where first you stand a decent distance away, so that the sitter's silk dress or frock coat looks intricately detailed, and then slowly step forward until the buttons and embroidery dissolve into wild, indisciplined splashes, and you wonder how he ever got away with it. It is even more fun in reverse, when you stand up close to the splashes and then move slowly back until they magically coalesce into a perfect garment.

I did not know much about Gainsborough's life, though,

so I started reading biographies, and then his own letters, gradually realising that he was a larger-than-life character – likeable, sociable, irascible, opinionated, funny – whose full-throated approach to the world contrasted dramatically with the rule-bound stodginess of his principal rival, Sir Joshua Reynolds.

He was ripe for a novel, I thought, and my friend Arabella McKessar, of Gainsborough's House gallery, egged me on. The trouble was, I could not see how to make it work. If you are trying to make a narrative tale out of a historical life, you need to find a story within that life that you can hew into a novel-sized shape. Gainsborough's life is littered with good yarns, but I struggled to see what that main story might be.

It was Arabella's husband Malcolm (although he denies all memory of the conversation) who pointed out that it had to be a comedy. In my first novel, *The Hopkins Conundrum*, I did not seek comedy in the biography of Gerard Manley Hopkins; rather, I lightened the gloom of the poet's difficult, frustrated life by wrapping it in a comic modern narrative. But with Gainsborough, as Malcolm persuasively argued, the comedy was staring me in the face: his long-running professional rivalry with Reynolds, sometimes confected by the media, sometimes real, and the two men's contest for the affections of the Royal Family. The po-faced Reynolds was inherently comic, with his ear trumpet and his earnest lectures on precisely how paintings should be made, even though he was notoriously incompetent when it came to mixing his own paints. Gainsborough himself was no less fruitful a subject, telling anyone who would listen how much he hated painting the faces of toffs, yet cheering up miraculously if the face had a crown on it. Playing it for laughs seemed all the more fitting given the era in which these men lived. This was the age of fops, dandies and courtesans, an anything-goes epoch of pre-Victorian decadence which was a heyday of comic or satirical literature – think Swift, Fielding, Sterne, Thackeray and Austen.

The process of writing biographical fiction with an eye to comedy is no different to the straight-faced version: it involves a lot of research. I have tried to be no less true to the characters and what we know of their lives than I would have been in a serious novel. I have changed a couple of minor details for chronological convenience, which only the most hardcore scholars will notice, but otherwise I have been faithful to the available sources, and used creative imagination in the gaps. We do know, incidentally, that Sir Joshua sat once for Gainsborough, but that nothing came of it. Speculation as to what ensued is where I have had some fun. Otherwise, the main licence I have taken is to tell part of my story through the eyes of the footman David. Gainsborough did have a servant by that name, but we know nothing about him, which is why backstairs staff are a novelist's friends: we can allow our imaginations to colour them in without fear of contradiction.

If there is any serious point to the book, aside from the basic aim of bringing Gainsborough the man to a wider audience, it was to try to write honestly about the production and consumption of art.

There is a common assumption in fiction that looking at art involves trembling and swooning in front of masterpieces, which never matches my own experience – nor, from what I see in galleries, most other people's. In Gainsborough's day, there was a great popular appetite for looking at paintings, which were the only images available in a pre-photography world. Going to the Royal Academy exhibition had the buzz of going to the cinema, but it was actually more like buying a celebrity magazine, because you got to see what the most talked-about people of the day were supposed to look like. There was plenty of review space for art in the newspapers, including of individual paintings, but this 'criticism' often meant taking issue with the colour of a sitter's frock or the distribution of the scenery. This was not a highbrow pursuit.

As for the artist, producing portraits was a business, providing status objects for those who were wealthy enough to commission their own likeness. For Gainsborough, if not for Reynolds, creating illusions out of pigment and oils was a skill rather than a noble aesthetic calling. Get good enough at it, and manage your career pragmatically, and a Suffolk boy of the middling sort could end up living the life of an affluent gentleman in Pall Mall. The objects he left behind became, for a while, the most valuable paintings in the world, although they are not that any more, because the market has moved on. Looking at them now is to admire the skill that made ground-up minerals look so convincingly like flesh and blood, and to peer at eyes made of paint that seem to take you into a long-dead sitter's soul. Who needs to swoon or tremble when you can do that?

To re-imagine part of Thomas Gainsborough's life, I have leaned heavily on successive generations of biographers: Henry Angelo, William Whitley, Jack Lindsay and, most recently, James Hamilton, as well as Ian McIntyre's comprehensive life of Joshua Reynolds. For reference to Gainsborough's work, I went back again and again to William Vaughan's Thames & Hudson book, Martin Postle's book in the Tate's British Artists series, and Nicola Kalinsky's beautifully illustrated volume for Phaidon. Rita Jones' technical analysis of Gainsborough's pigments, in her and Mark Bills' splendid catalogue to accompany the Early Gainsborough exhibition in Sudbury, was invaluable for the modern part of my story. Janice

Hadlow's compelling *The Strangest Family* was my bible for George III, Queen Caroline and their immense brood. Henry Hitchings' *The World In Thirty-Eight Chapters* provided a wonderful immersion into the Georgian sensibility, and James Woodforde's diary, *A Country Parson*, was a great linguistic and dietary resource.

The job of making the manuscript into a book depended on a familiar and trusted team: my editor Scott Pack, on our third such collaboration, helping me make this into the novel I wanted it to be; plus Dan Hiscocks, Clio Mitchell, Hugh Brune, Sue Amaradivakara and Ifan Bates, whose cover is a joy to behold. Thank you also to Liz Cooper at Gainsborough's House and to Liz Curry, who has known and loved Gainsborough country for much longer than I have.

A Right Royal Face-Off is dedicated to the memory of Nick Decalmer, whose path crossed mine at a very significant time in both our lives, and I am very glad it did.

Simon Edge was born in Chester and educated at Cambridge University, where he read philosophy. He spent many years as a national newspaper journalist and critic, and has an MA in creative writing from City University, London. He is the author of two previous novels: *The Hopkins Conundrum*, which was longlisted for the Waverton Good Read Award, and *The Hurtle of Hell*. He lives in Suffolk.

The Hopkins Conundrum

Tim Cleverley inherits a failing pub not far from the remote Jesuit seminary where the Victorian poet Gerard Manley Hopkins wrote his masterpiece, *The Wreck of the Deutschland*, about a real-life tragedy involving a group of nuns fleeing persecution.

To Tim, the opaque religious poetry is incomprehensible – as if it's written in code. This gives him an idea. Desperate to boost trade, he contacts an American purveyor of Holy Grail hokum – suggesting he write a book about the poet, the area and a recently discovered (and entirely fabricated) 'mystery'. The famous author is suffering from writer's block so he latches on to the project at once. But will Tim's new relationship with a genuine Hopkins fan scupper the plan?

The Hopkins Conundrum blends the real stories of Hopkins and the shipwrecked nuns with a wry eye on the Da Vinci Code industry in an original mix of fiction, literary biography and satirical commentary.

A splendid mix of literary detection, historical description and contemporary romance. Edge's witty debunking of the Vatican conspiracy genre will appeal equally to fans and detractors of Dan Brown – Michael Arditti

The novel seesaws between comedy and calamity, present and past. It pokes fun at pretension but also gives an insight into why a Catholic poet such as Hopkins – so weird, so spiritual and so intense – deserves his claim to greatness. The result is a novel enjoyable on every level – Jennifer Selway, Daily Express

A riotous read – Nicola Heywood Thomas, BBC Radio Wales

Also published by Lightning Books, price £8.99

The Hurtle of Hell

Gay, pleasure-seeking Stefano Cartwright is almost killed by a wave on a holiday beach. His journey up a tunnel of light convinces him that God exists after all, and he may need to change his ways if he is not to end up in hell.

When God happens to look down his celestial telescope and see Stefano, he is obliged to pay unprecedented attention to an obscure planet in a distant galaxy, and ends up on the greatest adventure of his multi-aeon existence.

The Hurtle of Hell combines a tender, human story of rejection and reconnection with an utterly original and often very funny theological thought-experiment. It is an entrancing fable that is both mischievous and big-hearted.

Simon Edge has given us a creator for our times, hilariously at the mercy of forces beyond even his control – Tony Peake

Part philosophical quest, part redemptive religious exploration, this is an original and witty look at religion and society seen through the eyes of a hapless and confused young man. The result is a clever and enchanting fable of self-discovery – The Lady

An unorthodox, comical and often deep story of rejection and reconnection with daft, challenging and fun plot twists. It's not what it seems, but then what is? Edge delivers a warm-hearted narrative of redemption that's never judgemental but is inclusive, funny and undoubtedly heretical. Read it or burn it, depending on your sense of humour – Gscene

Also published by Lightning Books, price £8.99